Each one of us has been "Geena" at some point in our lives. We've loved, been let down, and have almost lost our minds. This story is full of surprises. There are many twists and turns that take place that will have you jumping out of your seat. It will have you on pins and needles wondering what will happen next. As you journey through this era of Geena's life, be sure to keep your eyes, ears, and hearts open so you can see, hear, and feel everything Geena experiences. So turn off your cell phones, put the kids to sleep, and dive in head-first to see what happens When the Well Runs Dry.

ACKNOWLEDGMENTS

The responsibility of an author is to entice the reader to want more with each turned page of the novel. Life lessons have allowed me to gather the tools needed to lure my readers into a world of fiction that is foreign to some, heard of by many, and secretly wanted by all.

Relationships carry love, hope, happiness, excitement, brokenness, distrust, backbiting, sadness, hurt, and pain. Men and women experience one or more of these feelings at some point in their lives, whether in a marriage, friendship, etc.

Grief is optional… Growth is inevitable. Each of us can choose happiness over sadness, but what we learn in the process is up to us as individuals.

I would like to thank my husband, Mr. Bradley S. Hill, Jr. for being my rock and my best friend. Your love and support continues to push me to levels that I never imagined possible.

Veronica M. Lewis, Katina Rutledge, and Lawrence D. Dixon: I cannot thank you enough for your assistance and creativity during this project.

To my niece, Jerian Butler, thank you for breathing life into my young characters.

To each of my "quick" readers, you know who you are. Thank you for giving me a thumbs up during the hours I felt unsure of myself and needed reassurance that I was getting my point across. I appreciate you for taking the time out to give me the encouragement I needed to keep on pressing.

Last but not least, I must thank God for giving me this opportunity to share the gift that has been so graciously given to me.

My prayer is that each word found in this novel will somehow uplift, encourage, inspire, and ultimately bless the person that decides to dive into this world.

– KATRINA BUTLER HILL

I'm Geena
Chapter 1

It had been close to ten years since I'd gone on an all-girl vacation with my friends. Between getting married, the birth of my two kids, my demanding career, working in my church, actively participating with various social events for the community, and being the strong shoulder for my friends, I had absolutely no time to devote to myself, let alone go on vacation. Being that I was considered a social butterfly when we were in school, I missed hanging out with my girls but with the "Demands of Geena," I just couldn't find a way to add a get away with the girls into my plans.

Last Tuesday, as I was leaving the office for lunch, my best friend from middle school, Stephanie, called to try and persuade me once again to go on vacation with her and some of the ladies that we grew up with. I hadn't seen them in ages. This was her yearly ritual, so you would think she would have given up on me by now. Like clockwork, each year between May and June, Steph would be calling trying to scheme me into taking some time away. It was always tempting and Stephanie knew exactly how to make it sound like it

1

was going to be the best trip ever. She had the same speech each time, but she'd add a small twist to give it some flavor. This year was no different.

"Girl, you're not getting any younger. That job, those kids, and that husband of yours will be there when you get back! You deserve to get away from it all. Besides, Jared is always working late hours, staying away from home, and going out of town on his business trips. You're left at home to hold down the house, do the cooking and cleaning, take the kids, pick the kids up, tutor the kids, feed the kids, and all the other million things you have to do. Let's not forget to mention that demanding office job that you have dealing with all of those bougie folks day in and day out! Girl, you NEED a break!" It was time for me to cut in and interrupt Steph before she gathered more evidence to plead her case.

"I know, Steph, but the life that you live is totally opposite to mine." She smacked her lips before she responded.

"Oh yes, honey! That is the truth if I ever heard it! I can come and go as I please, I make my own schedule, and I follow my own rules. When I feed myself, my family is fed, and I don't have to worry about anyone except me. When I leave, I don't have a specific time to come back. I, my dear Geena, can do what I want to do." Stephanie smacked her lips again. "Honestly, I don't see how you do it. You have totally lost yourself in their world, Geena, and you know that is NOT fair. I mean, think about it. What's left for you?"

I sat there, holding the phone to my ear for a few seconds while pondering that question. For some reason, it affected me differently than all the other times Stephanie and I had the vacation conversation. What was left for me? As much as I hated to admit it, she was right. But how could I take the time away? What about my obligations?

"Okay, Steph, I love you and would love to chat a little more, but I've got to go. I only have time for a quick bite then I am off to my 1:30 conference call. We'll talk more this weekend, okay?"

She sarcastically responded, "Promise?"

"Yessss, Steph, I promise."

Leaving the office that evening, I had to stop by the grocery store to pick up some broccoli to go along with the Rosemary chicken and wild rice I was preparing for dinner. While standing in line waiting for the cashier to ring up my food, I noticed a group of girls that must have been in their early twenties. I was standing close enough to hear them as they laughed and talked about their plans for going out later that night. I began to reminisce on how much fun we had in college and how much my life had really changed. Steph, Rachel, Kim, and I had been friends for a long time. I met Stephanie when I was in seventh grade and we latched on to Rachel and Kim when we entered high school. I consider my girls to be more like my sisters than just my friends.

I smiled thinking back to how the four of us were always on the go... meeting up at my house, getting ourselves together to go out, in my bedroom with the music blaring, shoes and clothes everywhere. It was a ritual for the girls to bring a bag of shorts and tops for us to rummage through and try on. I giggled to myself thinking about how we would put on a pair of short shorts, pairing them with some kind of shirt we had cut up, put ribbon or strings through and tied all the way up our backs. Before we could head out the door, we had to take turns turning towards the mirror to dance, shaking and dropping it low making sure our pongs, as my mother affectionately called our booty cheeks, weren't in full view. The four of us were considered to be kind of wild in our day, but we didn't mind because we believed in not allowing anything to step in our way of having a good time. We were responsible young women; we were serious about our education and securing our futures, but we didn't let our journey to success stop us from enjoying every day of our teenage and young adult years. I missed those times, but I realized that time in my life was over and it was time for me to move on. Don't get me wrong, I am happy with my life and I know that there is a time for every season, but that season of my life was over.

Later that evening as I stood at the sink washing dishes, I thought about the conversation Steph and I had earlier that day. Although this was the same conversation we had every year, I began to question whether I should seriously consider taking this all-girl vacation. That thought didn't last long because I was interrupted by a cry of, "MaaahhhMaahhh!" quickly snapping me back to reality.

"Yes, Lily!"

"Can you help me with my math?"

From the other side of the house, I could hear another shout of, "Mommy, I can't find my gym shoes and I can't get another zero from Coach Wilcox."

"Just a minute, Frances."

This was a usual night in the Howard household, the kids screaming my name, me cleaning the kitchen and fulfilling any other household chores, all while Jared sat in his office in front of his computer as if he didn't have a care in the world. Although I knew he was focused on everything except us, I still screamed upstairs trying to get his attention to help me with the girls.

"Honey! Jared!"

"Yes, Geena, what is it?" This was his usual reply in an irritated voice.

"Could you please tear yourself away from your office just long enough to help one of the girls out while I help the other?" I mouthed his response as it came from his lips.

"Geena, I have a million things to handle before my meeting with the corporate office in the morning."

This was his answer to every question I had for him when it came to helping around the house or with the girls. Jared was very successful in his firm and respected amongst his peers. He had received numerous accolades for his attentiveness and commitment to the projects that he led for the company. His focus had become being the best at what he did for the firm, which I was proud of but it had taken away the partner that I once had and still needed. After taking a deep sigh, I threw the dishtowel into the sink and marched upstairs to rescue my girls from their misery.

Walking into Lily's bedroom, I almost tripped over her hot pink book bag lying in the middle of the floor alongside her Juicy Couture purse and leopard print flats she'd worn to school that day.

"Lily Alexis Howard, how many times do I have to ask you to keep your things off the floor?"

She didn't even look up to respond, acting like another Howard that I knew.

"Oh, sorry, Mommy, could you please move it for me? I am really into this next problem. Ms. Jamison gives us the toughest assignments to only be 3rd graders."

"What are you working on?"

It looked as if she was working on some new information from the way she was seated at her desk with her math book, worksheets, sticky notes, pencils, and index cards all over the place. She had Willow Smith's cd playing in the background, and her television turned to FOX, watching *Everybody Hates Chris*. Whenever Ms. Jamison introduced a new chapter in math, Lily panicked. Being only nine years old, full of life, spontaneity, and I must add, major attitude, the school placed her in all advanced classes. This was a great honor, but it put a lot of pressure on her since she was always striving for perfection. Math was her weaker subject so anything unfamiliar had her all in knots.

"Well how about we let Willow rest before she snaps her neck and let Chris go find somebody to like him?"

I knew that if I tried to turn off the CD player and television I would get her attention. "No, Mommy. Wait, it helps me to think. I need my outside sources of energy, see, it helps if I can do my homework and whip my hair back and forth."

"Well if you want my help with this assignment young lady, you better start using your inside sources of energy before I have to whip something. And it won't be any hair."

"Yes, Ma'am."

"Now what is it you need help with?"

As soon as I sat down to look over the directions, Frances burst into the room. "Mama! I need my gym shoes. I don't have time for Coach Wilcox's mouth tomorrow!"

Frances, while only two years younger than her big sister, tried her best to be her total opposite. It tickled me to watch her sometimes. I always wanted to have a sister, so it bewildered me that she didn't look up to Lily. Although they could pass as twins with their tiny frames and long thick hair, Frances prided herself on doing whatever she thought Lily wouldn't like. This meant wearing her long curly black hair pulled back in a ponytail every day instead of wearing it straight like her sister, or wearing a pair of ripped jeans or basketball shorts to accompany her freshest pair of kicks, as she called them. The only thing they had in common was dance, which still always ended up as a competition.

"Frances, did you look in the closet beside the garage? Check there and let me help your sister with her math, I'll be down in a minute."

"But, Mama! You always help her first. "

Lily dragged her attention away from her worksheet to say, "That's because I'm the smart one."

I had to thump her on her ear. "Uhm, get your eyes on your paper, smart one. Frances, what did I ask you to do?"

She turned away before I could complete my sentence. "Yes, Ma'am."

"And fix your face before it gets stuck like that."

I could hear her laugh as she went down the steps. "Yes, Ma'am."

It was always so hard to try and accommodate both girls at the same time, which was another reason I wished Jared would be more hands on. The girls had become so accustomed to the way things were in our house that they didn't even ask Jared for help. They always relied on me, so I stopped relying on him.

As I sat there going over the math with Lily, I began to drift back to the conversation I had with Steph earlier that day. Once the girls were taken care of and I had completed all the nightly chores, bedtime arrived and that meant it was time to yell out my usual,

"Okay, girls, it's about that time! Make sure you brush your teeth and say your prayers."

From one end of the house I could hear, "Goodnight, Mama."

And from the other end I could hear, "See ya in the morning."

And my nightly response was, "Good night, girls, I love you."

Walking into Jared's office, I stopped in the doorway watching him as he pecked away at the keys on his laptop. I missed the nights when I walked into his office catching him off guard, kissing him on his neck and taking him away from his work. Nowadays when I walked in, he kept his head down focusing on whatever he was working on. Walking in tonight, I tried to get his attention the best way I could. I walked in front of his desk, rubbed my finger across the top of his laptop, made noises as I moved some papers, and pushed his prized little league trophies around on his desk. I felt like picking one of them up and throwing it against the wall in hopes that would get him to look up. After all of my efforts, nothing worked, so I decided to just stop wasting time and talk.

"Hey! Whasssup, still working on the big proposal?"

While his head was still buried in his work, he responded, "Geena, baby, give me just a few more minutes. Go ahead and get ready for bed, pull the covers back for me, and I'll be up to join you. I'll be finished shortly."

And at that moment, I felt my nightly pain, as we continued a ritual of me cleaning up the kitchen, helping the girls, and walking into Jared's office only to be sent to bed alone. This had become the life for us; although I longed for more intimacy, I continued to be silent and not complain. The weight on my heart made it a struggle to put one foot in front of the other, but I made my way to the bedroom and prepared myself for bed. Walking into my cozy, beautifully decorated bedroom, all of the memories flooded back of when Jared and I were madly in love. I pulled the edge of the comforter back then plopped down on the bed. I thought back to the beautiful spring day when Jared and I went shopping together for bedroom furniture and the beautiful chocolate and teal bed linens and accessories. Back in those days, I used to get butterflies in my stomach whenever he looked at me, with the belief in my heart that the feeling would last forever.

After a few moments, I stood up to turn on the bed lamp before pulling the covers back, fluffing the pillows, and then heading for the bathroom. As I watched the water fill the tub, my mind shifted, thinking about how much Jared's love for me had faded. It was a sad ugly truth, but I had learned to live with it. I dropped my robe, took off my slippers and climbed into the bubble-filled tub, allowing the pillow of suds to cover my body like the clouds filling the sky on a stormy night. As I rested my head on the back of the spa tub, I began to really look at my life, taking off my paint-stained glasses that had allowed me to ignore the pain so prevalent in my heart. With my vision clear, I finally found the courage to stare my reality right in the face.

I felt my heart pound as I realized how much my truth hurt; I confessed to myself that my pain was unbearable. I thought about my life choices, the paths I'd chosen to take, and the promises I had made for myself that I found myself so willing to break. Tears fell from my face as I sank deeper into the pillow of bubble suds draped over my lovesick, weakened body. I began to question where my choices had led me and if there was any hope for me to capture the life I had always dreamed of. A life filled with love, adventure, and intimacy. Feeling the coolness of the water, I took my right toe and turned on the hot water to reheat my pool of emotions. I didn't realize how long the faucet had been on because, before I knew it, the water was about to spill over. As I stood to grab my towel and dry off, I heard my cellphone ringing from inside my purse.

"Hello?"

"Hey, Chick, whassup?"

"Steph, it's 10:30 p.m. You know this is my wind down time."

"Yeah, yeah, I know, but I was sitting here thinking about our conversation from earlier and I really want you to go with us, Geena. Every year, you turn us down, and we're not getting any younger! I spoke with a travel agent today, and I've been on the web looking for deals; I just found a hotel in Miami that is a five-star luxury suite and I just want to know if you're down or what?"

"Steph, look I told you..." She interrupted before I could finish.

"Look, Gee, I hate to just stand by and watch as you allow your life to pass you by! You are my very best friend, and I don't like what's happening to you. You have allowed life to take its toll on you. I have one full week to confirm the reservations, so you take your time, but not too much, and let me know what you want to do. No more pressure. I love you, BFF."

I felt her heart smiling through the phone as I replied, "Love you more, Steph, good night."

Drying off, I could hear Jared walk into the bedroom and take off his cuff links and watch, placing them on the dresser. He came into the bathroom to brush his teeth without even taking a look back over his shoulder to acknowledge my presence. I stood and watched him for a few moments, hoping he would utter at least a word to start some type of conversation. When he didn't, I sat down on the stool in front of the Jacuzzi to put on my lotion and wondered what had happened to the warm and compassionate man that I met, fell in love with, and married ten years ago. I was used to him complimenting me, touching me, holding me, and making me feel like a woman. After he put his toothbrush away, he turned around and noticed that I was watching him. His demeanor was cold and uncaring. As he turned on the shower, he finally asked, "Anything wrong, Geena?"

As my heart screamed out from pain, I wanted to say yes, but my stubborn mind just balled up like a shy girl on her first date. "Nooooo, Jared, nothing's wrong. I'm just tired. You have a nice shower. I'm going to bed."

As I walked through the bathroom door and headed to the bed, my heart longed for the passion we once had. I wanted desperately for him to ask me to join him in the shower, but he didn't. Instead he stepped in the shower without me, just like I felt he had stepped away from my love.

After Jared finished up in the bathroom, he climbed into bed beside me, reached to turn out his lamp, nestled his head onto his pillow, put the covers around him, and quickly drifted off to sleep. I lay there in cold silence, looking into the mirrored clock that showed my reflection staring back at me, tasting the salty tears that were falling down my face. I didn't dare to let Jared hear me as my emotions ran wild inside my body, so I remained in place and cried myself to sleep.

I must have been asleep for only three or four hours when I was awakened by the sudden movement I felt beside me. Although I wanted to jump up and ask Jared what he was doing, I just kept my eyes closed and listened. I could see him walking towards the bathroom through the dresser mirror, so I sat up in the middle of the bed to wait for his return. As he walked back into the bedroom he noticed I was awake.

"Whoa! You scared me! You okay, Geena? Is there something wrong?"

I told him I was okay as he looked at me confused and turned on the bed lamp to be certain that I was.

"Okay, well why you are sitting up in the middle of the bed at four in the morning? "Although my feelings of mourning from a dying marriage were on my mind, I held back and only mentioned the conversation I had earlier with Steph.

"Honestly, I am fine. I just wanted to talk to you about something. How do you feel about me joining the girls in Miami for an all-girls vacation?"

Without hesitation, Jared responded, "I feel like you should go! What's holding you back?"

I paused with a blank stare, not knowing what to say next. "Well for one, I thought we'd discussed vacationing with friends once we got married and how we didn't think married people should go out of town on trips without their mates." For assurance purposes, I took another pause to gather my thoughts, "There's just too much temptation out there and traps ready to slip you up, and I just don't feel comfortable."

Jared took me by the hand, scooted himself closer, and looked into my eyes as he spoke. "Geena, listen to me. You work hard, you take care of the girls, you handle the house, and you are always on the move. You deserve a vacation, and on top of that, I trust you, so there's no reason for you to feel that way. Besides, your friends constantly ask you to travel with them, and you always turn them down. I can handle things around here, and it will be fun to spend some quality time with the girls."

"But, Jared. I just don't think it's a good idea to be away from you and the girls for an entire week. I can see maybe going to have lunch or drinks, but out of town for a full week, I just don't know."

"Okay, Geena, what's the real issue? You know I trust you so why deprive yourself of something as special as spending time with your friends?"

"That's just it, Jared. I don't feel as If I am depriving myself of anything. I'm afraid that changing certain dynamics in any relationship can lead to something else. I mean if it's working the way it is, then why the need to make a change? Change is not always good!"

"Go on, babe. Listen, you deserve it."

As flustered thoughts ran through my brain, I finally agreed. "Okay, Jared, if you insist on it. I'll call Stephanie tomorrow. I guess I'm going to Miami."

While giving me a gentle kiss on the forehead, Jared stated, "You'll have a great time and you deserve it, Geena."

"Goodnight Jared," I replied as I returned the kiss to his lips.

Just Me and My Girls
Chapter 2

On the plane to Miami I couldn't help but think about my husband and my girls. I guess Stephanie realized it and that's why she stopped the stewardess to give me a double shot of Grey Goose to help me get loose.

"Geena, you're on vacation, baby! No time to be worried about what's going on at home. I'm sure Jared has everything under control. Sip on this, sit back and enjoy the ride. We're about to parrrrttyy!"

Steph was right. It was my time and I needed to take full advantage of it. The plane ride was smooth, that double shot sent me right off into dreamland. Once we landed, Stephanie nudged me to look out the window. There's something special about the Florida sun. For some reason, it seemed like it shone brighter than any other part of the world. After we checked our luggage, it was off to enjoy the sunny streets of Miami. I was really excited. I was thirty-two years young and hadn't gone out with my friends since I was twenty, two years prior to my wedding.

"Where's our first stop, Stephanie?"

"After we drop these suitcases off, I'll call the rest of

the girls so we can meet for lunch. They should be here by now."

"Okay, sounds like a plan."

Walking into the resort, we were greeted by two very tall, well-groomed, sexy gentlemen who had the pearliest white teeth and creamiest dark skin I had ever seen before in my life. They stood there looking like they had just walked off a magazine cover, with trays filled with cool beverages and cool damp compresses to put across our foreheads to help chill our bodies from the extra heat that we had stepped into as soon as we reached Miami.

Stephanie looked at me with that smirk she always gave. "Hhhooomm, and you worried about Jared and them chirrunz, girl, please." We chuckled, gave each other a wink, and took our drinks.

After the front desk attendant gave us our room keys, we were on the elevator to the fourteenth floor. It seemed like it took forever to walk down the hallway and my four-inch stilettos didn't make the walk any easier. Once we got to the door, we were ready to get inside and take a seat! The suite was gigantic and had room for us to have our own space, which I had been secretly praying for. We had our own California King-sized bed, a basket of wine was on the table near the couch, and a gorgeous view of the beach was in place to wake us each morning. I was in awe. Relaxation. No deadlines. No lost tennis shoes. No math homework. Finally! All I could do was stand in amazement, feeling like I was in heaven. Stephanie had left the room door wide open when she ran to the restroom, so I could hear some voices coming up the hall.

"Let's see, room 1408! Yep, this is it."

In walked Rachel and Kim, our other two friends that I hadn't seen in the last ten years. Once they entered the room, all the screams and hugs began.

"Ahhhhhhhhhhhhh! Geeeeeeeeena."

"Raaaayyychell! Kimmmmmmm!"

They both immediately started looking around. "Where is Stephanie?"

We all leaned forward when we heard Stephanie's sultry voice announce her presence.

"Here I am," she called in her southern drawl. In she strutted from the bathroom, wearing peep toe Louboutins, a cute black bikini, oversized designer shades, and somehow, she held a martini glass in her hand. Yes, it's true. On the low, we all despised Stephanie because she still looked exactly like she did in high school. I mean, I'm still fine and all for a woman who has had two kids. I got the flat stomach back, but just haven't been able to find those ripped abs again.

"Why aren't you all in your bikinis yet? We *are* in Miami, ladies!"

Kim and Rachel ran to hug Stephanie then Kim replied, "We need our drinks before we do anything."

Rachel chimed in, "I hate you and that little bitty waist! Now I really need a drink!"

Stephanie giggled as she turned to pull drinks for each of us from the bar.

"Rachel, you need to stop with that cute shape of

yours, girl! Shoot, I wish I had those big legs. Ya know a man don't want no bone."

"Well, if I can have that twenty-four pack you are still rocking, baby girl, you can have these thick thighs."

As we sipped on our drinks, Rachel turned to me. "So, Geena, how in the world did Stephanie trick you into a vacation this year?"

"Well, Rachel, to tell you the truth she helped me realize it was time to get away."

Rachel raised her glass then motioned for us to join her. "Well, I know all too well about needing to get away from it all. Everybody deserves a vacation. So, let's drink to that." We fell out with giggles of laughter then sipped some more.

Glancing at her watch, Rachel asked, "So what's up for the remainder of the day?"

Stephanie looked around from the mini bar where she was pouring herself another drink and said, "Well, my friend Robert that I told you about has already made an appointment for us to have manis and pedis at four this afternoon. We have a full body massage at six. It's only two now, so I guess we could grab a bite to eat then head on over. I saw a Cantina downstairs near the lobby and I heard they have the best veggie enchiladas. We can get something there."

We all looked at Stephanie confused, then Kim asked, "Uhm, excuse me but who is Robert?"

"Oh, he is my Miami friend that I met on Facebook. He's going to show us around while we're here. You know Miami has had a few more hot spots pop up since we've been down, and I'm trying to hit every one of 'em."

"Stephanie!"

"What, Gee?"

"Have you lost your mind?"

"What do you mean?"

"I am, no, WE are not going anywhere with Robert that you met on Facebook! He could be a fool."

Kim and Rachel burst out laughing.

"Geena, calm down. Robert is a really cool dude. We chat almost every single night, and we've exchanged pictures and everything."

"Ya'll chatted and exchanged pictures. What? When are ya'll going to realize how dangerous that Facebooking mess is? Didn't you see the pictures of that girl who met a guy on Facebook and he came to her house and killed her?"

"Geena, that wasn't true. It was just something that a non-Facebook user made up trying to deter people from using it."

"Yeah, Geena, and what about the fact that you are able to connect with people you haven't talked to in years? Kim and I have been in touch with girls that we were with in elementary school."

"My point exactly. If you haven't talked to them since kindergarten, what difference is it going to make now? And on top of that, it's messy. Folks trying to figure out whatchya got, whatchya don't, starting rumors and trying to take ya man."

Stephanie took over the conversation. "Well, I love it, Geena! Facebook has been very beneficial for me, and I, for one, am happy that it's around. Because of Facebook, I'm able to meet nice guys like Robert who should be here in just a few minutes." I immediately started putting on my shoes.

"Wait! Geena, what are you doing?"

"I'm leaving. Girl, you are not going to have me down here away from my husband and my children and I get killed…" All three of the girls started rolling around on the bed wailing with laughter. "What's so funny?"

"Geena." Stephanie had to catch her breath from laughing so hard, holding her chest as if she was having a heart attack. "Calm down, put ya Louis back down, chile. You're not going anywhere."

"Yes I am. I don't play with that…"

"We know, we know, you don't do Facebook and you hate for us to use it too, so that is why we planned to trick you!" They all started laughing again. "There is no Robert. We just made it up to see how you would react and sure enough, you reacted exactly how I thought you would… like a damn fool."

"That's not funny, Stephanie." I was mad at them for tricking me. They knew how I felt about that social networking mess, but I couldn't stay mad long 'cause they were laughing like some hyenas. After a few minutes, I started to giggle too. "Well, I guess it was kinda funny." I grabbed a piece of ice from the bowl on the dresser and threw it at Stephanie. "I can't stand ya'll."

"Awhllll, well we love you too, Geena, now go get that teeny-weeny bikini on and let me see what all of that working out has been doing for ya!"

Kim and Rachel stood up, still trying to compose themselves long enough to make it out of the door. Rachel took her room key from the dresser, struggling to speak. "Okay Steph, Geena, we're out. That was so funny! Oh Lawd! That Geena is serious about not using Facebook. Girl, you are a mess. We'll see ya'll in a bit. This is going to be an awesome week. I can feel it already."

Lunch and pampering was awesome! We all had a great time catching up, laughing, talking, and of course, gossiping! It was getting late so we all decided to get back to the hotel so we could change and get ready to go out for our first night in Miami, minus Robert! It had been a very long time since I went out to a club and I was kind of apprehensive, but of course I had Stephanie there to help me on my way.

Raw Reality
Chapter 3

Although I fought tooth and nail for years to avoid vacationing with my friends, I had to admit I was having the time of my life. I was clubbing, drinking, hanging out, and having a ball doing all things that I never really do anymore. I felt like I was in college again. For three nights in a row we hit the club scene, and I loved every minute of it. I danced so much that my hair had lost all of its luster and had to be pulled back into the infamous "Frances ponytail." I didn't know it at first, but this night would be the night that would change my life forever.

Sitting at the bar sipping on my favorite blue bottle of Moscato, I bobbed my head to one of my favorite songs, *So Fly*. By the time I took the last sip from my glass, the bartender came up and set another one in front of me and said it was compliments of the gentleman sitting across the club. I was shocked and pretty blown away to tell the truth. I had never experienced anything so sexy. I smiled and asked the bartender to send my regards to the nice gentleman. As the bartender turned to walk away, the girls came back from the dance floor.

"Hey, Gee! Whatchya sippin' on, girl?" Rachel asked as she sat down on the bar stool beside me.

Smiling, I replied, "I am enjoying my second glass of Moscato Di Asti that a nice gentleman sent to me from across the club."

"What? A nice gentleman? Now I have been walking around this club all night, eye-balling different dudes and ain't nobody bought me a drink yet! Who is it, Geena? Where is he?"

As we all giggled at her craziness, I responded, "I don't know, Rachel, calm down! I paused and looked around the room, but I didn't see anyone. I decided to just sit back and enjoy it. Besides, I'm not here to meet anyone."

They all sang in unison, "Because you have a husband at home. We know, we know."

Now Stephanie and Kim were single, but Rachel had been married just as long as Jared and I had, but you would never believe it when hanging out with her. Since the day she married, neither of them really respected their wedding vows. She had "friends" on the side and was always hanging out with the girls. I never understood her relationship with her husband because my belief was that married folks just didn't' do certain things.

"Hey, Steph, I've been meaning to ask you what's up with Rachel and Ced? Are they still together?"

"Girl you know how they do. Ced is still up to his mess, so Rachel just does her thing."

"Does her thing?"

"Yeah, she has her friends... he has his friends."

"Wait, so she is staying in a marriage knowing that her husband is cheating on her?"

"That's exactly what I mean."

I paused and look around the room in disbelief. "So if they are both cheating, why stay in the marriage?"

"They stay to save face. You know Rachel wouldn't hear the end of it if she left Cedric. Her cousin is sitting back waiting on that day, so she can say 'told ya so!' And you know Rachel is not about to have that."

"That is so sad."

"What do you mean sad?"

"To be in a marriage where there is no love left." I had to stop because I started thinking about my own marriage and the game of charades I had been playing. Wow, I guess it happens more than I thought. What happened to being happily married and in love?

"A lot has gone on that you know nothing about. Come on. Let's go to the lounge so I can fill you in."

Rachel reminded most people of a beautiful African goddess. She was short in stature with gorgeous dark skin and thick kinky hair. She always stood out from the rest of us and was not shy to make herself known with her loud mouth and vivacious personality. In the past five years, she had opened three shoe boutiques and was doing very well for herself. Looking at her, you would think she had it all together in all aspects of her life, but the act that Rachel put up about her marriage was just that: an act. She was miserable in her marriage and remained in it only to prove a point.

Rachel's husband had been caught cheating on her on multiple occasions and in order to somehow pay him back, she had reasoned that she needed to fight fire with fire. She was tired of being used and treated like a doormat.

Rachel met her husband, Cedric, while he was already in a relationship with another woman. The other woman just happened to be Rachel's cousin who was pregnant with his child. Cedric and the cousin were having some relationship issues and constantly argued and fought about anything under the sun. She didn't like the fact that he stayed out late with his friends, drank, and smoked; he didn't like the fact that all she wanted to do was spend money. The two of them weren't compatible at all and anyone that spent any time with them could tell. Each day that passed pushed them further and further away from one another until finally they found themselves in a relationship that was spiraling towards a dead end. The daily arguments proved they had nothing in common with one another, and the fighting had begun to escalate to the point where the cousin had become violent. Being that Cedric wasn't a man that believed in hitting a woman, he would push her away to avoid fighting her back. The fights became so frequent that he found himself getting mad enough to actually hit her back. To top everything off, they were about to share the load of parenthood. Living together had become unbearable and they both hated the sight of one another. Cedric had even started to leave the house for days without coming back home just to get some relief.

Rachel's cousin had started to confide in her about her relationship woes. She eagerly searched for answers to the many questions that danced around in her head about Cedric and where their relationship was headed. She told Rachel how she continuously begged Cedric to stop drinking and to spend more time at home with her, but his response to her would always be that he was young and didn't want to be tied down. Rachel was aware of how easily influenced her cousin was by others and how she set her goals according to someone else's dreams and aspirations. She only wanted to do what she saw worked for others, hoping she would reap the same rewards without putting in the same amount of work. One of her friends opened a day care center and was very successful at it, so Rachel's cousin started putting in the legwork to open one too. Another friend of hers started an in-home cooking service and was very successful at it, so she closed down the day care center and tried to start one as well. Rachel tried on numerous occasions to help her cousin figure out what she was good at, find her passion. She explained to her she could do what she really wanted to do and be successful at that because copying somebody else and chasing their dream wouldn't work for her.

Due to the direction the relationship was headed, Cedric was only concerned with getting paid on Friday and how much he could spend shooting pool and betting on cars at the race track after work on Friday night. The daily discourse was almost unbearable for Rachel's cousin. She found herself losing weight and her physician told her she was doing an injustice to her unborn child.

Often times, she would ask Rachel to talk to Cedric to see if she could figure out where his head was. Did he want the relationship or had too much damage been done to even try to repair it? Rachel didn't want to get in the middle of their relationship because she knew how those situations played out. One minute they hated each other, then the next they were ready to walk down the aisle and she didn't want any part of that confusion. Rachel told her cousin to try to work it out on her own. The cousin insisted that she help because Cedric had turned a deaf ear to her lips. After listening to her cousin gripe and moan for so long, Rachel decided she would try to help them sort things out.

Rachel and her friends often frequented one of the bars down town each weekend to have drinks and play pool. One night after work, she noticed a guy walk into the bar that resembled Cedric. Cedric was a big guy, tall in stature and built like a professional boxer so he stood out in a crowd. As she adjusted her eyes to figure out if it was him or not, she realized that it was definitely Cedric as he went to sit alone at the bar. The bartender was giving him a shot glass and a bottle of Remy. It looked like there was something bothering him, so she figured this was a good opportunity for her to talk to him about her cousin and their situation. She walked up and tapped him on his shoulder to get his attention.

"Hey, Ced. What a surprise to see you in here tonight. How are you?"

Cedric turned his attention away from the Remy bottle and towards Rachel. "Hey, whassup, Rachel." He took a deep breath. "If you want to know the truth, I'm not doing so good."

She could tell he was frustrated and very upset, so she decided to go deeper. "Well, what's wrong? If you don't mind me asking."

"Man, what's not wrong? It seems like the more I try to do right by your cousin, the further apart we push each other. You know how she and I fuss and fight. There is never a day that I can come home from work and have a peaceful conversation with her. Every day she is nagging me about something or other. It is sad that when the bell rings for my workday to end, my co-workers are happy and excited about being able to go home.I am the only one left with a sour taste in my mouth because I would rather stay at work! She wants to question me about my drinking even though my drinking is linked directly with what I am going through with her. At least when I drink I can tune her out and just pass out till the next day. I think it bothers me so much because I promised myself that after I left my parents' house, which was filled with bitterness, arguing, and discourse, that I would make my home a place of solitude. I understand that in certain situations I will have to deal with chaos, and I am cool with that.

I can accept the fact that I may not be able to have peace at work. I can even accept taking BS from the jokers that are there, but in my own house I feel like I deserve to have peace. And you know as well as I do that as long as I'm dealing with ole' girl,that may never happen.."

Rachel tried to get up on the side of the bar stool beside Ced to take a seat, but her short legs wouldn't allow her to do so.

"You need some help getting up there?"

Embarrassed, she replied, "Well if you don't mind."

To find clarity with what Cedric was saying about her cousin, Rachel asked, "What was the argument about this time, Ced?"

"I don't even have to tell you Rachel, it's some of the same ole' stuff. She wants to make all of these Big Girl purchases with Little Girl money. She has this idea that I should give her my paycheck each week to do what she wants to do, and I don't agree. Maybe if she showed some type of responsibility I would reconsider, but as of now, no deal!" Cedric poured another shot of Remy. "Then she wants to gripe and moan about how I choose to spend my flow and I am tired of it. She compares herself to those women that she hangs around with and I tried to tell her that wasn't a good idea. I warned her that she was going to let them talk her right up out of her relationship. with all of that, 'my man does this' and 'my man does that.' I wanted to tell her if she was so in love with what their men are doing for them, then she might need to get with them. I have told her over and over again to stop comparing me to those dudes. Evidently, those women are handling their business like they should, and maybe if she handled hers, things would be different. She wants to get married and have a large family, but doesn't know how to balance a checkbook. She'll spend her last dime on a pair of shoes, shopping online, and breaking her neck to go out of town. As long as we have been together, she has never been able to save any money. Check this. Now, she wants to buy an $80,000.00 car, and we are renting a house. Her priorities are all jacked!"

" Cedric, look, every woman wants a man that is going to support her, physically, mentally, financially, and spiritually. We need that safety net. We need to feel like we are wanted and appreciated. Once we are secure in our place, a real woman will make sure you are the king of your castle and you rule over the kingdom."

Cedric sat in silence before taking another shot. He gave Rachel's comments time to soak into his head then he stated, "See, Rachel, I need a woman like you."

Rachel was stunned; she lost her breath at the thought of Cedric's comment. "Hold on, Cedric. What do you mean?"

"I mean what I said, Rachel. You know I have always admired how you handled your business, being one of the popular girls in school, going off to college, opening your boutiques, and just being a successful sister. And from what you just said to me, you know how to treat a man."

To change the awkward twist in the conversation, Rachel explained, "We all have flaws, Ced. None of us will ever be perfect. In relationships, it is all about finding someone that accepts you for who you are and is willing to help you grow past any shortcomings.It is not important what a person has or can give, but how two people can bring out the best in one another."

Cedric explained to Rachel that he understood what she was trying to explain, but he didn't feel like her cousin was going about things like she should. As far as Cedric was concerned, it just didn't seem like she would ever change. And what made matters worse was that they had a baby on the way. He expressed how much he wanted to be a father, but he just wished he could re-pick his baby's mother. Cedric poured himself another shot before he continued. As he did so, Rachel asked him if he was planning to leave her cousin. As another shot went down, he gazed into Rachel's light grey eyes and responded, "Yes, tonight was the last straw. I have taken all I can take."

"Hold on, Cedric. What about the baby?"

"I'm going to do what I am supposed to do when it comes to my baby, but taking care of my baby has nothing to do with her."

Rachel's jaw dropped as she looked up at the ceiling wondering how she could tell her cousin about this meeting. Surely she would be crushed, devastated, and in total shock. She had already been dealing with too much. She was losing weight, battling depression, and now this? Rachel didn't want to give her cousin that kind of news while she was pregnant.. She was supposed to be meeting Cedric in the hopes of changing his mind. What had gone wrong? Although Rachel was appalled at what she was hearing and wondering how she should respond to him, instead of replying she just remained silent and continued to listen as he poured his heart out. Cedric didn't stop there. He continued to confide in Rachel about many of his innermost secrets. As the night continued and the drinks kept flowing, Rachel and Cedric shared the ins and outs of their relationships, giving each other intimate secrets from relationships in their past.

This conversation was the first of many to follow that started their close friendship. After a few months of being friends and continuing to learn more about one another, Cedric finally made the decision to move on without Rachel's cousin, so he packed his things and moved out of the house that he shared with her and baby-to-be and moved in with Rachel.

It was madness from the jump. Rachel's cousin couldn't believe the chain of events that had taken place. Towards the end of the cousin's pregnancy, Cedric and Rachel flossed around the city like they were the next Will and Jada Smith. Everywhere they went, they made a statement and it infuriated Rachel's cousin to hear the reports that would find their way to her ears night after night. She was a control freak and and decided she would do everything in her power to try to make Rachel and Cedric's relationship a living hell.

Once the baby was born, the dynamics of Rachel and Cedric's relationship took a critical turn. They were starting to argue a lot because Rachel didn't trust Cedric to go visit his child without her coming along, and since Cedric lived with Rachel, Rachel's cousin wouldn't allow the baby to come over and spend time with Cedric. She gave Cedric specific instructions not to have her baby anywhere around Rachel, so it became a continuous struggle for Cedric to see his child. Of course, this made him angrier and caused a great stress on his relationship with Rachel.

He was almost at his wits end with both of them and Rachel knew that he was about to throw in the towel. From the many heart-to-heart conversations she shared with Cedric, Rachel knew how much he cherished his child and understood that she was about to lose him because of the constant tug of war, so she decided to back down and let him start going over to see his baby. Plus she had started to feel guilty about how he wasn't able to bond with the baby because of the differences she and her cousin had with one another. Trying to be the bigger person, she agreed to step back and let him handle his business. Rachel had a lot to deal with in this relationship because ever since she and Cedric moved in together, she had not communicated with her cousin about anything that had gone on. It was almost like she was trying to avoid seeing her in the hopes that time would help to diffuse the situation.

Each time Cedric would get ready to visit the baby, it would infuriate Rachel. Although going into this relationship she knew it wouldn't be easy, she was becoming more and more insecure with each visit. She noticed how each time he would go visit, the visits would take longer and longer. But in order to try and keep the peace, she remained silent and never questioned him about the amount of time he spent over there.

One Saturday morning, Cedric got up and asked Rachel if she wanted to take a jog together then go out to have breakfast. She had just finished washing and twisting her hair, which was a three-hour job and really didn't want to mess her hair up all over again. However, just to have some alone time with Cedric, she opted to join him. A morning run was nothing unusual for the two of them being that they both were big on appearance and enjoyed working out. After they got back home, showered and started to lounge around the house, Cedric received a phone call. He got up and walked out of the room to take the call which made Rachel suspicious because he had been doing this for the past few weeks. He was gone so long that Rachel eventually dosed off to sleep. It was around 1:30 when she was awakened by Cedric nudging her to tell her he was about to go spend some time with the baby and would be back in a couple of hours. Rachel was pissed by his sudden need to go visit because it was interfering with her plans with him. She learned that day the true meaning of "grin and bear it."

As soon as he pulled out of the garage, Rachel called Kim to pick her up. She needed to get out of the house before she blew a head gasket. Kim obliged her, picked her up, and they went shopping to try to get her mind off of Cedric's visit with his baby. While they were out, Rachel decided to go lingerie shopping to surprise Cedric with a romantic night with him once he came home. He loved to see her in white lace panties and *Victoria Secrets* had the perfect pair. Rachel and Kim were having so much fun they decided to have dinner and drinks after shopping, but while sipping on her apple martini, Rachel noticed the time; it was getting late and time for them to go.

"Wow! Where did the time go? It's almost 10 p.m. I am so ready to see Cedric. Come on, Kim, let's go."

Riding down the street, Rachel and Kim's favorite song came on the radio. Rachel turned the radio dial up loud so she and Kim could sing along with the song. As they pulled into the driveway and opened the garage door, Rachel noticed that Cedric's motorcycle was not parked in its place. She instantly felt an empty feeling come into her gut, telling her that something wasn't right. She sat there in Kim's car allowing all kinds of crazy thoughts to run through her head. She turned to Kim and asked her to please drive her over to her cousin's house. Kim hesitated before driving back out of the driveway, asking Rachel if she was sure she wanted to do that. With all the pain that filled her eyes, Rachel looked at her and said she did.

The closer they got to the house, the emptier the pit

in Rachel's stomach felt, her heart ached, she started to perspire and felt like she was about to lose the spinach egg rolls she had eaten earlier that evening. As she suspected, Cedric's motorcycle was in the driveway. To add insult to injury, the lights were off inside the house. Rachel sat in the car, staring at the motorcycle in silence. It actually looked like her small body was sinking into the seat. It was so quiet in Kim's car that the absence of words had made a cold and cloudy film appear on the car windows.

Kim finally broke the silence. "Rachel, are you okay?"

At that very moment, tears filled Rachel's face like the water from a rainstorm filled a pond. "No, Kim, I'm not okay. I cannot believe Cedric would do this to me! After I trusted him! Gave him his space like he asked me to! Respected his wishes and supported him in being a good father! I should have known that this trick would use his love for his child to her advantage! All of those extended visits and private phone calls."

Kim then tried to convince her that things may not be as bad as she thought. "Well maybe they are sitting in the back of the house and the baby is asleep so they turned the front lights out trying not to wake him."

Rachel looked at her. "Well if that is the case, why in the hell is Cedric still over here? He is supposed to be visiting his child, not his trifling ass baby mama."

Before she could even register her thoughts, the rage of a scorned woman made her sling the car door open and head for the front door of her cousin's house.

Rachel was pissed off. And she was also devastated by Cedric taking her heart and stomping on it with these actions. He had taken her trust and torn it into shreds after she was finally able to work through her insecurities. Once at the door, she pounded and rang the doorbell continuously as hard and as loud as she could, not caring that it was late and it may disturb the neighbors. In her heart, she prayed that Cedric would answer the door to fill the void of her insecurities, but that wasn't the case at all; instead her cousin answered the door in a short little robe showing off Cedric's name that had been tattooed on the top of her inner thigh. This added fuel to the fire.

"Oh, you must be here for Cedric? Just a minute. He's rocking our baby to sleep."

She turned and called for Cedric. Rachel then saw her cousin's naked body as her robe swung partially open. Rachel became livid, pushing her way through the door and knocking her cousin on the floor. It seemed as though she was walking through a spinning tunnel trying to make her way to the bedroom with her heart pounding and tears forming in her eyes. When she finally got to the bedroom, the lights were out, and the darkness was disorientating. Rachel was trying to focus, but all she could see were tea light candles all around the room. Rachel stood there squinting and trying to look for Cedric. There he stood, trying to hide in a corner, jumping up and down with one leg in his jeans, trying to get the other one to go in. To make matters worse, the baby wasn't even in the room. Emotions took over and Rachel charged after him, her small body flying across the bed and landing on top of him. Her tiny fists pounded on Cedric's chest, her nails scratching his bare chest as she cried and screamed, "HOW COULD YOU DO THIS TO ME? I TRUSTED YOU!"

Shortly after, her cousin stormed into the room flipping the light switch on, yelling at Rachel to calm down before she broke something in her house. By this time, Kim had made her way into the bedroom trying to get Rachel off Cedric. When she finally calmed down, she continued to cry and ask Cedric why. He was silent, of course, standing there like a lost puppy, looking simple and clueless, not uttering a single vowel to plead his case. Then all of a sudden, Rachel's cousin walked up to her and got right in her face, full of sarcasm.

"Oh, you're crying now? Poor, poor Rachel? So now you're hurt? Upset? Disappointed, maybe? Let me guess. You are embarrassed and heartbroken? Yeah, I know each of those feelings all too well! 'Cause you see, cousin Rachel, I have had to wear those same shoes you are standing in and have had to walk in them for the last seven months! No matter how hard I tried to pull them off, they would NOT escape my feet. She got choked up. "It has been hard and I have hated every minute of it. There have been times when I couldn't even raise my head from my pillow because of the tears that felt like weights holding down my face, binding me to sadness. I couldn't stomach the thought of food and even water was hard to keep down. I was unable to love and nurture my newborn baby like I wanted to because each time I looked into his eyes, all I could see was Cedric. I think that was my breaking point."

Rachel's cousin sat down on the bed, picking up the baby's receiving blanket that was hanging on the bedpost, clutching it, holding it to her chest. "How could I allow my love for a man take away from the love I am to give to my child?"

She looked up at them before she continued, "To think that my own cousin would connive and scheme to have the one man on this Earth that I have loved and cherished for as long as I can remember. I have been so pissed at you, Rachel, because I shared with you my innermost secrets about him, how I wanted to spend eternity with him, how I wanted to have his babies, and how I prayed for the day that I would be his wife. You have sat with us, laughed with us, shared special moments with us, and this is what I get in return? Your betrayal did more than hurt me, Rachel. It crushed my spirit and I had no life left inside of me. You are my FAMILY! Our mothers are sisters and on top of that, you were supposed to be my friend."

She turned to Cedric, and sarcastically stated, "I hope she is worth it and I hope BOTH of you get all you have bargained for. The pain that I have experienced made me very angry, and that anger soon festered into bitterness. I was so bitter that I started to allow my life to go into a downward spiral and I was headed towards destruction until someone saved me.

"About two months ago, I met an older lady at a church function that I was forced to attend for work. The lady took one look at me and asked if she could pray with me. At first I was reluctant, but out of nowhere, I felt a calmness that reassured me that it was okay. Never has anyone ever done that and in that instant, God moved me. During that prayer, I was allowed to let GO of the baggage that was weighing me down. Many nights I prayed that the two of you would live a life of sorrow and that God would keep His blessings far from your reach. After I was able to acquire a strong prayer life and relationship with God, those prayers soon changed. I understand now that God will fight my battles and He can take care of any situation far better than I ever could.

"You see, it took some time for me to realize that I don't need you to be a good mother to my child. I understand the dynamics of family and yes, I would much rather raise him in a household where the father is present, but at the same time I don't want to raise my son to live a lie. You hurt me, Cedric, and for the first time in my life, I was broken."

"I know that things were not the best in our relationship. I know that there were things that we BOTH could have done better, but when you told me you loved me, I believed you and I thought you meant forever. When I met you, I never would have imagined that you would put me through this kind of pain. One thing is for sure, through this ordeal I have come to truly know God for myself. I can openly and honestly admit that my heart was torn to shreds, but by God's grace, my heart has been mended and I have no doubt that I am going to love again. The hardest thing for me to deal with has been forgiveness. For how can I forgive the two people that I trusted the most, but let me down the hardest? I had to come to grips with forgiveness, and even with all the pain I endured, I am able to forgive you.

"I used to think forgiveness would be a gift to the two of you, not understanding that forgiveness was for me. Now that I forgive you, I am no longer bound. Forgiveness is inevitable, but a relationship with the two of you is optional. And for that reason, a relationship with either of you is no longer needed."

She stood and took a manila folder from her nightstand and handed it to Cedric. "Here are your child support papers. I was going to let the case worker mail them to you, but I decided to give them to you myself."

She walked to her bedroom door signifying that she had made peace with the situation and was ready for them to leave. As she stood there with her arms folded, still gripping the baby blanket, she stared back at Rachel and with tear-filled eyes, she added, "I do not want to EVER see your face again."

The night of the big fight, Cedric wanted to explain himself but Rachel was too emotional to hear him. Rachel told Cedric to leave and she would have his things boxed up and ready for him to pick up sometime later in the week. She could not stomach his betrayal. She replayed the night in her head over and over, wishing that she had never agreed to his meetings and private phone calls. But she realized that being a 'Monday morning quarterback' saying what she could have or should have done wouldn't change the position where she then stood. That night she had to do some self-reflecting. She was confused, hurt, and disappointed because of Cedric's decision to treat her the way that he did. Trying to do the right thing had backfired in her face and left her with a broken heart. She felt that her efforts were pointless and his actions unwarranted. She tossed and turned all night wondering if she deserved what had happened to her. Was she really at fault for the demise of her cousin's relationship with Cedric? Was Karma paying her a visit? Tears soiled her pillow as she was reminded that love was tricky and it wasn't always fair. She couldn't help that she loved the man that once loved her cousin. Each time Rachel tried to pack Cedric's things up, she would find herself back in a pool of tears, missing his voice, his touch, his smell, and his smile.

Rachel was drowning in her self-pity, not able to function like she needed to. After a few weeks had passed, Cedric started sending her flowers, putting notes in her mailbox, and sending messages to her through some of their mutual friends. As mad as she was, Rachel started to miss Cedric and, against her better judgment, she called Cedric to come over so they could talk. Once he arrived, they talked, argued, and disagreed. He apologized over and over again for what had happened. He told her that hurting her was never his intention and that he wanted to make it up to her. As the weeks passed, Rachel's anger lessened and Cedric's visits to her house became more and more frequent. After about two months or so had gone by, Cedric surprised Rachel and asked her for her hand in marriage. She didn't even hesitate with a response of yes. Although she had lost all trust in him, she agreed to marry him because she felt like their union would somehow signify a win for her and a loss for her cousin.

With all the drama Rachel and Cedric had going on, they went forward with the ceremony. Early on in the marriage, Cedric was caught cheating again and again and again. Rachel started checking behind him, following when he went out with his friends, checking his voicemail messages, and accusing him of sleeping with any woman that he held a conversation with. She finally realized that cheating was a part of who Cedric was and that he had no plans to change. Although it killed her to think of how he lay with other women, she couldn't bear the thought of losing him. Their break ups and make-ups had become like a ritual because they did it so often.

***

I had never understood how Rachel could remain in a marriage where she knew her husband had outside women and disrespected her. Rachel told us she would stay in the marriage forever even if she was miserable. Her union to Cedric, in her mind, made her feel as if she had won and her cousin had lost. But in essence, she was the loser. We all thought she was crazy for marrying him with all they had gone through, but she assured us that this was what she wanted.

I sat there for a second allowing what Stephanie had spilled out to me. to register in my brain. I couldn't believe that Rachel had gone through so much. Now I was able to understand why she behaved the way she did. I felt sorry for Rachel. Learning about her situation reaffirmed that when people behave in a certain manner, nine times out of ten, there is a reason behind it. How awful is it to live a lie? Stephanie looked at her watch and motioned for us to finish our drinks and rejoin the girls at the bar. When we arrived, they were standing in the same place where we left them. Kim turned to ask what took so long. I told her that we walked to the restroom and got sidetracked talking with some ladies about some nearby outlets and restaurants.

Rachel started looking around the room and pointed out some guys that she met on the plane coming to Miami.

"Hey ya'll! There go my boys, Travis, Ray, Dee, and Nard." As she waved at them, they began walking towards us.

I was thinking, *WAIT, four of them and four of us, not a good combination.* Before I could get up and get away, they were standing in front of our seats.

"Good evening," the guy named Dee said to each of us, giving a special smirk to Rachel as if he already had plans with her later that evening. We all smiled then engaged in small talk. I didn't say much because I really wasn't interested in getting to know these men. I was in Miami to kick it with my girls and relax before I made it back home.

Embarkation
Chapter 4

The next night, we went back to the same club because evidently Rachel wanted to run into the plane guys again. This time I had something for them though. While they walked around in search of their new-found friends, I took a seat at the bar in a corner, alone. I was hoping I would fade into the background and not be bothered by anyone. I ordered my usual and began to sip and enjoy the music. I was having a ball watching Stephanie, Rachel, and Kim on the dance floor. You couldn't tell those girls they weren't jamming out there. I sat in my seat laughing inside while watching them make fools of themselves; out of nowhere, the bartender from the night before came to give me another drink from a gentleman from across the room. This time, I was drawn by curiosity so I asked the bartender if he could point out the "secret Santa."

He smiled and told me, "The gentleman asked me not to, BUT I can let him know that you are requesting to know who is being so generous."

"Okay, I guess that's fine. I would like to say thank you to him for being so kind."

The bartender smiled and walked away. Fifteen minutes had passed since I had heard anything else from the bartender, so I figured the drink dropper would remain anonymous. As soon as I lowered my head to take out some cash for the tip, I could feel someone walking towards me. I lifted my eyes to see the bartender standing in front of me in his street clothes. In his bartending get up he looked like a regular ole' guy, but in his True Religion jeans and white V-neck tee he looked kind of scrumptious.

"Excuse me, Ms.?"

"It's Mrs."

"Oh, it is. Please accept my apology, I didn't see a ring on your finger, so I wasn't aware you were married."

I had taken my wedding ring off to make sure I wouldn't lose it while I was out; I had lost a few pounds for my trip and my ring was slipping on my finger.

"Yes sir, I am, is there something I can do for you?"

"Well…. wow, this is embarrassing."

"Embarrassing?"

He took a deep breath and looked around. "Yes, uhm… you asked me to send a message to the nice gentleman that was sending you drinks, so I was coming back to let you know that I was the nice gentleman."

I was stunned; the bartender was trying to hit on me. Lord, and how cute of him to say that a gentleman from across the club was sending me the drinks. I hadn't ever dated a white guy, but this bartender looked a lot like Chris Cuomo from Good Morning America, and I love myself some Chris Cuomo.

"As flattered as I am, and believe me, I am flattered, but I am a married woman, so I couldn't..."

"No, no, no, there's no apology necessary. I understand."

I extended a handshake and money for his tip. "Well thank you for your generosity and kindness."

He took my hand, turned it over, rubbed his thumb across a few times then gently kissed it. "You can keep the tip, and I really hope you accept my apology. I am very, very sorry."

I tried my best to reassure him that I was okay. As a matter of fact, I thought it was pretty cute.

"I promise you, it's no problem."

He stepped back preparing to walk away. "Well, goodnight, Mrs."

"It's Mrs. Howard, but you can call me Geena."

"Geena? What a beautiful name." He looked up with one eye closed then looked back at me. "Your name stands for genuine beauty, did you know that?"

I blushed. "No, I did not."

"Well it fits you perfectly because, my sweet Geena, you are a beauty. I must leave now. Have a nice night, and enjoy the rest of your stay in Miami."

As he was walking away, Steph, Rachel, and Kim were coming over to check on me.

"What was that all about?"

"What? Talking about White T?"

Rachel put her hand on her hip and replied, "No,

I'm talking about Whitey."

"Girl, stop it! How about that. It was the bartender!"

Kim jumped in. "What! Stop it, Geena! The tall doofy lookin' dude with the black vest and bowtie?"

"Yes! That was him, I'm not lying. That penguin outfit doesn't do him any justice, but doesn't he look like my boyfriend?"

"Your what?" Rachel interjected.

"She's talking about Chris Cuomo," Stephanie answered with her mouth turned all up.

A light went off in Rachel's head. "Oh, the anchor that used to be on Good Morning America? I hated it when they took him off. I don't even watch it like I used to. That Chris is a sexy ole' something."

"Well he was my mystery Moscato man."

"No!"

"YES! Stephanie. Tried to holla, too!"

"What?"

Laughing and talking with my girls, I caught a glimpse of someone that I hadn't seen in a very long time. I was moved to silence as I sat and watched my first love, my high school sweetheart, the man that I planned to spend the rest of my life with, who I had not heard from, heard of, or any of the sort since I met my husband and got married. Steph noticed my sudden change in demeanor and asked what was wrong. All I could do was point. She looked but said that she couldn't see anything because it was so dark. There was just enough light shining on his face from the dance floor to see exactly who he was. I knew that face from miles away.

"No, Steph, not anything. It's someone."

I pointed again, this time moving her face over to where mine was. After she adjusted her eyes a bit, she spotted him, sitting with a group of men, talking, having drinks, and laughing from time to time.

"Geena! That's Michael!"

"Yes, Steph! It is! I wonder what he's doing here. In Miami? At the club? The same club that we're in?"

"Calm down, Gee!! Hold your horses. Why, oh why are YOU, Mrs. Married, acting so giddy about Michael? What would Jared say?"

I wasn't really paying any attention to Stephanie because I had my eyes glued on Michael.

"Geena, wait, please don't tell me that you are still in love with that man after all these years, a marriage, and two babies? What is up with you?"

"I don't know, Steph. I haven't even spoken to him yet and I'm already about to hyperventilate."

"Wait! Did I hear you say you haven't even spoken to him yet?"

I sat in silence for a few seconds unable to put my finger on what I was feeling, but whatever it was, it had me warm. I had tingles all over my body. The emotion that had taken control of me was one that I had screamed for in silence at home for my marriage.

"Geena! Hey, hey, hey! Earth to Geena. Are you okay?"

"Yes, Stephanie, I'm good." By this time, Rachel and Kim started to wonder what we were whispering about.

Kim asked, "Hey, what's with all the hush hush?"

"Geena here has spotted her first love across the room over there and she is in a trance."

Rachel joined in the banter. "No! Michael Sullivan is not here! Mr. MVP himself! Where is he? It's been years! We should all go say hello!"

"No!" I screamed.

"Wait a minute, Gee! Didn't you just say you wanted to say hello? Well, here is your opportunity!"

"I won't know what to say to him after all these years."

Stephanie yanked me by the arm, pulling me towards Michael. It was a tug of war between Steph and my bar stool because I was holding on for dear life. After she realized the bar stool was about to defeat her, she let me go and walked over to talk to Michael without me. As I watched them all converse, I remembered what love was like with Michael. At that moment, my heart began to press against my skin for a simple hello. However I tried to hide. I was hoping that he wouldn't turn around to see me andwishing that I had a Genie bottle near that I could rub and instantly escape the events that would follow next. Of course, none of those things happened and, in a matter of seconds, Michael was walking my way. I sat in my seat like a piece of stone. Not a muscle on my body moved. I watched as the distance between us became shorter and shorter. When he arrived only inches away from my seat, all I could focus on was the smile that had once made a sweet innocent girl grow into a woman.

"Geena! I cannot believe out of all the people in the world I would come to Miami and run into YOU." He reached down to hug me asking how I had been. As he hugged me, I closed my eyes, living in the moment. "What have you been up to?" As he continued to talk, all I could do was stare at him. Somehow all of the giddy girly feelings that I had for this man close to fifteen years ago all came back instantly. I was blown, had no words to express what I was feeling, and I stared in amazement at this beautiful structure of a man. As he took the seat beside me, he touched my hand and I melted like a piece of chocolate that had sat in the sun on a warm summer day. We tried to talk over the music, but it wasn't working so he asked me if I would like to get some coffee so we could get out of the loud club to talk. I don't know where all of my morals went, but I watched as they marched out of the door. I agreed to leave with him, and I had no regrets about my swift decision.

"Uhmmm, could you hold on for a few minutes, Michael? I need to speak with the girls before I leave."

As I walked towards them, I had to clear my throat and make noises to get their attention because they were so intertwined in conversations with Michael's friends.

"Hey, Stephanie. Uhm, Michael wants to take me for coffee so I'll meet back up with you girls later on tonight."

Stephanie looked at me, smirking, and I knew all too well what that smirk meant. "Well, Ms. I'm going to get coffee. It's already two in the morning. What time do you plan to get in?"

"Steph, come on, it's not like that. He just wants to talk, and all I want to do is go listen."

"Okay, Mrs. Jared Howard, I will see you in a little while after you talk with Michael over coffee."

I hugged her neck before walking back to meet up with Michael. Everything in me was telling me that this was wrong, but it felt so right.

Excuses or Explanations
Chapter 5

The next morning, I tried to sneak back into the room, hoping Stephanie would remain asleep. I tip-toed to the bed and tried to slide in without her waking. But as soon as I pulled off my heels, slipped off my clothes, slid into the bed, and lay my head on my pillow,Steph sat straight up in her bed like an alarm had gone off.

"Uhhmm, where in the hell were you all night long?" I sat up on my side to answer her.

"I was out catching up on things with Michael."

She then got out of her bed to join me on mine. "What all did you catch up on?"

"Well, we talked about a little bit of this and a little bit of that."

I guess my sarcasm and huge Cheshire cat smile annoyed Stephanie by the way she snapped at my answer. "Geena! Stop playing and tell me what happened. Where did ya'll go? What did ya'll talk about? WHAT did ya'll do?"

"Okay, Stephanie! Goodness! Calm down, I'll tell you. Michael escorted me to his car and we drove about twenty minutes out to a small quaint coffee shop that was empty and quiet. We laughed and talked about things that I honestly had forgotten about like prom, football games, and all of the silly things we used to get into when we were in school. He made me laugh and it felt really good to have a man laugh with me again." I paused to see Steph's reaction, hoping she didn't catch the 'laugh with me again' statement, but like I thought she would, she did.

"Wait, excuse me. What do you mean, have a man laugh with you again? Are there problems in the promised land with you and Jared?"

I really didn't want to go into detail about Jared and I so I just played it off like everything was fine. But in my head, all I could think of was the joy Michael had given me in the few hours I had spent with him. I was happier in those few hours than I had been with Jared in the past few years. Michael made me feel like a woman again that night.

"Uhmm, no. I didn't mean it like that. Jared and I are fine. It's just different with Michael because he knows how to make me giggle and have a good time. You know how everything with Jared is so business-like." I had to hurry and change the subject before Stephanie dug any deeper. "Anyway, Steph, I had a great time and Michael is doing so well!" I sat up on the bed to continue. "And get this! He is the CEO of a Fortune 500 company. He has a home out west, and he still loves to work out, which is apparent since he is still as fine as he was when we were in school. He serves on various boards in his community, he's single and he doesn't have any children!"

Stephanie stood up from my bed and walked to the window before turning back around to me. "Geena! Slow down! Okay that sounds good and all, but uhhhmmm, why does the fact that he is single and doesn't have any children excite you?"

"It doesn't excite me, and stop judging me! I'm talking to you as a friend, a sister, why am I getting so much flak from you?"

Stephanie realized she was upsetting me so she changed her tone and sat back down beside me on my bed. "Okay, Gee! You're right, my bad. Tell me some more of this good-good!"

"Well, it was amazing. We talked four hours straight, catching up on old times. He was great company." I paused before I made my date announcement. "Matter of fact, Michael has invited me out for another date today. I only have two more days here in Miami and I would love to kick it with ole' MVP."

Stephanie stared at me with a look of uncertainty. "Uhmm, you're gonna do what now?"

"Michael is picking me up around noon, or so, and we're going to spend the day together."

"Geena, are you certain this is something you should do? I mean what about your life back home? Do you think Jared would be okay with this?"

"Stephanie, look, I didn't say I was going to elope with Michael. We are only going out to see a few sites, grab a bite to eat, and catch up a little more.

Remember, Steph we were more than lovers. We were true friends. He helped me grow to be the woman I am today and I appreciate that. I just want to hear more of what he's been up to and…"

Before I could continue, Stephanie cut me off. "Okay, Geena, no more explaining. You get some rest. I know you don't want him to see you with those huge potato sacks under your eyes, and do something with that ponytail too. You're walking around here looking like Frances after a basketball game. I'm meeting the girls for brunch and shopping. I guess we'll talk with you later."

I smiled at her as I lay my head on my pillow for a brief nap. "Thanks, Steph. I'll call you later."

Not more than a few hours had passed before I heard what sounded like someone trying to break into my room. I awoke to my cell phone almost jumping off of the nightstand as it vibrated from one side to another. I jumped to answer it.

"Hello?"

"Did I wake you?" I had to gather myself and clear my throat before I could continue the conversation.

"Hey, Michael, I was just about to take a shower. What's up?"

"I was just calling to find out the best time to pick you up."

"Uhhmmm, it is about noon now and I know we said noon but I overslept. I'm sorry. Would 2:00 be okay?"

"Cool. I'll be out front waiting for you at 2:00."

"Okay, I'll see you then."

After I put the phone down, I fell back onto the down comforter on my bed smiling thinking about the first day I met Michael. I tried my best to drift back off, hoping to get rid of what was left of the potato sacks Stephanie had warned me of. No matter how much I tossed and turned, I couldn't fall back to sleep. I couldn't get up from the bed and I couldn't move. The longer I lay in that spot, the more I began questioning myself. What was I doing, planning to spend the day with my ex? Was spending this time with Michael really a good idea? Did Stephanie's concerns have some validity? Should I call him back and cancel? All of these questions continued to float around in my head like a bird circling the sky. I finally forced my way to the shower so I could get dressed, still thinking. *I'm about to spend the day with Michael. He's just a friend. There can't be too much harm in that.*

Date... Destruction... Delight
Chapter 6

As I walked down the stairs to the foyer of the hotel, I could see Michael standing with his back towards me looking down at the coy fish in the lobby aquarium. He was dressed to impress just like I knew he would be. Michael was voted Best Dressed for our senior class and from the looks of it, he hadn't lost his swag, with his khaki and cream seersucker slacks, olive-colored short-sleeved Oxford and tan Cole Haan loafers. He stood over six feet tall with broad shoulders, long lean legs, and muscled arms. I wanted to surprise him so I slowly tip-toed my way behind him.

As I approached, I whispered, "Are you waiting for someone, sir?"

Michael turned to look at me with his creamy pecan tan skin, neatly trimmed beard, and thick curly hair. His warm eyes lit up as he looked at me from head to toe. "Geena, you look beautiful."

I knew I was looking good. My freshly flat-ironed hair was sweeping my shoulders, my make up was soft and sexy, hiding those sacks Stephanie had warned me about, and my lips were glossed. My shoulders and back were accented with warm copper undertones from my body lotion, and my strappy sandals were showing off my nicelytoned legs.

"Thank you, Michael. You're looking pretty dapper yourself."

"Well, shall we go and start our day?" Michael opened the door, being the gentleman that he always was.

"Yes. Thank you, sir, I am ready!"

Walking to his car, I felt like I was walking on a cloud. I hadn't felt this way in a while and it felt good to have that feeling again. Michael took me to an amazing restaurant that had a gorgeous view of the ocean. Spending time with him again was a dream come true. My mind was far from reality, and I didn't mind at all.

"So, Geena, what's next? Would you like to go site-seeing, to the galleria, or the beach?"

I smiled from ear to ear just for the simple fact that he was giving me so many options.

"You know what, Michael, how about we just go with the flow? The day is young and we have all night."

Michael winked at me and stood to push his chair away from the table, then came around to pull mine out too.

"Sounds like a plan. Come on, little lady. Let the festivities begin."

We left the restaurant and went riding around West Miami. As the hard top dropped down on Michael's black-on-black Mercedes, our designer shades went up, signifying it was time to ride. He took me to some of the resorts that he was part--owner of and some of the land he was in negotiations to purchase. Michael was indeed successful and very accomplished. We then went to the galleria where he purchased a red one-shoulder dress and a black strapless dress for me. I watched as some of the ladies in the shop marveled at the way Michael and I shopped together. That was another thing I had always loved about him. He didn't mind spending time shopping with me. He liked to watch me try on clothes, and he always gave his honest opinion on what worked and what should remain on the rack in the store. After all of the dress shopping, I picked out a sexy pair of heels to match the red dress and we were on our way to our next destination.

Later that evening, we ended up on the beach with a bottle of wine, sipping, talking, and watching the sunset. I was enjoying Michael's company a lot, but I had a burning question that was about to singe a hole in my throat if I didn't get it out. After a few moments, I finally broke the silence.

"Michael, would you mind if I talk to you about something and ask you a few questions?"

"Not at all. What's up?"

"Well, first I want to thank you for an awesome day. I really enjoyed everything and I appreciate you for taking this time out with me. I'm so proud of your many accomplishments. I knew even back in high school that you were going to be successful. All of the dreams we shared came true for you, but I can't help but wonder about something. What happened to the wife and kids you had written into your plans?"

"Well, Geena, if I can be totally honest with you, after we broke up I never really found any woman that could take your place. I dated a lot of nice young ladies and even loved a few. No matter how much I tried, I couldn't find anyone that could fill the void when you left me. Along with that, I vowed I wouldn't have children with any woman I couldn't foresee being my wife. So you see, my Sweet Geena, my heart still belongs to you."

I was totally shocked to hear Michael talk that way because it wasn't the answer I was fishing for. I sat there unable to believe what he was saying. Could this be true? After all these years, he had saved himself for me? All I could do was lay my head on his chest. I closed my eyes as I let the cool breeze dance across my face and allowed his words to sink in. I don't know what happened but I felt a shift in my heart. I was falling in love with this man all over again. After a few minutes passed, I raised my head, sat up and looked him in his eyes.

"Michael, you mean after all these years, you're still in love with me?"

"Geena, I never stopped loving you and I never will." Michael sat up straight and put his wine glass down before he continued, looking directly in my eyes. "When I got word that you were married I was pretty upset.No, let me be honest,.I was devastated. When I heard you had kids, I was even more heartbroken because you marrying and having children with someone else meant I would never have the chance to make you my wife. After a few years of dealing with other women and realizing they weren't you, I knew in my heart that someday I would find you again and that I would make you my wife."

"But, why? How? I mean, I don't understand. You never told me how you felt."

"No, Geena. I told you how I felt. You just chose not to listen. I can still remember the day like it was yesterday. You had just finished your last class, and you were preparing for graduation. We talked about marriage. I suggested you start your career before we got married, save some money in an attempt to make our lives as secure as possible before taking it to the next step. Remember that?"

I could remember it like it was yesterday. "Yes, Michael, I remember, but you weren't being fair! Why would you make me jump hoops in order to be your wife? If you loved me and wanted to be with me, have a life with me, why didn't you JUST marry me?"

Michael took me by the hand. "Geena, it's not that I didn't want to make you my wife, I just wanted to make you the happiest wife in the world. I witnessed firsthand how so many of my friends got married early, had children early, and had to struggle to make ends meet. I didn't want that for us, so I figured my plan was the best, but found out later that my plan got me put out of the running."

"Michael, you're right, and now I can remember that day like it was yesterday. You HURT me and the pain was unbearable. I felt like you were making excuses and trying to find reasons to leave me. You had moved away, started doing well for yourself, and I felt like our lives were moving in two different directions." I felt myself welling up with tears, my heart was pounding through my chest, and my throat began to close as I continued to express my feelings and get some understanding. "As time passed, it felt as if our love drifted farther and farther apart until one day I just couldn't take it anymore. I knew that it was over and faced the fact that it was time for me to move on. After everything was said and done and we broke up, I had about a year before my degree was complete. I took that year to really find out who Geena was and what would be best for me. For so long, I did what I thought was best for everybody else, putting myself on the back burner. When I went off to grad school, that was when I met Jared." I dropped my head and closed my tear-filled eyes as I thought back to that time in my life. "I never thought I would see you again."

Michael reached with his index finger to lift my head. "Well, Geena, I'm here."

Michael pulled me close, taking me into his arms and I melted. He held me tight and I embraced him more. The compassion was real and my feelings were true. After a while, I had to tear myself away from his grip.

"Well, Michael, what am I supposed to do now? I'm married, I have two children, and I have a wonderful life. What am I supposed to do?"

"Geena, listen, I'm not asking you to do anything, I'm here to tell you where I stand. I still love you like I always have, and to be frank with you, I will never stop."

Silence filled the space between the two of us.

"Michael, for the past few years, I've asked myself why? Why didn't we work out? Why did you leave me? Why did we allow the relationship to fade? I thought you had gone on and just forgotten about me and to hear you say that you love me, it's just... I don't know."

Michael looked into my eyes with a sweet calmness to reassure the anxiety building in my heart. "Come on, Geena, let's go. I have something to show you."

"Where are we going?"

"Somewhere we can talk out of the elements,. It's getting chilly out here and I think we have a lot of unresolved issues that we need to deal with."

Without any reluctance, I agreed with him. "Okay, let's go." We took a ride about fifteen minutes away from the beach and arrived at a beautiful villa.

"What's this?"

"This is what I wanted to show you. This is one of the properties that was owned by one of the first partners in my firm. It's been refurbished and now is used as a guesthouse for myself and my colleagues whenever we're in town. This is where I'm staying for the week. Let's go up, have a drink, and continue our conversation."

We walked into an enormous foyer ordained with marble floors, a winding staircase, and a chandelier that was fit for royalty.

"Michael, this is beautiful!"

"Thanks, Geena, come on in and have a seat while I make us a drink."

As he walked towards the kitchen, he stopped and turned on some soft music. I sat waiting for him, anticipating what was about to happen next, anxious but excited at the same time. The room was gorgeous. The ceilings were twelve-feet high, the furniture was plush and comfortable, the walls were painted a deep cranberry, the paintings on the walls looked like murals, and the atmosphere was smooth and soothing. I felt like I was sitting inside a magazine cover for Better Homes and Gardens. As I was admiring the scenery, Michael walked back in wearing a smile that could captivate anyone's heart.

"Here we are, sweetheart, a glass for you and one for me. Now where were we?" I started to speak, but was cut off by Michael answering his own question. "I know. We were here." He held his glass up to toast. "To Geena, the woman that captured my heart over fifteen years ago and never let it go."

Michael tapped my glass and sipped some of his drink while I sipped from my glassand we stared into each other's eyes. He then pulled me close to him in the dimly lit room. He closed his eyes as he enjoyed the melodies softly ringing from the system. I continued to sip on my wine, nestling my head on his shoulder.

"Michael."

"Yes, Geena?"

"I still love you, too."

I could feel my body warming up to his. As our eyes met, our lips soon followed. Taking our glasses and placing them on the table in front of us, Michael began to kiss me. With no hesitation, I kissed him back. Before I knew it, his hands were all over me and I watched as he undressed me with his eyes. I felt alive and vibrant. It was a feeling I hadn't experienced in a very long time.

His soft lips ran down my neck as his strong hands ran up the middle of my tingling thighs. My white strapless dress didn't stand a chance with all that was going on in the room that night, and I knew it would soon be on the floor. The smell of Michael's cologne was putting me in a trance, taking me back to a time in my life where love was all I needed. His soft skin felt warm and I loved the way it felt rubbing close to mine. He stood, staring back at me with his light brown eyes, unbuttoning his shirt and exposing his broad chest and chiseled abs. I was in awe of this perfect specimen that stood right before me and the anticipation of what was about to happen next was killing me. As I reached out to touch him, he pushed my wrists back, pinning them to the couch as he continued to run his tender lips from my chin down my neck to my exposed, full and sensual breasts. I could feel my body explode wanting more of him. He took his knees and parted my legs, pressing the weight of his body on top of mine. I could feel his erection as it grew harder and longer, making me spread my legs even wider. He flipped me over on top of him, placing my legs around his waist as if he was a horse and I was the jockey. He continued to undress my sex-craved body with his eyes while using his hands to complete the deed. Once our bodies were completely naked, Michael was inside of me, fitting perfectly, like a hand in a glove. We became inseparable, our love for each other oozed from our bodies and in those moments we became bonded just like we had been all those years ago, while our hearts were caught somewhere in the middle.

The next morning, I awoke to the sun shining on my face through the shade of the upstairs window. I could hear pots and pans clanging in the kitchen. I grabbed Michael's short-sleeved Oxford shirt from the chair and went to the restroom to freshen up before walking downstairs. As my foot took one step after another, I could see him standing in the kitchen cooking breakfast. Before I could utter a word, I stood in amazement at how much I still loved this man; after all these years I actually still had true feelings for him.

"Well, good morning," Michael called to me as he turned to catch me watching him.

"Hey, Michael. Good morning." I walked over to him, standing behind him in front of the stove, peeping to see what he was cooking.

"Did you sleep well, Geena?" I reached my arms around his waist, resting my head on his broad, smooth back.

"Yes, sir, I did, but how did I end up in the bed upstairs?"

"I carried you up after you fell asleep down here."

I smiled girlishly thinking about the events of the night before as I pecked him on the cheek to thank him for the deed.

"What do we have for breakfast? You have it smelling good down here."

"We have a little bit of this and a little bit of that." I smiled remembering how we both used to use that phrase. He turned away from the stove to look at me, taking me by the hand. "Has anyone ever told you how sexy you are?" I tried to hold back from blushing. "I know what you like, Geena, so I've got you covered. Take a seat over there and breakfast will be served in a few minutes."

I was impressed. Me being spoiled? All I get at home was, 'I'm hungry! When are you gonna cook? Are you finished yet? How much longer?' Being with Michael, I was in another world where I was the star of the show. I had to admit that it felt good. Coming to the table, I couldn't help but stare at his shirtless body as he placed plates of fresh fruit, wheat toast, and scrambled eggs before me.

"This looks great, but aren't you going to join me?"

"No. I had a protein shake already and I have a meeting at noon. So you enjoy while I get cleaned up.

I'll be back as soon as I can." Michael pecked me on my lips before heading towards the stairs. He turned and winked at me before he was completely out of my sight.

My breakfast was delicious. I couldn't believe that he remembered my favorite breakfast meal after all this time. After I finished, I walked upstairs to talk with Michael while he finished getting dressed. I love a man in a suit and I especially love one that can wear it like it was made for them. I took a seat on the ottoman in front of the bed.

"So, are you taking me back to my hotel before your meeting?"

Michael answered me as he laced his shoe. "I figured you could just chill out here. I'll only be gone for a few hours. When I get back, I'll take you then." He stood to look into the mirror, adjusting his navy and grey polka dot bowtie, which was the perfect accent to his grey suit, while looking back at me. "Are you okay with that?"

"Sure, I'm cool, if you're cool." I smiled at him for reassurance.

Once Michael left, I lay across the bed looking at the ceiling, thinking about the night before and how good it felt to be in his arms again, and how alive he made me feel. Soon I drifted off to sleep.

I faintly heard a door open and keys falling down on a table then footsteps coming near me. A few minutes later, I felt tugging at my leg.

"Hey, Geena, wake up, babe."

I turned around to find Michael holding a bouquet of fresh flowers in front of his face.

"Michael! How sweet of you. They are gorgeous!"

Michael placed them in my hands then sat on the bed next to me.

"And so are you." I blushed as I smelled each of the flowers, as if I was looking for a different scent to come from each one. "Passing the florist, I saw them in the window and had to stop so I could bring them to you."

"Thank you, Michael. I really appreciate this."

"I couldn't think of a more deserving woman. What would you like to do today?"

"I don't know, Michael. Surprise me."

After answering his question, I immediately thought about the promise I had made to Stephanie. What was she going to say about this? I didn't want to break my promise to my girls, but I really wanted to spend some more time with Michael. We decided to have lunch and walk along the beach before I arrived back at my hotel to meet Stephanie, Kim, and Rachel. Knowing she would be upset with me, I decided to contact her once I was on my way back.

Bittersweet
Chapter 7

A s Michael drove me back to the hotel, I picked up my cell phone to call Stephanie. I noticed that she had been calling and texting me for the past four hours. She let the phone ring a few times before she answered; I guess it was to pay me back for staying away for so long.

"Hello?"

"Hey, Stephanie."

"Geena! Girl, where are you?" I could hear the attitude in her voice.

"I'm on my way to the hotel, and I just wanted to make sure you were there alone."

"Yes, I'm here alone. How long will it be before you arrive?"

"I'll be there in an hour or so."

"Hurry, Geena, because we need to talk."

"Oh, Stephanie, talk about what? I'm just having some fun, so stop with the 'we need to talk' stuff. Okay? I'll be there shortly, hold tight."

Driving closer to the hotel, Michael's conversation began to die down. I turned to him to make sure he was okay. "Are you alright? You've been quiet for the past twenty minutes."

"Everything is fine. I'm just thinking of some way to make you stay with me tonight." I giggled at him.

"Oh, Michael, you know I have to get back to my friends. They're gonna be so mad at me for coming on this trip with them and spending so much time with you. Besides, I need to start packing and get myself together to go home."

He drove in silence until we were in front of the hotel. Once the car stopped, he turned off the ignition and then looked directly at me.

"But that's just it, Geena. I don't want you to go home." I was stunned.

"Michael, you know I have to go home. What are you talking about?"

"Geena, I'm talking about us! I don't think it was a coincidence that you came to Miami the same week I was here on business. You said yourself that you haven't taken a trip like this for the past ten years or so. You admitted to me that I made you laugh and feel free again. And on top of everything else, you told me you still love me."

I didn't know what to say. I turned my head and looked out of the window trying to gather my thoughts, then looked back at Michael.

"I do still love you and I realize now that there's nothing in this world that can change that. We have history that can never be erased, but I also have a life that I can't escape."

Michael took my hands. "Geena, I don't believe

that's true. I think you can escape. I love you, Geena, and the past few days with you have proven to me that I'm supposed to be with you. I know you're married, I know you have a family and a career, but that doesn't erase the fact that you're supposed to be my wife. We made decisions that placed us in the positions that we stand, but that doesn't mean we can't make some new ones."

I couldn't take it anymore; I turned to open the door! Michael was saying too much too fast and I needed to escape! Before I could get my feet out of the car, he reached over to stop me.

"Geena! Wait. I'm sorry. I didn't know how else to express myself, please accept my apology if I am being too direct."

"Michael, I don't know how I'm supposed to feel now. I thought we were old friends, spending time together to catch up and have a good time. Things did go a little deeper than I anticipated, but we're adults so I didn't think it would cause such a stir."

"Geena, I thought the same thing, but making love to you reminded me of what I was missing. It was more than just sex to me, Geena, and you know that. It was a mental connection, one that I've never felt with any other woman."

"Michael, I didn't mean to belittle the situation. I know that we have a strong connection, but I can't relinquish the fact that we can't go further than we have. I've got to go."

"Wait, Geena, take my card and hold on to it; please

promise me we'll at least keep in touch."

I sat there, holding the card, staring down at it, then turned to look at him. "Michael, I just don't want to..."

He cut me off before I could complete my sentence. "Geena, promise me."

I took a deep sigh, looked him in his eyes, and assured him I would keep in touch, although in my heart I knew it would be impossible once I got back home. "You have my word that I will be in touch." He smiled and kissed my cheek.

"Would you like for me to walk you up to your room?"

"No thank you, Michael. I really need to get upstairs so I can prepare for my flight tomorrow. Take care, and it was great seeing you again. Miami was a great idea after all." I leaned in to give my last goodbye, kissing his soft lips for the last time. "Thank you again for everything. I will never forget it."

Going up the elevator I anticipated the million questions Stephanie was about to ask me. I needed answers fast so I could be quick on my feet! As soon as I walked into the door, I greeted Stephanie with a huge hug.

"Hey Steph!" Her hug was not as huge as mine.

"Okay, tell me all about it, where did you go, what did you do?"

"Well."

"Wait a minute, Geena! I haven't seen that kind of smile since high school, what's really going on, Gee?"

"Nothing! We just chilled out, talked, you know,

just caught up on life." She looked at me sideways, her eyes filled with disbelief. I knew that she was about to call me out on it.

"Okay, that is what ya'll supposedly did the day before. So you want me to believe that it took two whole days for ya'll to catch up? What else did ya'll catch up on?"

"Girl, please. I am a married woman." I couldn't keep a straight face when it came to Stephanie. She knew I wasn't telling the truth. "Okay, Stephanie, don't judge me when I tell you this. Please!"

"I won't judge you, Geena. Now come on with the come on!"

"Girl, Michael made love to
me like it was the first time. It was passionate, it was hot, it was sexy, and it was all that any woman could ever want or need. I realized spending time with him, Stephanie, that I still love him."

"You still WHAT? Wait, you mean you love him like in a Jesus way, right?"

We both burst into laughter. "No, crazy! I love him, Steph. I love him just like I did all those years ago. Michael is special and he will always have a place in my heart."

"Hi ho silver, hold on now! Did you forget that you have a husband, miss 'I got Love Under New Management'?"

"No. I didn't forget that I have a husband or children. I am completely aware that I have a family. All I said was that I still love Michael, and that doesn't mean that I can't love my family, too."

Stephanie snapped her fingers like she was trying to wake me from a dream.

"Earth to Geena! Can you hear yourself talking? How can you love your husband and your ex-boyfriend? I don't have a husband or a boyfriend and even I know that can't be possible!"

"Yes it can, Stephanie. My heart is big enough to love both of…"

Stephanie cut me off before I could go any further. "Wait, please don't tell me you plan to keep this up. You did say sayonara to Michael before he pulled off, didn't you?"

"Of course I did. He just begged me to keep his card and reach out to him from time to time. He knows that what happens in Miami STAYS in Miami."

"Uhhm no, Gee. That's Vegas. You ain't in Vegas." We burst into laughter, falling on the bed.

"Come on, start packing. We have a lot to do before the morning.Plus the girls are on their way over to have dinner with us so we can all say goodbye."

"Stephanie, look this is between us. Please don't tell them about Michael and I."

"Geena, do I look crazy?"

"No, but you look like someone who will tell my business so I am reminding you not too!" Stephanie picked up a pillow from her bed and threw it at my head.

"Hush, Geena!! Your lil secret is safe with me."

The Plane Ride Home
Chapter 8

"Ready to head back home, Geena?"

"Yes, I am. Thank you for talking me into coming, Stephanie. I really needed the time away, and I'm so glad I came."

We hugged as she responded, "That's what friends are for. Have you called Jared and the girls?"

"Good looking out. Let me call them before the announcement is made to turn all electrical devices off."

Jared answered the phone on the second ring. "Hello?"

"Hey, babe."

"Hay, Geena," he sarcastically stated. "It's so good to hear from you. You girls must have really been having a good time the last few days there because I didn't hear anything from you." He caught me off guard with his response. I had to be quick on my feet with an answer.

"Yeah, we've had a great time the entire trip. We did a few tours, and we got some massages, hit a few beaches and just enjoyed girl time."

"Well that's good, sweetheart. I'm glad you have

enjoyed yourself and even happier that you're on the way home. The girls miss you like crazy too. Hold on, here they are staring at me." I was so excited to hear my babies' voices in the background.

"Let me speak with them."

"Mommy!"

"Hey, sweetness, how are you?"

"I'm good, we're good. Daddy took us to the zoo, we went shopping, we had a picnic in the park, we helped him with the dishes, we met his friend Ms. Sharon..." All of a sudden, she went quiet as if the phone was snatched away.

"You met who?"

Jared's voice came back over the line.

"Hey, Geena, I'm late getting the girls to practice, we'll call you from the car. Love you, babe."

The phone signal went out. I sat holding the phone repeating over and over. "Ms. Sharon." Who in the hell was Ms. Sharon, and why did Jared snatch the phone away from Frances? Steph was already starting to doze off so I had to nudge her.

"Stephanie, wake up, listen. I was talking to Frances on the phone and she was going over everything they had done while I was away, and she mentioned someone named Ms. Sharon. When I was about to question who Ms. Sharon was, Jared took the phone away and quickly hung up."

Steph sat straight up for me to continue. "So, why didn't you call him right back?"

"Well, he said he was on the way to take the girls to

practice and they would call me back so I'm going to give him a few minutes."

Just like I thought, the loud speaker came on from the cockpit. "Attention passengers."

I whispered to Stephanie, "Oh well, guess I'll have to wait a little longer than a few minutes."

"Gee, try to relax. Close your eyes, and before you know it, we'll be back home so you can see your girls and talk to Jared then."

"You're right, Stephanie. I'll do just that." After closing my eyes, I couldn't get Frances' voice out of my head. Who was Ms. Sharon and why did Jared have my children around some woman that I didn't know? The more I tried to rest, the harder it was for me to do so. I decided to read a bit hoping it would calm my nerves so I picked up my tote to get my book. Michael's business card fell out onto the floor. I stared at it thinking. Michael. I took it from the floor and stared at it for a while till Stephanie turned her head in my direction and noticed what I was doing.

"Geena, I thought you were going to rest?"

"I was, but I couldn't so I decided to read a bit. When I reached for my book, his card fell out."

"I thought you said you were gonna leave well enough alone!"

"I am, Stephanie. Having his card doesn't mean I'm going to have his baby- Goodness! Lighten up a bit. I mean, I guess it's okay if we just remain friends like Michael suggested."

"Geena, you know as well as I do that being friends

with your ex, who you still love, is NOT a good idea. It's too close for comfort,.Bad things are gonna happen, Geena. Mark my words; you need to leave well enough alone."

"Stephanie, trust me. I know what I'm doing." By this time, the light came on allowing the usage of electrical devices.

"Geena, go ahead and call Jared."

"Good! It's about time! Here goes nothing."

I called Jared's phone six times only to get his voicemail.

"Stephanie, he isn't answering the phone."

"Call him back!"

I must have called him at least eight more times and still didn't get an answer. I sat there boiling over in my seat. I couldn't believe he wasn't answering his phone. I picked my book up from the floor and grabbed Michael's card. Steph snatched the card away.

"No, Geena! Do not call that man!"

"Why not? Jared isn't answering. He's probably on the phone with Ms. Sharon anyway!" I snatched the card back. "I am CALLING!" Dialing his number, I was apprehensive about the kind of reaction I would receive.

"What's up?"

"Uhm, Michael?"

He responded with great excitement in his voice. "Geena! Hey, baby, how are you?"

"I'm good. I hope I didn't catch you at a bad time."

"No it's never a bad time for you to contact me,

Geena. Where are you?"

"I'm still on the plane about an hour away from home. I couldn't sleep so I decided to give you a call."

We talked on the phone until it was time for us to land, laughing and reminiscing of the time we shared while in Miami.

"Well, Michael, I have to hang up now. It's time for us to get off the plane."

"When will I hear from you again?"

"Uhm, I'll try to call you back tonight." I hit myself on the forehead as soon as I said it. *How am I going to sneak on the phone to call him while I'm at home?*

"Promise me, Geena."

"Promise you?"

"Yes... I want you to promise me you will call me tonight even if it's to say hello and goodnight."

I couldn't believe I was setting myself up this way. "Okay, Michael, I promise."

"Have a safe landing, Geena!"

"Thanks, Michael."

"I love you, Geena."

My stomach quivered as I replied, "I love you, too."

Stephanie couldn't wait till I got off the phone with him. "You love him, TOO? What do you mean you love him TOO? Geena?"

I had to cut her off before she went on and on and we ended up being the last ones off the plane. "Look, Stephanie, it's time to get our bags. Let's go!" I hoped she would drop the conversation all together. After we got our bags and headed out of the airport, I could see my girls making their way through the crowd, running to meet me. Their arms were stretched wide, and they had balloons and flowers in their hands. Once they reached me, I was plastered with what felt like hundreds of sweet kisses.

"Did you girls miss me?"

"Yes, Mommy! We missed you so much."

Jared walked up behind them with the silly grin that I had grown to despise over the past few years. He hid behind his sports shades so he could avoid looking into my eyes. He leaned in to give me a kiss, but I gave him a look letting him know that we needed to talk and there would be no kissing until that time.

"Hi, Jared."

"Hey, Geena, we missed you." He pulled me away from the girls to hug me. I really wanted to knock him on the floor, but for the sake of my girls, I hugged him back and quickly turned my attention back to Lily and Frances.

"You girls will not believe how much Mommy missed you. Where's the car?"

Jared responded with the hopes that I would give in and talk with him. "It's parked around the corner, you ready to go?"

I didn't even look up at him. "Yeah, let me tell Steph goodbye. Could you take the girls and go get the car then drive around here?"

"Sure!"

"Girls, go with your daddy and I'll be ready in a few minutes."

"Yes, Ma'am." As I walked back to the double doors, I could see Stephanie coming out.

"Hey, did you see your family?"

"Yeah, they are going to get the car." We hugged, saying our goodbyes.

"Okay, girl. I had a blast, and I'm so glad you decided to go with us."

"I'm glad I came along too, Steph. It was a much-needed trip."

"You better get a move on, Jared just pulled up with those gorgeous girls of yours."

"Okay, I'm going, but look, Stephanie, I need you to give me your word that you will never breathe a peep of what happened in Miami to Jared or anyone else."

"Geena, I told you before, you have my word. Come on. I'll walk you to the car."

Jared stepped out to open the car door for me. "Hey, Stephanie, I heard you girls had a ball in the M.I.A."

"Yes, as a matter of fact we did. You and my little nieces didn't lose your minds while my girl was away, did ya?"

"We missed her, but we managed to keep it all together."

I turned to look at her with a smirk. She knew I was thinking about Ms. Sharon.

"Give me another hug, girl! I'll call you later."

Back Home…Back to Reality
Chapter 9

After getting the girls down for bed, it was time for Jared and I to finally finish the talk from earlier.

"So, Jared, can you tell me who this Ms. Sharon is that the girls had the pleasure of meeting while I was away?"

"Ms. Sharon is one of the new associates at the firm. She started this week and, as you know, I'm responsible for integrating all of the new hires that are new to the area. Since I had the girls with me at work a few days while you were away on your trip, they met her there. She was really nice to them and they liked her a lot."

"Does she know they have a mother?"

"Of course she knows about you, Geena. Come on. What's wrong with you? You never act this way?"

"No, I don't but it just threw me for a loop and I was shocked to hear Frances say she met Ms. Sharon and you know how I am about my children being around other women. Ever since the time we had the incident when Frances was going to daycare with your ex-girlfriend's son."

"Come on, Geena! Don't go there. That was forever

ago, and we have moved passed that."

"Correction, you have moved passed it! I still can feel that pain like it happened yesterday."

About seven years ago, I found out that Jared and his ex-girlfriend, Ebony, were meeting for lunch and spending a lot of time together while I was completing one of my certifications. He was being the good fatherbytaking and picking our baby up so I wouldn't have to do anything but focus on the certification. Lo and behold, while I was studying my butt off for the cert, Ebony was studying my every move in order to capitalize on my being away from my family.

One of the young girls that worked at the daycare, Keeta, was known for running her mouth. She was a character with her Dora the Explorer scrubs, purple weave ponytail, cherry-red lipstick and big gold hoop earrings that had dollar signs in the middle. I was shocked that the daycare manager even hired her with all the tattoos she had up and down her arms, but I guess the most important thing to management was how well she took care of the children, and the children adored her.

As I entered the daycare to pick up Lily one afternoon, I saw Keeta standing in the entrance window reapplying her lipstick. I tried my best to avoid her because I was in a rush and didn't have time to waste chit-chatting. As soon as she looked up and saw me come through the door, her eyes lit up like a kerosene lamp.

"Mihh. Howard, is that you?" She never was able to

get the "Mrs." out of her mouth quite right. I was trying to walk as fast as I could past the window trying to avoid the chatter so I just threw my hand up to wave and said, "Yes, how are you, Keeta? It's been a long time. Is my baby ready to go?"

"Yes ma'am, she just finished her snack and now she's watching TV with the other kids."

"Okay, well let me get in here so we can get out. I have a busy evening ahead of me. It was good seeing you again."

Instead of letting me be on my way, Keeta started putting her cosmetics bag away then stood to follow me to walk down the hall into the baby room. "It's really good to see you, Mihh. Howard, and I must say, you look really good with all that's going on."

I stopped in the middle of the hall and looked at her, trying to understand what she was talking about. "Excuse me?"

She put one hand on her hip and the other on my shoulder, leaning closer to me and whispered, "I mean, most women that lose their husband to someone else are really bitter, faces all frowned up, mean to everybody, don't want to talk to nobody, just angry. But look at you, coming in here looking good, all professional, make-up flawless, hair sweeping all down ya' back, take it from me, Mihh. Howard, it won't be hard for you to find a man. I can promise you that!"

I stood there with a lump in my throat trying to figure out what this girl was talking about, why was she talking to me as if Jared and I were no longer a couple? I had to catch myself before I exploded, I had to keep calm so I could get some more information so I just played it off and played along. "I'm maintaining, Keeta, I have to, for my daughter's sake."

"That's what I'm saying, Mihh. Howard, see I look up to women like you, ya know, with ya fancy degrees and stuff. I have a cousin right, her old man left her for this other chick and she just lost it! I'm talking about stop combing her hair, started eatin' like a pig, gained a whole bunch of weight, wearing nothing but big ole' t-shirts and sweats every day, looking a hot Damn mess. I tried to help her, but ya know some people just can't be helped. I guess the difference between you and her is that you got your stuff together, with your big office job and fancy clothes and cars. Yeah, see you don't need a man to be happy. I'm more like you, yeah, I been to school too. I told my cousin to enroll in the nursing program with me. I've been in now for about eleven years. I'll be finished soon though. I'm just working at the daycare until I can get my financial aid back on track."

"Oh, that's good, Keeta. Uhm, how is Mr. Howard doing? I haven't had a chance to talk to him lately."

"Your ex? Oh he seems to be doing well to me. He ain't skipped a beat, come in here all suave and stuff. You know how he do it. Tell me this, Mihh Howard, how well do you get along with the new girlfriend? Ya'll talk?"

My heart dropped to my toes, my head began to

hurt, and my knees almost gave out, my stomach filled with knots. His girlfriend? I had to get out of there, get to Jared, and get some answers. It took everything in me to keep my composure. "Hey, Keeta, let me get in here and get out. I'm going to be late. It was good seeing you again."

"You too, Mihh. Howard. You take care now."

Evidently, Keeta thought Jared and I were separated because she hadn't seen me at the daycare in so long since I was studying. It must have been meant for me to go to the daycare that day and talk to Keeta. Otherwise I may have never found out.

I later heard the truth from Jared. His ex-girlfriend, Ebony, had a son in the same class as Lily. Jared and Ebony saw each other from time to time when dropping off or picking up the kids. One afternoon, Ebony had asked Jared if he and Lily would like to join the two of them for a bite to eat. Eventually, they started making plans to take them to the park, movies, and various restaurants near the school. I was dumbfounded after hearing all of this. My husband, who I had made vows with before God, was taking his ex-girlfriend around, not considering if people saw him or not. It was the lowest blow I had ever received.

Jared and I had argued and fussed and almost came to blows. I was just furious with him! How dare he play house with my child! How dare he jeopardize my reputation! How dare he do this to me! Jared pleaded with me for weeks to forgive him. It was a hard road, and although I tried my best to forgive him, I never could. I wasn't able to relinquish the fact that people thought I was no longer his wife and that this chicken-head girl was my replacement! I thought long and hard about being a single mother; it was something I never wanted to be. I decided to stay with Jared for my baby's sake. I didn't want her to grow up in a home like I did with one parent here and the other one there. I wanted her to have stability at home if she didn't have it anywhere else, in the hopes that stability would spill over into all areas of her life. So I stayed. Unhappy, but I stayed. We argued about Ebony for close to a year before I realized I was giving this imbecile power. From then on, I vowed to never bring her up again and Jared gave me his word that an episode like that would never happen again.

Now, Jared and I found ourselves rehashing the Ebony ordeal once again because Ms. Sharon had surfaced.

"Geena, I know that's still a thorn in your side, but it seems like all I have done is soothe the pain. I need for you to tell me what to do in order to take it away."

I really didn't want to discuss it any longer, so I walked away andheaded upstairs to the bedroom. After a few minutes, I heard the office door close. Soon thereafter, I drifted off to sleep. After about an hour or so, I woke up to use the restroom. Walking back to the bed, Michael crossed my mind. *I thought, I gave him my word that I would call him, but should I? With all that's going on with Jared and I, should I complicate things more?* I lay in the bed watching the clock contemplating whether or not I should make that phone call. As the time got closer to midnight, I decided to at least call him to say goodnight. I got up, took the card from my reading book, and called him. My heart began to beat faster and faster as the phone rang. Then finally, he answered.

"Hey, Geena!"

"Hey! How did you know it was me?"

"Let's see, modern technology allows us to take phone numbers and save them in our phones." We laughed together.

"Oh, so you saved my number, did you?"

"Well of course I did. How was your flight home?"

"It was nice. I rested well and was excited to see my girls when I got to the airport."

Michael cleared his throat. "Was that the only thing that made you excited?"

"What do you mean by that?"

"I mean was that the only reason you were excited?"

"Come on, Michael, why are you going there?"

"Geena, I'm just asking a simple question. Were you happy to see your husband? And I ask it because the last time I saw and spoke with you, you were happy, but to hear you say you were only excited to see your girls lets me know that something isn't right."

Michael always did have a keen sense when It came to my feelings, which was something else that I loved about him. I took a deep sigh and thought hard if I should share my true emotions with him. Wanting to share my thoughts with someone was leading me to do so. "Okay. I really need to get this off of my chest. While I was on the plane..." I shared the 'Ms. Sharon incident' with Michael.

"Well, Geena, have you talked to him about it to get some type of clarity?"

"Yes, we talked but I'm still not clear."

"Do you TRUST him, Geena?" It took me a minute to answer the question, because honestly, I didn't.

"I want to trust him, but I just don't know if I should."

"And why Is that?" Feeling that I was going in too deep with my personal business, I tried to change the conversation, but Michael was persistent and wouldn't allow it. "Geena, in situations like these, it's best to talk things over. If you can't get through to him, let me help you."

"And how are you going to help me in this situation?"

"For starters, I can be a listening ear, not here to judge you, him, or the situation. Sometimes, hearing yourself talk allows you to question if you should or shouldn't react to certain things. I know it has helped me in the past."

As we continued to talk, I started to feel even more comfortable with him. "I want to trust him, but the incident that happened when we first got married has stuck in the back of my mind every single day. I hate that it happened because it put a damper on what should have been a great marriage. I admit that he tries to make things work, but I just replay that day in my head over and over and over again."

"Geena, what exactly happened?" I went into to detail about the daycare situation.

"Okay, I understand why you're having trust issues with him, but in order for your relationship with him to be mended and made strong, you're going to have to make things work. It's easy to throw in the towel, but who wants something that's easy?"

I couldn't believe my ex was giving me sound advice on how to salvage my marriage. "Michael, you know, you are right. I haven't given him a fair chance, and I need to do better."

I could hear Jared's footsteps so that was my signal to get off the phone. "Hey. I gotta go."

"Why?"

"Jared is coming upstairs. I'll call you tomorrow." I thought to myself, *Why am I making this promise?* It was too late and I had to go!

"Okay. I'll talk to you then, Geena. I love you."

With a slight hesitation, I replied, "I love you, too."

Jared came in and went straight to the restroom, giving me just enough time to slide Michael's card back into my book and put my cell phone away. Minutes later, he crawled into bed without a word to me. I lay in bed thinking about the conversation I had with Michael, confused about why he had such a great interest in salvaging my relationship with Jared, until I fell asleep.

Things Are NOT the Same
Chapter 10

It had been a complicated six months. Jared and I spoke less and less, while Michael and I talked more and more. On top of everything, I started to notice a difference in Jared's scheduling. He had increased his client base, which was good for the business, but because of the influx he was spending more and more time at the office, which completely got under my skin! Late-night business dinners and weekend business meetings had become the norm, and I noticed that Jared was practically never home. Was it his work responsibilities keeping Jared away or was I falsely accusing him of wrong-doing because I was carrying around some guilt of my own? It was apparent that there was a problem and it needed to be addressed, but I wasn't going to be the one to start the conversation.

One night after I came up from cleaning the kitchen, Jared caught me coming into the bedroom and broke the ice. "How long are we going to do this, Geena?"

"Woah! You scared me! I thought you were still in the office. How long are we going to do what?"

"Act like two ships passing in the night? It's been

weeks since we even parted our lips to talk to one another, unless it was about the girls, and months since we touched each other."

I was growing angrier just thinking about how much time had passed since we addressed this issue. "And whose fault is that? Mr. 'I have a meeting' every time I turn my damn head."

"Look, you know my job is demanding, as yours is, but there's no need for you to raise your voice and definitely NO need for you to curse. We can talk this out without raising our voices and going there."

I walked right up to him and stared him in the face. "NO, you went THERE when you started taking your ass out to business meetings three or four times a night per week. All these new venues you have to visit with God knows who! Probably out hanging with Sheila, or Shelly, or whatever her name is."

"Oh, that is what this is about, Geena? Sharon? You still feeling insecure about Sharon?"

"INSECURE? Why in the world would I be insecure about her? I have a Bachelor's degree in business, a Master's degree in finance, and a Specialist in management! This trick is a rookie trying to sleep her way up the ranks in your firm."

Jared responded with dry laughter and subtle undertones.

"I knew it! Sharon HAS intimidated you!" He continued to snicker and smile. "For your information, Miss I-got-a-Bachelor's-Master's-Specialist, Sharon is educated as well, she has…"

I cut him off before he could utter another word.

"Wait, I know like HELL you are not about to sit your ass up in my face and take up for this hoe!"

Jared threw his hands up in a 'whatever' gesture and strolled out of the bedroom, down the hall, and into his office. I marched right behind him.

"Where in the hell do you think you are going?" Jared stopped midway in the hall to respond,

"I don't have time for this, Geena. I told you we can talk things out, and here you go with all of this yelling and talking loud, cursing. I am not about to get into a shouting match with you about something you have made up in your mind and that you know NOTHING about."

"Oh well, you are the one walking away from me, Jared! I'm not running from the conversation. I can hold my own because I have nothing to hide so go ahead and finish what you started. you said you wanted to talk, so let's TALK!"

"But you aren't talking. You're shouting and making a FOOL of yourself. Besides, the girls are trying to sleep. You're going to wake them with your ghetto antics."

Oh. I had to pump the breaks because he was about to make me go in on him. "GHETTO what? Hold on, please tell me you aren't calling me ghetto, as if you didn't come from the projects, too."

Jared backed past me and headed towards the bedroom. As I followed him, he turned back around to speak.

"Yes, we both know the struggle and came from the same place, but because you CAME from the projects doesn't mean you have to act like it."

He turned toward the closet, grabbed a travel bag and began filling it with clothes.

"You know what, Geena, I've had about enough of this for tonight."

"What do you think you're doing?"

"What does it look like? I'm packing some clothes because I think I should leave before things escalate and get out of control."

"LEAVE? Leave and go WHERE?"

"I don't know, but I know it will be AWAY from you!"

Jared briskly passed me, bag in hand, as he headed for the stairs. I chased behind him.

"How dare you leave? Jared! Jared! Jaarrreedd!"

By the time I reached him, he was picking up his keys and heading for the door. He turned to me before opening it.

"Look, Geena. I don't know what's going on with us, but whatever it is, it isn't working. I need some time to myself to think, I'll call you later."

I stood there alone in disbelief as Jared closed the car door, pulled out of the garage, and drove down the driveway. Never once in ten years had we spent a night away from each other because of an argument; we had always been able to work it out, no matter the issue or situation. I felt like I was standing in the shoes of one of my close friends calling for help, longing for me to give her the right advice, to make everything all right. What was happening to us? I was confused! I was mad! I was infuriated! I ran upstairs and threw myself into the pillows, accidentally bumping the night stand with my leg. The hand-painted ceramic wedding picture frame given to us by my recently-deceased aunt, wobbled from side to side. I hurried across the bed with all that I had to reach out for it, trying to rescue the picture from the destruction it would face if it hit the floor, but I was too late. It bounced and rolled in slow motion, my fingers touched it, but I wasn't fast enough and with my arm extended, I watched as my favorite picture of Jared and I, on the happiest day of our lives, shattered all over the cherry wood floor. I gasped, looking down at the picture of us all broken into shambles; I was left realizing that love is a gamble. Overwhelmed with emptiness, I crawled off the bed to the floor with tear-filled eyes, earnestly picking up the broken pieces, trying my best to piece it back together, while praying I could do the same with my heart.

The next morning was Saturday so that meant I had dance class, soccer, and grocery shopping with the girls, but with all that went on the night before, my mind was far from worrying about any of those things.

"Mommmmyyyyy!"

The girls were coming into my room to fulfill their Saturday morning ritual, and asking me what was for breakfast. That was one of the fun things the girls and I loved doing together since the weekday mornings were always so hectic with schedules and planning. They could tell immediately that something was wrong with me. I was in the bed with my clothes still on, my hair all over the place from tossing and turning all night, and my eyes red from crying. They also noticed that their daddy was not in bed next to me.

"Morning, Mommy," Lily hesitated after looking at me. "Is everything okay?"

"Hey, girls. Oh goodness! What time is it?" I turned to look out of the window trying to do something with my messy hair. "It's morning? WOW! I must have really been tired. Look at me, I slept in my clothes!"

Frances sarcastically interjected, "Yeah, something that you FORBID us to do!"

"What did you say, Frances?"

"Ohhhh nothing, Mommy. I was just asking if you wanted us to start breakfast or would we be going OUT to eat on this lovely Saturday morning?"

I popped her on the bottom, and we all laughed and, for those few seconds, I was able to escape from the pain of the previous night's events. My girls knew how to make me feel better, even when they didn't know I needed it. As I got up to use the restroom to get cleaned up, the girls followed me.

"Hey, Mommy. Where's Daddy gone this early?"

I paused trying to think of an excuse for the absentee dad.

"He left a note saying he had to meet with some clients today, and he'd be back later on."

I didn't know anything else to make up. "You girls

go ahead and get dressed. We're going to skip dance and soccer today and go shopping."

"Yay, whoohoo! Yes! I need some more Chuck Taylors, I need some gloss from Bath and Body Works, and I need a new..."

A laundry list was called out each time we took a 'mommy and me' shopping spree, and it never failed. They had a million things they needed. Ushering them out of my room, I turned on the shower and sat on the side of the tub thinking. I still couldn't believe what had taken place the night before. I was more numb than I was shocked. In all the years Jared and I had been together, we had never allowed anything to get us so upset. Even with a broken heart, I had to put my hurt feelings aside to spend some quality time with my girls.

"Are we ready to GO?"

"Yes, Ma'am."

They were all cute and ready to ride, so we locked up and were on our way. Driving down the street, I started to drift off, thinking about the fight Jared and I had and wondering where in the hell he could be. He hadn't called me like he said he would. I felt myself getting a little too upset so I turned up the radio trying to find some music for the girls and me. Having a mini-concert like we always did would help take my mind off things. It was always a fun time with my girls, laughing and singing. Bonding was important to me, and my first priority was being a great role model and excellent Mommy for them. We shopped for a few hours before stopping for lunch; the fruit I had packed for the trip was escaping our systems so it was time to eat.

As we sat eating our lunch in the food court, Frances noticed the Chick FilA cow walking in our direction, giving out free samples.

"Mama, can I go get one?"

Before I could answer her, Lily chimed in. "You're going to be fat. You have food on your plate already. Stop being so greedy."

"I work out and I eat in moderation so, NEXT." It wasn't too often I had to come to Frances' rescue. She could handle Lily, and Lilly knew it.

"Can I, Mama? Please."

"Go ahead, Frances. Lily, go over there with her."

"But Ma…"

"I didn't ask if you would like to go with her, I said for you to go."

Frances took Lily by the hand.

"Come on, Lily. You won't have to eat yours. Just give it to me. I wouldn't want you to get fat or anything like that."

Lily gave Frances a look that should have singed a hole in her forehead…

"You get on my nerves, ooooohhh! Mama, where did ya'll get her from?"

"Don't worry about where they got me from. Worry about where you are about to take me to."

"Take you to? Can you please use proper English, Frances."

"You know what I mean, Lily! Take me to, take me over, let's just go and get this chicken. Come on! Make it snappy, nappy! You heard Mama! Let's move it!"

Frances was a character. She loved pushing her sister's buttons. I loved HOW they loved each other. Watching them as they walked over to the Chick FilA cow, I finished the rest of my salad with thoughts of Jared popping into my head.

I had a gut feeling that he was with "Ms. Sharon". and I couldn't shake it no matter how hard I tried. After lunch, I took the girls to pick up a few Red Box movies so we could head back home. I drove up to the house hoping Jared's car would be there. To my dismay, it wasn't. It was tough walking into the house on a Saturday night without him. I told the girls to put their things away, take their showers then once we were settled, I would set the dvd player for movie night. I took a long hot bath before joining them, in the hopes that Jared would come in at any time to join us, but that didn't happen either.

It was close to 9 p.m. when I started the second movie.Lily looked up from the television and asked, "Mommy, what time is Daddy coming home? It's getting late."

Frances chimed in with, "Yeah? Where is he? We haven't talked to him all day."

Not knowing how to respond, I told them to call him. They didn't get an answer, so they left a message instead. About twenty minutes later, he returned their calls, telling the girls that he loved them and hated that he was missing movie night, but he had to leave for a business trip and would be back Monday afternoon. I was fuming on the inside! Monday afternoon? Who in the hell did he think he was? Frolicking around with that skank while I sat home and twiddled my thumbs! I couldn't wait till that last movie ended so I could march upstairs, call him, and let him know what was on my mind. I couldn't dial those digits fast enough. I called him over and over, only to get his voicemail. On my last attempt, I left him a message telling him exactly how I felt.

"How dare you tell the children you will be back Monday afternoon, refuse to talk to me or give me an explanation! You need to call me, Jared. ASAP!"

I sat there in the bed fuming with anger. I was so pissed. As I was about to pick up the phone to call him again, my phone rang. Without looking at the caller ID I picked up the phone. "You really have some nerve."

The voice from the other end replied, "It's only been a day since we talked, babe. I miss you, too." It was Michael and I had to admit, I was relieved to hear from him. I took a deep sigh.

"Hey, Michael."

Then out of nowhere, I began to cry.

"Geeena! What's wrong, sweetheart?"

"I'm an emotional wreck. I'm angry, sad, confused. I'm upset and I'm…"

"Hold on, Geena, let's slow down. Take a deep breath, calm yourself, and tell me what's bothering you."

"Okay. Remember I was telling you about my suspicions about Ms. Sharon?"

"Yeah."

"Well, Jared and I finally talked about it Friday night and it turned into a huge fight, he got upset, and left the house and hasn't come back home. Then he told the girls that he had to leave on a business trip and wouldn't be home till Monday! Now what kind of B-S is that?"

I burst into tears retelling Michael the events that took place Friday night. He listened and didn't say a word until I was finished.

"Geena, I think you need to really sit down and talk things out before the situation gets worse."

"Well, I tried to talk to him, Michael, but he left."

"Do you mind if I ask you something, and don't take this the wrong, but how was your delivery?"

"My delivery? What do you mean? I told him what was on my mind."

"You see, it's not good to discuss matters like these when you are already upset because you will more than likely say something you'll regret later. It's best to calm down and talk things over in a civilized manner. It sounds to me like he got fed up."

"Wait? So you're taking HIS side?"

"No, Geena. I'm just telling you how we men think. We don't want to hear a lot of yappin' and it sounds to me like that's what went down last night."

I was catching an attitude because what Michael was trying to cook up, I wasn't trying to eat, so I told him I would have to call him back.

"Now, Geena..."

"No, no, no. Let me call you back, I'm tired and I need to try and get some rest. I'll talk to you later."

After we hung up, I tossed and turned thinking about Jared and where he could be. I was so angry at him, at myself, and at everything that had something to do with Jared. I cried because I was sad, and then I got mad. I was an ocean of emotions and I just felt like balling up in a knot and disappearing.

The next morning, I got the girls and myself ready for church and we were off to hear the Word; my spirit was always lifted when I was able to get in some praising. I didn't speak a word about Jared and, thank God, neither did the girls. Church was powerful. Pastor Riggins talked about how we had the power to change any situation because it was all in our attitudes. As I listened to his sermon, I began to reflect on how my relationship with my husband had changed over the years and the role that I had played in the changes. I had always blamed Jared for all of the grief we experienced in our relationship, never taking ownership of my shortcomings and downfalls. After the service was over, I was even more ready to speak with Jared about what was going on. The girls and I had a great dinner, played a few games, cleaned up a bit, and started to prepare ourselves for the week that awaited us. As the time on my clock drew later, I began to think about Jared, wondering if he was thinking about me. I wanted to call him so badly, but wanted him to call me even more. I waited hoping he would call, but he never did. Before I went to bed, I decided to call Michael. We talked for an hour or so and I thanked him for being so honest with me and helping me to see my faults, and how after talking with him and listening to the sermon at church, I was able to admit that I made some pretty big mistakes too.

It's Over
Chapter 11

During a meeting Monday morning at work, I received a phone call from Jared letting me know he would pick the girls up for me, take them to practice, then meet me at home later that night for dinner. I was anxious to see him; after all those months of ignoring one another and barely speaking, I was ready to lay it all out on the line and judging from that phone call, he must have been feeling the same way! I promised myself I wouldn't badger him about where he was, what he was doing, or who he was with. I just wanted to talk about starting over with a clean slate and try to make our marriage work. That night after dinner, I cleaned the kitchen while Jared did his usual. After the kids were tucked in, I went in hoping Jared and I could sort things out. As I opened the door, I noticed he was on the phone and abruptly hung up.

"Who was that?"

"Who was who, Geena?"

"On the phone, weren't you on the phone?"

"Oh, yeah that was one of the guys from the firm."

"Oh. Well, uhmm, I guess."

"Wait, Geena. There's something that I need to tell

you." As my heart was sinking, I knew that there would be bad news coming next.

"Okay, I'm all ears." I sat down on the couch next to his desk, giving him my undivided attention.

"You know that I love you, right?"

I kept my head hung as I responded yes to Jared's question.

"You know there is nothing I wouldn't do for you or the girls?" Jared got down on one knee in front of me.

"Yes." My heart began to race even faster and I could feel my underarms getting wet.

"Well, I think we can also agree that our relationship isn't where it should be in order for us to have a productive life and happy marriage."

I immediately looked up at him and stared him in the eyes. "Wait a minute."

"No, Geena, this time you're going to have to wait. Through our entire marriage, I have allowed you to take the lead, make the decisions, say what we will or won't do, talk when you want to, and silence me until you have finished with your point.

"I've had to take a look at myself, and if we are honest with each other, we can admit that you're not in love with me. The girls are your first priority, then your career, next are your social activities, now your friends have been added back to the equation, and I'm left to be last. That's not the kind of life I signed up for! I'm tired of living this way, Geena, and I've made the decision to speak with a divorce attorney."

"Wait, wait, wait? Are you kidding me, Jared? A divorce attorney? To do what?"

"Come on, Geena. I'm certain you know what a divorce attorney is used for with all of the "degrees" you've acquired."

It took everything in me to ignore his sarcasm. I could feel my temperature rising and my heart beating in my throat. Then out of nowhere, I burst into tears.

"Jared, wait? Why are you doing this to us?"

"Geena, listen. This was a very hard decision for me to make. I've pondered long and hard about which route I should take, praying, trying to figure out what more I can do to make our marriage work. After months of beating my head against the wall, I finally realized that my sanity is imperative for me to be strong for my daughters, and for their sakes I must take myself out of this situation."

"This situation? It's not a situation, Jared, it's a marriage, but I guess that explains why it's so easy for you to throw it all away! We took vows to stay together until death do us part!"

"And we said some other things too, like forsaking all others, loving each other in sickness and in health. I don't know the last time you even asked me how I was feeling, let alone taking care of me when I was sick!"

"You are a grown man, Jared! What do you mean, take care of you? I have children I am responsible for taking care of."

"You see, Geena! That is what I mean. You don't even see anything wrong with how things are around here. Although I'm not a child, I still want and need nurturing too!"

"Well, you didn't need any nurturing when you left the house on Friday. You didn't even call to check on me or the kids or let us know you were okay."

"Geena, I needed that time away from the house to be alone, to clear my head. I'm coming to you now ready to do what is best for both of us."

"How is this BEST for us, Jared? We have a home, a family, and a future. What am I supposed to do?"

"I guess you'll be doing what you always do. Cater to the girls, go to your meetings, and work on your reports, you know. Those things. Did you notice there was nothing about me on that list?"

"How dare you insinuate that I don't care about you or our marriage."

"Geena, let's be realistic. You have pushed me into a corner. You don't talk to me, you don't touch me, you have pretty much taken over everything that concerns Lily and Frances, and by the time you're finished with them at night, I can't touch you."

"Okay, Jared, that is not fair. Maybe if you would help me around here with the girls, then maybe I would feel like touching you or being touched. All you do is WORK! You are the last person in the building almost every night, and when you come home you hide away in your office and do more work!"

"See, this is what I knew would happen, I would talk to you about one thing and you would turn it into something else."

"Well, Jared, let me give you a news flash, I am a mother of two growing young girls so NO, I can't stroke your ego every time you would like for me to."

"Stroke my ego? Are you serious, Geena. Is that what you think this is about? I don't need anyone to stroke my ego, but it would feel good to feel appreciated and wanted some times. You treat me like I'm not even around!"

Before I knew it, I got so upset that I lashed out at him. "So you mean to tell me you are comparing yourself to two innocent little girls that YOU helped bring into this world?"

"All I am telling you is this: when we took our vows ten years ago, we BOTH uttered these words, 'forsaking ALL others.' Now that didn't mean we aren't supposed to love our children, family members, or friends, but it was clear to me that I was to put you before all of them and you do the same for me. If we had BOTH put each other first, then everything else would have fallen into place. After the birth of the girls, everything began to change."

"WAIT, you wanted to start a family just as much as I did, so don't act like it was my choice alone."

"No, I'm not saying that either, but if we want to be truthful and honest, neither one of us wanted to be parents as soon as we did. We had a plan, Geena, and you didn't stick to it!"

"I didn't stick to it? What are you talking about, Jared?"

"We agreed we would be married at least five years

before we had children so we could work on us, build on our relationship and have a solid foundation to build a lasting marriage and continue to cultivate our friendship. But after that first year, you stopped taking your birth control pills, under the direction of your mother and aunts, which may I add have no man of their own, in order to I guess trap me and you got pregnant."

I stood up from my seat, pushing Jared back away from me. "TRAP you? Are you serious right now? And what reason would I have to trap you, Jared?"

"Come on, Geena. I've heard ya'll talk about how having a baby seals the deal and guarantees you'll never go broke because child support alone will pay your bills . As irritated as it always made me, I never spoke on it."

"Well, for your information, Jared, I don't NEED you to take care of my girls. My salary will cover everything that we need, so please don't think you're doing us a favor by sticking around."

Jared walked away then made a semicircle, looking at me in disgust. "You see, that's just it. What kind of wife tells her husband she doesn't need him? If you don't need me, Geena, why did you marry me? I acknowledge the fact that you have a great career, you make a lot of money, and financially you and the girls would be okay without me, but what about the emotional and physical? Does that account for anything?"

"You started this, Jared, and besides all that B-S,

what do you mean by what happened when I got pregnant? When I got pregnant, I was married and had a husband, so why not start a family?"

"That's my point, Geena! NO communication! If we made the decision to wait TOGETHER, why did you change up on me without letting me know? I felt like I was being forced into something that I didn't sign up for."

"WHAT? So you're telling me that you didn't want our first-born?"

"No, I'm not telling you I didn't want her. I'm telling you that I didn't want to have children that soon. Now don't get me wrong, I love my daughters with everything that's inside of me, and I love being a father. I just miss being a husband."

"So, what do you want me to do, Jared?"

"There's nothing you can do, Geena, because you don't see a problem in what you are doing! When things get to that point in a relationship, it's best if the two parties separate, and I think it's about that time."

"Two parties? Uhhmm, this is NOT one of your business mergers, Jared. This is our marriage and our future we are talking about."

"Geena, it's time we faced facts. Our marriage is over.I'm sorry, but as of today, we don't have a future anymore."

It felt like an iceberg had entered the room and sat between us. I was dumbfounded; it felt like my heart was cracking into a million pieces. Tears rushed down my face. "So,okay, you are leaving your responsibilities as a father because we can't see eye to eye on a few things?"

"We don't see eye to eye on a LOT of things and NO, I never said I was leaving my children. Trust me, when I say they won't skip a beat. I plan on talking to them about this in the next week or so. They are smart girls and I don't want to keep anything away from them to learn on their own, and I don't want them growing up in a household where the husband and wife barely speak. I want them to really know what love is, so when their time comes, they will know that it is true."

"So. Just like that, Jared? You're throwing away ten years of marriage? It's that easy for you to turn your back and just walk away?"

"I'm not throwing it away, Geena. I'm only doing what has to be done."

"So where do we go from here?"

"Well, this weekend I went looking for a condo."

"A condo?" I instantly got sick to my stomach. "You're moving out soon?"

"Geena, the sooner the better. The longer I prolong things, the longer it will take us to move beyond the anger and pain in order to be strong parents for the girls."

I plopped down on the couch in the study, head in my lap, and began to weep. I couldn't catch my breath, and I felt like I was in a dream and I prayed that somehow I could just wake up. Jared walked up to me, got down on his knees, and took my hands away from my tear-soaked face.

"Geena, look at me. We both know in our heart of hearts that this was bound to happen. Please know that I still love you, but it's time we found our own direction. Who knows, maybe this split will give us the time we need to grow as individuals. I don't hate you, Geena, and I don't want you to hate me." I continued to weep, looking into Jared's eyes hoping there was something that I could say or do to change his mind. His body language remained the same, which told me any plans to sway him wouldn't make a difference. Jared could see the torment I was dealing with so he offered to stay with me that night. For the last time. "If it's okay with you, could I hold you while you fall asleep?"

I was reluctant at first, but with all the sorrow that filled my heart, I really needed to be held, even if it had to be by the person who caused me such agony and pain. "Yes, Jared, I would appreciate it if you would."

That night, as I lay in bed, I couldn't stop crying. I could feel Jared's arms around my waist and it felt natural for me to relax my body into his like I used to do when we were first married. The night continued to play over and over in my head; all I could think about was my husband of ten years leaving.

The next morning, the breeze from the bedroom window ruffled some papers that were sitting on the nightstand near my side of the bed, waking me up. I sat up in the middle of the bed and noticed there was a note beside me. I picked it up with my eyes closed, hoping and wishing it was a letter from Jared saying he was reconsidering his move and we would try to work things out.

"Dear Geena, I know you didn't get any rest last night, and neither did I. I know we were both thinking about this new phase in our lives. I have the girls and I'm taking them to school. I called Brittany and told her you weren't feeling well and would be in later today or tomorrow. Get some rest, Geena, and I'll call you later. - Jared."

My wish was washed away with the words I read. A burning rage came over me. I stood in the middle of the bed and screamed to the top of my lungs, throwing the pillows all over the room, stomping around until I was so weak, I fell to the floor.

I screamed out, "Why! How could he do this to me?" I was a pitiful mess. My body was limp as if each of my bones had been taken away. I couldn't cry. I couldn't muster any more tears. I prayed and asked God to take the lump out of my chest that I couldn't remove on my own.

He Is Gone for Good
Chapter 12

After falling asleep, I was awakened by the garage door opening. I jumped up from the floor, immediately gathered myself, ran to the restroom, locked the door, and turned on the shower. That was where my tears found me again. I didn't know where my tears began or where they ended. I could hear my girls talking to each other, standing at my restroom door, knocking to get in. My heart was so heavy that I couldn't even muster enough strength to respond to them.

"Mommy! Mommy! Open up!"

"Just a minute girls. Let me get out of the shower. Could you ask your dad to turn the oven on and put the chicken breast on for me?"

"Uhhmm, Mama. Daddy just dropped us off. He didn't stay."

Hearing those words made it feel as if my heart was falling down the drain along with the water drizzling from my body. I had to fight through the pain to answer the girls.

"He didn't stay?"

"No, Ma'am, he said to tell you he would call you

later."

"Okay. Uhm, give me a second and I'll be out."

I sank down in the tub, letting the water from the shower pound all over my body in the hope the pressure would erase the tears I'd shed. I couldn't catch my breath. My head hurt. I felt like I was about to explode. I was angry, I was hurt, and I was ashamed. Just like that, my marriage was over and there was nothing I could say or do to change it. After I began to resemble a prune, I gathered myself to get out of the tub to head downstairs and start dinner.

The girls and I talked about their day at school and we completed homework just like any other school night. They could tell that something was wrong because I came downstairs in my robe, no makeup, hair pulled back into a ponytail, and slipper socks. Frances couldn't keep her eyes off of me.

"Mommy, are you feeling okay?"

"I'm okay, baby, just a little under the weather that's all. I'll be back to my old self in the morning. I just need some rest."

I couldn't relinquish the fact that the upstairs office was empty and, sadly, so was my heart. That night I climbed into bed alone, clutching my pillow as tightly as I could, praying and asking God to help me understand where I went wrong. How did I go wrong? Was it my fault that Jared left? I gathered that God was on another call because at that time, I didn't receive an answer.

That night I had a dream that Jared and I were

summoned to court to plead our case. The judge asked each of us to speak and explain to the jury what happened in our marriage and why we thought it was ending.

Standing here all alone, thinking how could this be? What did she do for you to up and leave?

I am pinching myself trying to understand. How could you love another?

Does it move you in the least that I am your children's mother?

My heart is aching and the tears, they fall, how could you do this to me after all I have done for you?

What did she whisper in your ear to make you leave me this way, and break my heart in two?

I thought we would share our lives and together we would spend eternity.

But now I am alone, sad and confused, because you chose her, not me!

You see, I bore your children, they share our same blood, and I believed you would be a good father.

You shared stories with me about how your dad left home and how you witnessed the struggles of your mother.

How could this happen? What did I do to deserve this kind of hurt and pain?

I have toiled and toiled to try and figure out how I can make you remain.

Have you even considered the children, you once claimed them as your priority?

That no one in this world could make you turn your back and leave them nor me.

You have broken my heart into pieces and now my life is left in shambles.

Thinking that our love was endless, realizing that love is a gamble.

Jared speaks.

In the beginning you were everything that I hoped and dreamed of in a wife,

But I found myself at a crossroad wanting more splendor in my life.

Yes I promised you that when we had children, I would be a good dad.

Staying with you and being mistreated was some dream that you must have had.

And hold on a minute, don't go blaming me what is mostly all your fault.

You were the one that claimed to be fed up and threatened that we should part.

Now I tried my best to be a good man and I broke my back for you.

I worked real hard to pay all the bills to come home to a selfish you.

You never tried to lift me up; you continued to tear me down.

Each time that I tried to be intimate with you, all I got was an ugly frown.

What did you expect me to do? You practically pushed me into the streets.

You pushed and pressed and pressed and pushed till you pushed me into her sheets.

I don't mean to sound hateful or mean to you, but this

may sound harsh to hear me speak to you like this,

But you know for yourself it has been several months since we even had shared a kiss.

I told you I was growing weary and that I needed compassion from you,

You pushed me away and told me to grow up because you had more important things to do.

True we both made mistakes in all of the years we shared,

But when the cycle started, you broke me down like you never cared.

Even after this, I still remained directly by your side,

Giving you emotional support and still I tried to provide.

Yes you have my children and that one fact is true,

But the love and intimacy we once shared is over and well past due.

We had started living together as strangers; no love between us was shared.

We had separate lives and different agendas, neither of us cared.

So as I thought and prayed about it, I realized it was time for me to go.

Once the trust and love is gone, the bond will never grow.

I will pray for you so pray for me, there is no reason we should hate each other.

Besides, no matter what happens from this day forward, you will be my children's mother.

The Adjustment
Chapter 13

It had been close to six months since Jared moved out and the girls and I were finally getting some control back over our lives. Although I didn't like what was going on between Jared and me, I was pleased to see that Lily and Frances were adjusting fine. Scheduling was quite simple. Jared would pick them up every other weekend, which gave me a break and time to do some things I hadn't done in a while, like shop alone, have lunch with my friends, and rest. We alternated drop offs and pickups from school and practice, and things were going pretty smoothly. We both did a good job of explaining to the girls what was going on and why the decision for Jared to move out was made like it was. For the girls to be so young, they handled the separation prettywell. This surprised me because I figured they would be torn about the decision since all they had ever known was Jared and I being together. It made me happy because their happiness and sense of normalcy was my focus.

One weekend after Jared brought the girls home, we were upstairs in the laundry room folding clothes, talking about their escapades with Daddy, catching up like we always do. Then out of the blue, Frances announced, "Ms. Sharon is so much fun."

Lily nudged her in the side as if to hush her. I was stunned but didn't want to react foolishly, which would make them shrink back and stop talking so in order to gather some information, I spoke jokingly.

"Oh, Ms. Sharon was at your dad's house?"

"Uhhmmm. well…"

They both were stalling for time, afraid I may blow a gasket or something so I had to assure them that I was cool with the Ms. Sharon situation, even though I knew nothing about it.

"Look, girls, your dad can have friends. It's okay, and I want you to always remember that you don't have to hide anything from me."

Although I was boiling inside, I didn't want to let the girls know. I always tried to make sure they felt comfortable talking to me about anything, so I just hurried them out of the laundry room so I could get to my bedroom. I couldn't wait to get to the phone to call Jared and question him about my girls being around this woman with our divorce just being finalized.

"We had a ball, Mama."

They continued saying how much fun they had and I knew that my first responsibility as their mother was to make sure they were safe and treated fairly; the selfish part of me didn't want them enjoying time with another woman, especially with Ms. Sharon.

"That's good, baby. What do you all want to do for the remainder of the night? Movie? Game?"

Both of the girls decided to go to their bedrooms to watch movies on their televisions, so that left me to find something to do on my own.

"Well I guess I'll get a bubble bath prepared and enjoy the rest of my night. You girls go ahead, and I'll see ya in the morning."

The anticipation was killing me! I was so ready to call Jared. Of course when I called him, he let the phone ring a million times before he answered.

"Hello?"

"Hey, Jared." I tried to speak as calmly as I could.

"Whassup, Geena?"

"Uhmm, I just wanted to talk to you about the girls."

"Why? Is something wrong? They seemed fine when I dropped them off."

"No, there's nothing wrong. They are fine. I was talking to them and they mentioned Ms. Sharon."

Jared immediately snapped at me. "Look, Geena, I'd appreciate it if you wouldn't call me questioning who I spend time with. We've been divorced for quite some time now so when the girls are with me, they are safe and that should be your only concern."

"No, that is not my only concern. I have to be concerned with everything that concerns my children, and them being around HER concerns me!"

"Okay, Geena, that's enough. I don't have time to entertain your screaming tonight. I have some things to handle before I get to the office in the morning. I'll talk to you later. Good night."

All of a sudden I heard the phone click and then a dial tone.

"Hello? Hello? Jared. Hello?"

I sat there holding the phone thinking to myself, *I know like hell this man did not hang up on me.* I was outdone! No explanation for the mother of his children? How dare he treat me this way. I immediately called Michael and before he could say hello, I was already talking.

"You are NOT going to believe this!"

"Believe what?"

"Jared had my girls around Ms. Sharon."

"Calm down, Geena. What's done is done and there is no need for you to beat yourself up over something you have no control over. It isn't healthy to remain angry over something that happened over a year or so ago. I think you need to get away to take your mind off of things. When is the next time Jared gets the girls?"

I was really not in the mood to respond to any questions. I was so PISSED!

"Since he had them this weekend, I'll have them next weekend."

"So that means the following weekend, we'll meet up."

"Uhhmm, I don't know, Michael."

"What do you NOT know, Geena? I hear the change in your spirit every single day. Some days you're happy, but the majority of the days you are upset or sad, and that bothers me."

He was right; ever since I came back home from

Miami I had been agitated. it was time for me to take MY life back.

"Michael, make the arrangements, let me know what they are and I'm there."

"Sounds like a plan, Geena. I'll get on that in the morning and get back with you. Now do you feel better?"

I giggled like a weight had been lifted from my shoulders.

"Yes, Michael. I do, thank you so much. I'm excited about our date. It's late. Let me get to bed, and I'll call you tomorrow."

"Good night, Geena. I'll talk with you then."

The next morning, I had to call Stephanie to give her an update.

"Hello!!"

"Hey, Stephanie, how ya doing, girl?"

"I'm good and HOW are you?"

"I won't complain, although I could."

"Why? What's wrong? Jared again?"

"Yes, of course! Found out last night Ms. Sharon was at his house while Lily and Frances were there."

Stephanie didn't respond.

"Steph. Did you hear me?"

"Yeah, I heard you." Stephanie took a deep sigh before she continued. "I didn't want to say anything, but they have been spending time together for quite some time now."

"WHAT? Wait, what do you mean?"

"Well, remember I told you I joined the new gym up

on Riverside last spring?"

"I remember."

"Well evidently, so did Ms. Sharon."

"Huh?"

"Okay, Geena. check it, about a month ago I was coming out of the gym and noticed a black BMW that looked like Jared's, but since there were rims on the car and the windows were tinted, I couldn't really see who was driving it. For the next couple weeks, that same car would be out front when I would leave and I would see a tall, light-skinned lady get into it. I was curious to see who the mystery driver was a few weeks ago so I watched them. I realized it WAS Jared's car. When the car door opened, I saw the birthmark on the cheek, and nobody else has that birthmark like Jared. I just figured the woman had to be Sharon."

I had a lump in my throat, and wondered why it sickened me so much to hear about this woman being with my ex-husband when I was happy with Michael.

"So they are dating or something?"

"I don't know, Geena. That's why I didn't want to bother you with it."

"Stephanie! You're my best friend. You're supposed to tell me things like this."

"I knew you would say that, but I wanted to protect you. I hoped it would be a short fling and you would never have to know. I'm sorry, friend."

"Stephanie. I don't know how I should feel."

"Geena, it's time you let it go. Move on, have a life of your own. Jared has done just that. He's made his move, has a new player on his team. Now the ball is in your corner. WHEN are you going to make yours?"

I tried to fight back the tears. "I am so upset!"

"Geena, it's been like months since Jared threw you the deuces. Girl, get a grip! I know he yo baby daddy and all."

"NO, he is the father of my children. I am not a baby mama."

Stephanie started giggling. "I knew you would say that. Okay, Geena, it's time you get your own life and FORGET about the father of your children!"

"Well, as a matter of fact, I have made some arrangements to get my mind off of everything."

"Oh yeah? Speak, my sista, speak."

"You are so silly. Okay. You know I've been spending a lot of time talking to Michael."

"Yeah, that's another thing, why are you so adamant about Jared and Sharon when you have been all in Michael's stuff since Miami?"

"I don't know to tell you the truth. I think talking to Michael is why I didn't lose my mind after Jared left. I have such a good time talking to him. He always knows how to make me smile."

"Well, what's the plan? What are ya'll going to do? Where are you going to go?"

"I don't know, he said he would SURPRISE me."

"Sounds like FUN!"

"Yeah, I hope so. I'm excited to see him and just get away from it all."

Michael and I Again
Chapter 14

Michael surprised me with a weekend getaway to Aruba. When I say this man knows HOW to treat a lady, I am NOT exaggerating! We had a ball, and being with him gave me the confidence to walk around the resort like I didn't have a care in the world. We arrived on Friday afternoon and had to fly out Sunday evening, so every moment we had together had to be spent doing something worthwhile. The beach was beautiful and each time that I looked at Michael, I felt gorgeous. It was the way his soft, light brown eyes danced all over my body that made me feel like I was the only woman in the world. The physical attraction I had for him was overwhelming and all I wanted to do was stay in his strong arms where I felt safe, complete, and secure. I watched as passersby stared and smiled at us. Many of them even asked if we were newlyweds. On the last night of our trip, we had a long talk over dinner.

"Geena, I need to ask you something."

"Yes, Michael?"

"How long will it be before we can move on and take it to the next level?"

Giggling, I replied, "Uhmm, I think we've already done that."

"Come on, Gee, I'm being serious."

"Okay, I apologize. I am all ears."

Michael pulled his chair close to mine and took my hand. "For the past six or seven months there hasn't been a day gone by where we haven't talked to one another. I don't know about you, but each day I feel like we're growing and evolving into so much more than just friends."

I sat quietly staring into his eyes, hoping that he wasn't telling me a bunch of lies. "Like I told you in Miami, Geena, it wasn't a coincidence that we ran into each other at the club, spent time together like we did, and kept in touch like we have. I'm in love with you, Geena, and I don't want another day, week, or month to pass that we can't be together."

"So what exactly are you asking me to do, Michael?"

"All I'm asking for you to do is love me. In my heart, I believe that if you love me, everything else will fall into place."

I sat there thinking about what Michael was saying to me and although I was in love with him, I didn't know where we could take the relationship, especially with him living out of town and me having the girls.

"Michael, trust me when I say that I love you, but have you taken into consideration everything that comes along with me?"

He answered back to me. "What, the girls?"

"Not only the girls but my career and my..." I stopped myself. For the first time I heard myself repeat what Jared had always said to me; he was right, although I never wanted to admit it. I put everything else in front of my relationship with him an,d because of that, my marriage suffered. I instantly grew saddened because I was realizing that everything he said about me was true, and there was nothing I could do to change it.

"You know what, Michael, spending time with you always affords me the opportunity to look at myself, and for the first time in a long time, I don't like what I am seeing. For years I have put romance on the back burner, consuming myself with the needs of everybody else - my children, my employees, my partners, my family, and my friends. The one person that I took vows with suffered because of me." My eyes filled with tears just thinking about the hell I must have put Jared through all those years, and how treating him poorly had turned me bitter towards him.

"Geena, don't beat yourself up too bad. Over the years, I have witnessed marriages fail because they didn't start with a strong foundation. Couples get married for all the wrong reasons sometimes and that's why they end up in ugly divorces or they last but lack love, intimacy, excitement, and joy. These are the things I feel a solid marriage must have.

"One of my good friends from college met a young lady at a frat party we all went to one night. She was gorgeous and came from a well-to-do family Her Mom and Pop owned a lot of land, had a home on each coast, and she was set up to literally have it made with or without a successful college career. Her major could easily have been Party and Pledging Management.

"He knew that things could never go too far with her, but against his better judgment, they began to date anyway. For a while, things seemed okay. They had a lot of fun and they had a lot in common. All of a sudden, she started to show a side of herself that my buddy didn't really like. She had a really nasty attitude when things didn't go her way. She had maybe two friends because females despised her. The thing that kept him around was the 300 series BMW he was able to drive, the fully furnished condominium he was able to live in, and the access to however much money he liked. He was accustomed to spending a lot of time with her. I don't think there was a weekend that passed where they weren't traveling out of town.

"Eventually she started talking to him about moving in. My boys and I begged him to get out before he got in too deep because it seemed like everybody we knew who moved in with their girlfriends ended up with a kid. He wouldn't listen because he was blinded by all the fringe benefits. Lo and behold, after maybe five months of dating her, she got pregnant. Her father was a minister and they didn't believe in abortion. Before my boy's head could turn, they were planning a wedding. Her parents pretty much pressured him into marrying her because they didn't believe in the 'baby mama, baby daddy' deal.

"I can still remember it like it was yesterday. As soon as that baby came, EVERYTHING changed. Prior to the baby arriving, he used to brag to us how she catered to his every whim, but all of that became null and void. He went from ninety to none in the happiness department right before our eyes. I tell you, Geena, he was miserable. Always pissed off, mad, and every time he would get with the fellas, it would be the same ole' story. 'Man, Kristy gets on my nerves, she be pissin' me off, she never cleans up, there's baby stuff all around the house, she doesn't cook, and I don't know the last time we had sex.'

"Now let me give you a bit of advice to live on. Never withhold sex from your mate, you may be mad, you may be angry but never withhold the booty. And I will tell you right now, Geena, if a wife isn't having sex with their husband, I can promise you there is somebody else that is. I know you're thinking if you don't want to be with the person, why cheat? Just leave. But it isn't that simple. When you have made an investment in someone, you don't want to just throw it all away, so you'll take some attitude and unhappiness. But you will be getting the sex elsewhere. You see, we men gotta have it. Women are emotional creatures, and men are physical fools."

I started to think back to the conversations I had with some of my friends and how we all joked about how we were holding out on our husbands in order to make them complete some type of task or fulfill some type of need we had. I was sick! So instead of us making a fool out of them, they played us like some fools!

Michael continued talking. "I'm not telling you this stuff to make you feel bad or have any regrets, but I'm just telling you that if you don't have chemistry with a person, the relationship is going to suffer; having a few kids doesn't make a marriage successful. In my heart, I'm certain that God has somebody for everybody. He made each of us, so He knows what we need. The reason we see so many unhappy marriages is because folks are walking around here married to somebody else's husband or wife. Marriage is supposed to be beautiful, not full of arguments and disgruntled feelings. Your mate is supposed to bring the best out of you and vice versa. When you are weak in one area, God has given your mate what they need to be strong. That is how the two become one. God has to be the matchmaker, not your "mama 'nemor your friends.

"A few years ago, I met a wise old couple that had been married for over forty years and were still madly in love. It was something very unique about them that I had never seen in a couple before. Forgive me if I sound crazy, but it was like I could see love all over them. It was in every move they made, even at their ripe old age. The gentleman touched her as he spoke, they held hands, looked at each other, and love exuded from their eyes each time they looked at one another. The conversation that we shared was one I would never forget, and I knew that one day I would use it to benefit myself greatly. It was so good that I wish I could have recorded it. It sure taught me a lot.

I guess the older gentleman noticed my interest in them because as I stared at them, he looked at me and asked, "Uhmm, is there something I can do for you, son?"

"Startled, I laughed and explained to him that I had never seen a couple interact the way they did. I further explained how intrigued I was and the conversation just went from there. We spent two or three hours talking. Well, they talked, I asked a few questions and just sat in silence to listen. They were so willing to share their life stories with me that I missed two very important meetings that day. It was almost like God had ordained that moment. I had never taken that route before, but for some reason that day I did, and I can assure you that I was happy I did so. The older gentleman, Mr. Harold, started the conversation that would impact my life forever.

"You see, son, when I was in my prime, I used to run the streets HARD. Out of all the years that I dated, I never had just one woman, because one woman couldn't supply all of my needs." He stopped and chuckled a little while adjusting his black neck tie, accompanying his crisp white shirt and burgundy sweater vest. "I had to have the pretty girl, the smart girl, the fast girl, the church girl, and the working girl. I was pretty greedy if I do say so myself. You see, as a young man, I witnessed how many of my friends got married fast for, in my mind, all the wrong reasons. I made a personal vow that I would never fall into those same traps."

Mr. Harold stood to take his wallet from his back

pocket before continuing. "The lifestyle that I made for myself dealt some cards, so I had to quickly learn how to play with a full hand. My choice to deal with so many different women led me to becoming a parent at a rather young age, which pushed me to grow up faster than my peers. Instead of going off to college and having the career I had planned, I had to get three part-time jobs, buy diapers, formula, and deal with baby mama drama."

He took out some pictures before returning his wallet back to his rear pocket and taking his seat next to his wife.

"I never complained about the road I was treading because I understood that my decision to be with so many different women led me down the path to being a young father. Instead of fulfilling my dreams, I dropped them to be there for my children." He set the pictures of his children in front of me.

"Because of these innocent youngins being brought into the world, I was constantly under a lot of scrutiny and pressure. I don't know if you have any children, young man, but take it from me, having children with different women is a constant struggle. There's always something more somebody thinks you should be doing. Everybody has their opinion of what they feel is a good father. Spending time with my children strained me because I had to divide my time between two households. Neither of my children's mothers allowed me to take the children away from their home, which meant I was constantly trying to figure out a schedule to accommodate each of them, knowing full well that no matter what kind of schedule I presented to them, somebody would have an attitude. There is nothing worse on God's green Earth than a baby mama with an attitude. They can make your life miserable!" He laughed, taking his hand and shaking Michael on the shoulder.

"On a scale of one to ten, Deborah, the first young lady I had a baby with, was a fifteen when it came to nasty attitudes. Instead of listening to reason about how funds should be handled, she used the money I gave her for my son to keep her hair, shoes, and clothes done. We constantly fought about money because she felt like I owed her a paycheck for having my baby. Eventually, all the bickering pushed me away from her, which in turn took me away from my son, whom I loved very much. He was two months shy of turning three years old when I moved out.

"During the time I was living with Deborah, I met a friend named Shae. When I left Deborah, I moved right in with Shae and her two children. Living with Shae brought about my second son, Jeremiah. Things were good between Shae and I at first, until Deborah started asking me to come over and watch Harold Jr. while she studied or ran errands. Before I knew it, I had baby number three on the way with Deborah. Shae immediately threw me out. She was a woman scorned, not able to find it in her heart to forgive me for cheating on her with Deborah. Shae was always looking for ways to pay me back for my dirty deed each time we shared the same space. During the times I tried to spend time with any of my children, I was subjected to a speech on the mistakes I'd made. Because of the issues I had with both young ladies, there would be days, weeks, and even months that would quickly pass between the times I saw my children."

Mr. Harold looked down at the worn and tattered pictures. "I knew that was unacceptable and something had to change before my children were all grown and I had missed all their special moments as a child. I didn't want to be like my father who missed every school play I was ever in, never came to watch me play ball, missed my birthday parties, and never tucked me in bed at night,. Of course phone calls were also far and few in between. I made a personal promise to myself that all three of my children would know WHO their father was, how much I loved them, and I would be an influential part of their lives individually as well as collectively."

Mr. Harold went on to explain how important marriage was to him. He wanted to have a wife one day, but didn't want to rush into something he would more than likely regret later. He had so many people in his ear saying he should make one of the mothers of his children an honest woman and marry one of them, but he didn't agree. Although he had children with them, he didn't feel in his heart that either of them should be his wife. His main focus was his children and how he could make a better life for the three of them. His belief was that he didn't have to marry either of those women in order to be a good father. He went on to say that after praying for a wife, God delivered Mrs. Harold to him and he had never been happier. He loved his wife and was not ashamed to let anyone know it.

Mrs. Harold was a snazzy lil woman. Her soft silver hair was flawless, her burgundy and black dress fit like it was tailor made, and just by looking at her. You could tell she was all about her business. More importantly, looking at her, you could tell she was in love with her husband. Even at 67 years of age and after 43 years of marriage, she treated Mr. Harold like a king. She looked at him with glowing eyes each time she made contact with him. It was funny to me how she even giggled girlishly at his jokes. Their interaction with one another was amazing to Michael.It blew him away. It proved that true love was real and you can be happily in love.

After Mr. Harold was finished talking, Mrs. Harold spoke up. "Yes, honey, love can be tricky, but I can assure you that it is real. The kind of love that I have for Mr. Harold here is strong like the love that I have for the Lord. I honor my husband. I cherish the years that God has given me to share with him, and I praise God for our union. He treats me as his queen and he, my dear sweet young man, is my king." She looked up at Mr. Harold.

***

I interrupted Michael to comment on his story. "Wow! That's amazing, Michael. I've never heard anything like it. Did you ask them how they met? Did she have any children of her own? Do they have any children together?"

"As a matter of fact, I asked them those exact questions. Mr. Harold said he had gotten to a point in his life where he was tired of running the streets and running women. Running women had got him to the point where he was 26 years old with a nine-year-old son, a five-year-old son, and a three-year-old baby girl. He didn't have any plans of adding to his bunch, so he knew that some things were going to have to change. Although he could have his choice of woman, he was ready to settle down so he began to pray. He said that it had been a pretty long time since he'd talked to God, but that night he was reminded of a conversation he had had with his great grandmother as a young boy. She told him that whenever he got lonely, confused, sad, or upset and felt like there was nobody he could rely on, he should always remember that we all have our own private prayer closet where we are able to go to the Lord in prayer."

Michael went on to explain that Mr. Harold explained that his great-grandmother was the person that taught him how to pray. She was wise and had given him the foundation that he was now standing on. Mr. Harold said he could remember his great-grandmother getting down on the side of the bed onto her knees and having him close beside her; this was one of the rituals that had to be done each and every night before they went to bed. He said that he could remember how she called out to God then would begin talking to Him like she was talking to one of her best friends. When he was really young, he didn't understand why she would get on her knees and talk to the ceiling, but after years of sitting up on his knees next to her, he finally realized that prayer was just a conversation with God. We are supposed to talk to Him because He is our father. He is our friend. He is our everything. Our relationship with Him has to be nurtured in order for it to remain strong. Just like any other relationship, communication is the key. If the communication is dead, then so is the relationship.

Mr. Harold said that one night he sat on the side of his bed thinking about how he used to watch his great-grandmother pray to God and how each time he would hear her ask God to do something, give her something, or make something happen, a few days later it was done.

There were many things in his heart that he wanted to come to pass like finally getting his college education, starting his own business, and a few other things he had his heart set on that had to be put off in order to raise his children. Mr. Harold said he knew he needed a strong partner who was willing and ready to work herknuckles to the bone in order for those things to happen and finally come to pass. He continued on with his story.

"I recall one night coming home from one of the bars that I frequented with my friends and I was supposed to meet a young lady back at my apartment. I remember getting to the apartment and all of a sudden feeling sick, not ill from a sickness, but my heart had grown sick from all the games I was playing. When the young lady arrived, I apologized to her and asked if we could get together later because I needed some time to myself. Shocked that I turned her down for a late-night rendezvous, she fussed with me about coming over for nothing and firmly asked me to never call her again. After she left, I fell to my knees and cried out to God to rid me of my ways and send me a wife."

Michael said he was in shock when Mr. Harold said that because he had heard of people asking God for things, but since he had never done it, he didn't really understand the concept. He went on to say that not more than a month later, God saw fit that Mr. Harold ran into his queen at a local fair and they had been together every day since that one.

"So, what did she have to say?" By this time, I was all up in this story.

"Believe it or not, Geena, her story was similar. Although she didn't have any children, she had her share of boyfriends and acquaintances. She, too, had gotten to a place in her life where she was ready to leave the clubbing and partying life behind her and settle down, but she didn't think she would ever have a husband. She told me a few stories about how her friends were either already married or in long-term relationships about to be married and how she was disgruntled about the situation she stood in."

Michael explained how Mrs. Harold told him, "I still remember that time in my life like it was yesterday, young man. I prayed often, but never for a spouse because I felt that would be a selfish prayer. Until one Sunday, I heard a sermon at church that changed my life forever. The Pastor was talking about how prayer is powerful and how God wants us to come to Him with everything. Like the old spiritual says, 'All our sins and grief to bear. All because we do not carry EVERYTHING to God in prayer.' The Pastor encouraged us that day to remember if there is a burden we feel is too heavy, take it to God. If we have an illness the doctors have told us cannot be healed, take it to God; if we have a bill that we cannot afford to pay, take it to God; even if we stump our toe and want to curse, don't curse but just take it to God.

"That same night, I got down on my knees and talked to God about my future and the things that I wanted to accomplish. A few weeks later, I was on my knees saying my prayers before I got into bed and I began to weep. My heart was full and my mind was focused on God. I asked the Lord to prepare me for the mate that He saw fit to be my husband. I didn't want to have to go and find him like I had heard so many of my friends say they were going to the club to do. Because I knew the bible verse that reads, 'He that findeth a wife, findeth a good thing.' I knew the responsibility was not left to me. My husband was supposed to come and find me because that is what God said and I trusted God wholeheartedly. He had never let me down before. Lo and behold, not more than a month later Mr. Harold came knocking at my door."

Michael paused in his story and looked at me.

"WOW. Just like that?"

"Yeah, Geena, just like that. They both said they were blessed to be married to their soul mate. Mrs. Harold said she loved the fact that God prepared them for one another and they didn't have to go through years of turmoil and pain before realizing they were made for each other. She said she's heard so many of her friends say their marriages are strong because of everything they have gone through and they are thankful for their ups and downs because it made them stronger.

"Mr. Harold said he is thankful that they didn't have to go through a lot of nonsense in order to realize their love could stand the test of time. People are in marriages and suffering in silence because they have to fight with demons from their past. Either they have cheated on their spouse or they have been cheated on, and no matter how they try to act like those feelings never come up, they do. That's another reason why they talk to young people about love and relationships. If someone cheats on you, they don't love you, and if they love you, they won't cheat on you. Marrying someone that deliberately hurts you, hurts YOU!"

"Now that is deep. I guess that's why Jared and I never could get it together. I tried to mask my hurt, but it only caused more harm to both of us. On the outside looking in, we had the perfect life. Married, two successful careers, beautiful children, huge home, nice cars, fancy clothes, but underneath it all we were in pain due to the fact that we had married somebody else's husband and wife."

I placed my hand on Michael's knee, and then he placed his hand on top of mine, looked into my eyes and told me, "I've learned that it takes someone special to show you your flaws then help you to grow from them, and I'm willing to be that person for you, Geena."

I leaned in to kiss Michael and then took him by his hand. "Now let's go upstairs and enjoy our last night on this beautiful resort."

After our mini-excursion, Michael and I were pretty inseparable. There wasn't a weekend that passed that we didn't spend some quality time together. He would fly into town to see me, and I would fly out to see him.I was having the time of my life; I felt like I was in college again. Our days were filled with love, and I couldn't believe how alive I felt.

Frances and Lily were doing well in school and in their extracurricular activities. Even my relationship with Jared was going well. We hadn't argued or anything in what seemed like forever. I was finally getting to the point where I was able to deal with the demise of our relationship as well as our divorce. In celebration of that, I decided to do something special for Michael. He was always doing something out of the ordinary to surprise me and I wanted to at least try to return the favor. I called him and told him I wanted him to fly in, but instead of meeting at our regular hotel, I thought it was time he came to my house. He couldn't believe it and quickly agreed to the plan.

That weekend we had a ball! We went to an NBA game, shopping downtown, saw a Tyler Perry play, and spent time just talking and enjoying each other. As I was coming downstairs one afternoon, I noticed he was staring at my girls' pictures hanging on the wall.

"Hey, Michael! Whatchya doin?"

"Oh, hey! I was just looking at these pictures. You have some beautiful daughters."

"Thank you, sir. They get it from they MahMah." We both laughed.

"So, when do I get to meet them?"

"Uhmm, I really haven't given that too much thought, Michael. I don't want to rush them into anything."

"Rush? Geena, it will soon be a year that we rekindled our relationship. How much longer will I have to wait to meet them? Being that I will be a part of their lives, I think we need to do it sooner rather than later."

"You're right, but let me talk to them about it first. Fair enough?"

Michael pulled me close to him and kissed me then replied, "Fair enough!"

My World Turns Upside Down
Chapter 15

I should have known that all good things must come to an end. Things were just going too good for them to last forever. The day started like most Fridays, with Michael and I talking on the phone making plans for the weekend and catching up on any prior week's events that we'd omitted talking about earlier in the week. This Friday things seemed a little different. His conversation wasn't the same and I could tell that something wasn't right.

"Michael, is everything okay?"

He hesitated, cleared his throat, and then took a deep breath. "Well, Geena, there is something that's kind of bothering me, but I don't want to discuss it over the phone. Do me a favor. Go ahead and get dressed and I'll be over in about an hour so we can go to dinner and talk."

My heart sank. As always, I thought the worst! I couldn't swallow and my head began to hurt. "Huh? You tell me something like that and expect me to wait an entire hour to talk to you? Come on, Michael. You can't keep me hanging like that. Please tell me what's going on. Okay, at least tell me this. Are you planning to stop seeing me? You can just say that over the phone. There's no need for you to take me out in public to embarrass me."

Michael laughed. "Geena, baby, calm down and stop jumping to conclusions. Why do you always think of the worst case scenarios? Give me an hour and I'll explain everything to you when I get there. Will you please let me talk to you in person?"

I began to feel sick, almost like I had just heard a close friend or family member had passed away, even though he had tried to reassure me. I just had an awful feeling that something wasn't right. "Okay, Michael, but please hurry. You know how I hate to wait."

After we hung up, I scurried to get my things together and continued to torture myself by thinking the worst. What could be wrong? I kept questioning myself over and over again. The last year had been pure bliss with Michael back in my life; because of him the transition with the divorce was much smoother than I could have imagined. He was there to keep me sane during the times I could have gone crazy. He was my voice of reason, my listening ear, and my shoulder to cry on. I couldn't help worrying myself. Was it something that I did unknowingly? Had he decided the long-distance relationship was not going to work? Was he tired of me putting him on hold for my hand in marriage? Could it be another woman?

I paced the house waiting for Michael to arrive. I looked at the clock as it changed to 7:52. He had eight minutes to arrive. At exactly eight, I could see car lights from the blinds flash on the house. It was Michael. I immediately went to the door. By the time the lights on the Ranger Rover were out, my hand was on the driver side door. "Where's my explanation?"

Michael got out of the car giving me a warm hug and kiss like he always did. "Hey, beautiful."

I tried to ignore the soft scent that came from his baby blue Charles Tywart collar. "Don't 'hey' me Michael, you said you were coming over to talk. You're here, and I'm all ears. Let's talk. "

"Geena, we're gonna talk, but do you think I could possibly come in first?"

I wasn't up for wasting any more time. "Michael, come on. It's killing me!"

"What's killing you?"

"The news!"

Michael looked up at the sky, took a deep breath, then said, "Oh yeah, the news. Come on inside and let's sit down and talk."

My heart began to thump out of my chest as he held my hand walking into the house, not knowing what kind of words were going to escape his lips. We walked in and took a seat on the love seat in the great room. The television and radio were off, so we sat in complete silence. After a few moments, Michael pulled me close to him, looked me in the eye and began to speak.

"Geena, I got word a few months ago about a job offer that my Senior Director suggested I take."

"And the bad news is? WHAT? Michael, what are

you talking about? Advancement is always positive. Why the need to tell me this in person, and why am I just hearing about it if you got the offer months ago?"

"Well, that's part of the reason I wanted to talk to you face to face. I've been trying to find a way to turn the position down."

"Turn it down? But why?"

"Because, Geena, although it is a hell of a pay increase and a great career opportunity for me, I had my reservations."

"You HAD reservations or you HAVE reservations?"

"Well I had them?"

"So that means you are taking the new position?" Michael paused to gather his thoughts.

"Yes, Geena, I have decided to take it."

I was relieved! "So the big news was good news? You wanted to take me out to celebrate the BIG promotion? I'm so happy for you! That is exciting! Congratulations! And all this time I was tripping thinking it was something bad!" I stood up laughing at myself looking in the mirror to put on my lip gloss from my purse. "You work hard, Michael, and you deserve it. Your director knows you have what it takes to go to the next level, and he knew that you would be the man for the job. WOW!"

I turned to lean in to kiss him, but as I got closer, he held his hands out to stop me. "Wait, Geena, that's not it.There's more."

I was confused and didn't know what to think

about his refusal to kiss me, or what he was going to say next. "What's not it?"

Michael took my hands and pulled me back down to sit beside him on the love seat, staring into my eyes with a seriousness I had never seen from him before. "Well, there's more."

My heart skipped a beat and I held my breath. "Okay, Michael, continue."

"The reason I never brought the new job up to you was because I was contemplating really hard. You see, for the past few months I've been enjoying spending time with and getting reacquainted with a very special young lady that God allowed to come back into my life. During this time, I realized she was what I needed in my life and I decided that I would be marrying her in the very near future." I began to smile. "But with this job that may not happen." My smile disappeared. "This job will take me out of the country for fifteen months, Geena. Although we have done well with our long-distance relationship this past year, this will be a whole new ball game. We can't just jump on a plane to see one another. We will only be able to rely on the telephone and Skype."

There was an awkward silence sitting between us, and I didn't know what to say. "WOW. That is some news, Michael. I don't know what to say."

"I know, Geena, that's why I felt we should talk in person and not over the phone."

I dropped my head in sadness thinking about the news I was just force-fed. My eyes filled with tears as I tried to keep them from falling. After a few minutes, Michael took my chin to lift my head and saw the water as it crept down my cheeks.

"Geena, look at me. Listen, this doesn't mean that it's over for us. We will just have to find a way to hold on to what we have while I take this tour. Do you think you can wait on me?"

"Michael, I don't know what I... I don't... How am I... I just... Why is this happening to us? Things are going so well! Why all of a sudden does your job want to send you away?"

"Geena, baby, listen. This is why I contemplated for so long. I put our relationship before it all, but when I thought about it for the long-term benefits, I realized it would benefit us both. This could be the time you take to really sort things out with Jared without me clouding your judgment."

"Hold on. How did Jared get into this?"

"Geena, since the divorce the two of you still haven't come to terms with how the properties are being handled and I think you are kind of dragging your feet because you have gotten comfortable."

"Michael, that property is the least of my worries!"

"That's my point exactly. You need to handle that business, Geena, because when we're married, I don't want any outside influences on the decisions that we make for our future."

I paused, did he just say married? Briefly after his statement, he stood to take something out of his pocket then got down on one knee. Taking a deep breath, then extending his right hand to take my left, Michael uttered those four little words that every girl hopes to be asked one day. "Will you marry me?"

I was floored. There was a mixture of emotions. I was shocked! Excited! Happy! Blown away!

"Yes, Michael! Yes!! I will marry you!!" Michael slipped a four-carat diamond ring on my finger that sparkled like the stars in the sky.

"I love you, Geena."

My gaze left the sparkle in the diamond and went directly to the sparkle in Michael's eyes as I responded. "And I love you!"

For the remainder of the weekend, we talked about us and all that we wanted to accomplish as a couple.

When Michael left Sunday night, I had only a few hours before Jared brought the girls home so I had to make a dash over to see Stephanie. I didn't even call her. I was so excited I just went straight to her house. When I arrived, I noticed there was a Silver 6 series BMW and a champagne-colored Bentley in Steph's driveway. Both were unfamiliar cars. At any other time, I wouldn't barge in on someone that had company, but this time was different. I didn't care; my concern was showing off my bling and telling her the big news! I took the keys out of the ignition of my Vette and ran to her front door, ringing the doorbell and knocking on the door like someone was after me.

"I'm commmmminnnng. Whooooo issssssss itttttt?"

"It's me, Steph. Open up!"

She opened the door and greeted me with her ever

so sarcastic mouth. "So, uhm, we don't call no mo?"

We laughed and hugged each other while I made my way through the door. "What's UP, Geena?"

"Stephanie, I'm so sorry for coming over unannounced but, BaayyBeey, we gotta TALK!"

"Come on in, Geena. I have some company, but you're more than welcome to chill with us."

I walked in behind her thinking, did I NOT just tell this chick I needed to talk to her. I wasn't there for the social hour. "Stephanie, could we just go straight to your room and talk. I don't have much time before Jared brings the girls home."

"Hold on, Geena. Don't be rude now. I want you to meet my friends first."

I could feel myself getting irritated so I took a deep breath and agreed to meet these folks so I could get on with my announcement.

"Geena, this is Rodney." He extended his arm out to shake my hand.

"Hi Rodney."

"And this is Zack."

I shook his hand as quickly as I could, hoping to get to business. "Hi, guys, it's very nice to meet you, but I'm in a rush and just need to talk to Stephanie for a quick second. If you don't mind, we're going to excuse ourselves for just a moment. Thank you." I grabbed Stephanie by the arm and dragged her to the back room.

"What is your problem, Geena? Why are you being so rude?"

"Stephanie! Did you hear a word I said at the door? I need to TALK to you! LOOK!"I held my left ring finger up at her.

"Daaayyyyyuuuummmm! Don't tell me that's what I THINK it is!"

"Yes, Stephanie! We are getting married!" We screamed and hugged each other, jumping up and down.

"Okay, Geena! When did this happen? How did this happen? When is the big day? I know I'm the Maid, the Matron, the Flower girl, or something."

"Yes, Stephanie, you know you will be my right hand."

"Okay, Geena! Spill it! How did it happen? When did it happen?"

"Well, he came over tonight to tell me about this new job opportunity that he has overseas."

Stephanie gave me that look that she gives when she's about to curse. "Overseas? You mean like not in the United States?"

"Yes, Steph, that's what overseas means."

"So you mean to tell me you're about to marry a man that won't even be living in the States? I mean I questioned ya'll doing the long-distance thing before, but this is taking it too far."

"He isn't going to live there for good, Stephanie. He's only going to be gone for fifteen months. That will give us time to plan the wedding."

Stephanie looked at me cross-eyed as she walked around the room to get her glass that was sitting on her dresser. She sipped on it a few times, as she gathered her thoughts. "I don't know, Geena. Fifteen whole months with NO contact? That sounds kind of risky."

"How does that sound risky?"

"Listen, it's hard enough being faithful to someone that lives in the same house that you live in, let alone someone in another country. I think he's trying to trap you, Geena."

"Trap me? HOW? What do you mean?"

"Look, He's leaving right, okay. But he puts a ring on your finger right before he goes? Sounds like, looks like, smells like a set up to me. But hey! To each his own, my sister. If you like it, I love it."

I could feel myself getting angry. How could she talk to me this way when she was the one that insisted I get on with my life? "Wait a minute, Ms. Know-Every-Damn-Thang! I didn't come over here for this! I came over to share a very special moment with my very best friend! How dare you treat me this way?"

"Geena, look, okay, I'm sorry. I didn't mean to rain on your parade. I guess I'm just playing devil's advocate. I'm happy for you, Geena, but I just want you to be careful. Give me a hug."

Stephanie put her glass down before coming over to hug me. "You forgive me, BFF?"

We both laughed because that was what we used to always say to each other when we fell out as teenagers only to make up again in the next few minutes. Stephanie always knew how to push my buttons, but that's my girl and I loved her.

"Yes, heffa! I forgive you! Wait, what time is it?"

"Uhhmm, it's almost nine, why?"

"Oh goodness! Let me get out of here! Jared will have the girls home in a few minutes! Gotta go! I'll call you later."

As I rushed from the back, I passed the room where the two gentlemen were sitting and just threw my hand up in goodbye. I didn't realize the one named Zack was outside walking back in from his car. He caught my eye as I rushed past him. *Hhhmm*, I thought, *he's a cutie for a guy with a bald head.*

Later on that night after I got the girls settled in, I talked on the phone to Michael until I fell asleep.

Michael found out later that week that his office would be ready and they needed him sooner than later. I was upset of course, but looked at the situation as giving us more time to plan for the wedding and the sooner he left, the sooner he could get back home and I would be Mrs. Michael Sullivan; that name had such a nice ring to it. I remembered writing it all over my folders when we were in high school, accompanied with hearts, stars, and little zigzag lines. Just to think how life brings about such big changes.

The night before Michael had to leave, we made passionate love and held each other. We talked about our future and all the blessings we were asking God for. I drove him to the airport that day with a large lump in my heart. Tears filled the corners of my eyes and my head was hurting from trying so hard to keep them from creeping down my chin. Although I knew he was leaving, I still didn't want him to go. I was upset because I wasn't going to be able to speak with him until the following day; as soon as he got there he would have to meet with his colleagues and get straight to work.

To get my mind off of everything, I decided to call Stephanie since her house was on the way from the airport and the girls were gone with Jared.

"Hello?"

"Hey, Steph."

"Hey, Geena! What's wrong?"

Stephanie always knew when there was something wrong with me just from the sound of my voice. "I just wanted to come over and have a drink or something."

"Cool, come on over! We're about to start a card game and we need one more person. Kim had something come up so you can be our fourth wheel."

It sounded like an okay idea, and I really didn't want to sit in the house alone so I decided to join them; spending time with Stephanie, Rachel, and Kim always meant I was about to have a good time. "Okay, Stephanie, I'll be over in a minute. Is there anything you need for me to bring?"

"Uhhmm, nahhh. Just come on over." As I drove up I noticed there were no cars in the driveway. I didn't mind because that would give me time to mellow out before the others arrived. Before I could get to the door to ring the bell, Stephanie was there to open it up. "What UP, Gee!"

"Hey, Stephanie! Thanks for having me over, girl! Uhmm, where is everybody?"

"They are on the way, come on in. What's up with you?"

I plopped down in a chair at the kitchen table. "Girl, I just took Michael to the airport and I'm just out of my mind."

"Well, don't worry, we'll cheer you up." The doorbell rang. "Hold on, Geena, let me get that."

When the door opened, I heard two guys talking and laughing, then they walked in with brown paper bags covering their faces. As they got closer to the kitchen where I was sitting, I noticed that it was the two guys from a few weeks ago. I guess I had a nasty look on my face because when Stephanie took the seat next to me, she pinched me before reintroducing them.

"Geena, you remember my friends, Rodney and Zack?"

I reached my hand towards her leg, pinching her back before I answered. "Yes, I do. Hi, guys!"

"Hey, Geena. Whassup?" Rodney said as he placed the brown paper bags on the table in front of us.

"Nothing much, just stopped by to say hello to Stephanie. I didn't mean to intrude so I'll be on my way."

Stephanie looked at me like 'WHAT?' and as I tried to walk out she pulled me to the back room.

"Hey guys, go ahead and get the card table ready and the drinks blending. We'll be right back."

Once we got to the bedroom, Stephanie closed the

door and leaned against it. "What are you doing, Geena?"

"What am I doing? What are YOU doing?"

"Well, Ms. Gotta GO, I recall you phoning me stating you needed to get out of the house!"

"And I recall you saying I should come over for a card game because Kim couldn't come due to a change in her plans!"

"And that is what happened, so what's the problem?"

"Well, I assumed there were some more females over here. You know how I am about being around dudes that aren't my dude!"

"Like I always say, when you assume, you make an ass out of u and me. Look, Geena! Get over it! These are some cool guys that I've known for years. We went to school together, and had the same internship at the hospital. Rodney is a pediatric surgeon and Zack is a gynecologist. Their schedules are pretty crazy, so we try to hang out from time to time whenever we get a chance."

"So what happened to you?"

"What do you mean, what happened to me?"

"If you all are so tight and both of them are successful physicians, and you all interned together, then what happened to you?"

"Oh, well you know me, Geena. I'm an 'artist' ." We both burst into laughter.

"Girl, you are a mess!"

Stephanie came from money. Her mother had

married a very wealthy European man that came from a lineage of great businessmen and leaders who were serious about paving the way for their children and setting them up for prosperous futures, so my girl Steph was set for life.

"No seriously, Geena, you know my folks left me a bank full of money so I really didn't have a need to go into medicine."

"But all that time in school, Steph?"

"I know but at 33 years of age, baby, I can think of more things to do with my day than spend it in a hospital full of sick people."

"Stephanie! That wasn't nice. We need good doctors. You should be proud of your accomplishment and start a practice of your own." Steph's father wanted her to be a physician, so she only went to school to fulfill his wishes.

"I'm just kidding around, Geena. I respect the profession, but I don't think that's what I was called to do. Remember you taught me that? We got a calling?"

"Don't make light of my spirituality, Stephanie."

She giggled then continued. "No. I'm being serious. I really don't think I would be a good doctor because it's not something I could see myself doing and be excited about it."

"So what is it you feel you've been called to do, Stephanie?"

"Uhmm… shopping, going to the gym, hanging out with you, my BFF."

"I'm serious, Steph, Don't you ever get bored doing

the same thing, day in and day out?"

Stephanie looked at me with crossed eyes and said, "Uhmm, the question is don't YOU get bored doing the same thing day in and day out?"

"I didn't mean it like that. I'm just saying. I just want you to have a life of fulfillment. You know, get married, have a few babies."

"Now there YOU go with that! How many times do I have to explain to ya'll "married mothers" that is NOT my calling!" We both burst into laughter. "Geena, you know I cannot keep a man and I don't like lil' children, except yours, of course because they cool, but other lil' children, ohhhnooo. I don't DO them."

Stephanie was right, as beautiful as she was, she couldn't seem to keep a man. It seemed like most men were intimidated by her independence and ability to handle her own, so she dated a lot with no intentions of ever settling down. She didn't have any friends that she dealt with on a regular basis except for Rachel, Kim, and I. Since we were in school together, females either hated her and couldn't stand to be around her or loved her and tried their best to be her friend. She knew which girls didn't like her, but she could care less. If she didn't fool with you, you didn't exist to her anyway.

After we all finished school, she tried a few business ventures to keep her mind occupied and to have something to do during her shop time breaks. She opened a purse boutique for a little while, but couldn't seem to get along with the customers. She then tried consulting work for a little while, but couldn't seem to get along with the other consultants. After two failed businesses, she decided shopping and working out would fill her days. She had no real need for an income because she was living off of her inheritance. I suggested she could at least become a personal trainer, but realized that may not work because she would more than likely fall out with her clients. So being an "artist" meant she didn't have a job, and really didn't need one.

"You are so crazy, girl, but I gotta get out of here."

"Look, Geena, don't leave. Stay and have a few drinks, a few laughs. I won't let them bite you. I promise, you don't have to worry."

"If I didn't mind staying home alone, I would leave, but I guess one card game won't hurt anything."

It Wasn't So Bad After All
Chapter 16

I actually had a really good time that night and those guys were hilarious. Good company, good drinks and good fun! Stephanie and her friends helped me take my mind off of missing Michael so badly. A month or so passed before I heard anything else from those two characters. I was watching television in my bedroom one afternoon folding clothes when I thought about that night with Steph and the guys and how much fun we had. A few minutes later, my phone rang and it was Stephanie.

"Hey, Geena!"

"Hey, Steph. What's going on?"

"Nothing much. Are you busy?"

"No, just doing a little folding, what's up?"

"Do you remember the guy named Zack from the card game?"

"Yeah, I remember him! Funny you ask that because I was sitting here thinking about ya'll and how much fun we had that night."

"Yeah, we had a ball that night, didn't we?"

"Yes we did."

"Well, he's going to be giving free checkups and

medical advice to the ladies down at the shelter tomorrow and needs some volunteers to help fill out paperwork and greet the women. Will you have the girls this weekend?"

"No. It's Jared's turn to have them so count me in! You know that I love community service."

Stephanie snickered at my response. "Yeah, I told him you would be the best candidate for the job. I'm glad we'll be able to do this together, Geena. It should be a lot of fun. It always feels good to give back."

"You are right about that, Steph."

"Okay, go ahead and finish folding your clothes and I'll be over to pick you up around 7 a.m., so we can get there kind of early."

"All right, Stephanie, sounds like a plan. I'll see you in the morning."

Servicing More Than the Community
Chapter 17

It was freezing cold early that morning, and the sun was barely peeking out to say hello. As we arrived at the shelter, I was shocked to see so many women standing in line in need of medical attention. Just thinking about the situation they would be left in if these doctors hadn't decided to give back made me even more eager to volunteer. The ages ranged from ladies in their early twenties to women in their late fifties. There were black, white, Hispanic, and Oriental women standing in the cold with the hope of seeing the doctor that day. I felt more than fortunate that morning realizing that could have easily been me standing in their shoes. Stephanie and I entered the building ready to work our fingers to the bone for such a worthy cause. It seemed like the line continued to grow. There were women with children, women in wheelchairs, women wearing tattered and worn clothing, as well as women that resembled your average soccer mom.

By noon, we had filled out well over 84 forms. The doctors were working their butts off to see those women. One of the attendants that worked at the shelter went to the door to make an announcement that services would continue at 1 p.m. in order for us to take a break and get something to eat. I was so exhausted, but had an adrenaline rush from the excitement of helping others. While we sat at the break room table, Dr. Zack Stone came out to join us.

"Good afternoon, ladies." I guess I really hadn't paid much attention to him as a doctor, but but that white coat did wonders against Zack's dark skin. I skimmed the room and from the expression on the faces of the other ladies, they noticed too. Zack was tall and dark, with perfect white teeth. Even with his physician's coat, you could tell that he must work out seven days a week. He was bald, which was never a turn on for me. But his curly goatee and mustache set him apart from all the other bald men I had come in contact with in the past. He had a sexy confidence that would make any woman notice him.

"Good afternoon to you," we all sang in unison.

"I just wanted to speak to you ladies for a few minutes to thank you for your selflessness and for coming out this morning to help out with registering the women of the community."

I spoke up. "And we thank you for what you are doing down here. I wasn't aware that these kinds of services were even offered."

Zack pulled out a chair to sit with us as he explained the cause. "Well, Geena, this is something that we try to do twice each year, once in the winter and again in the summer. You wouldn't believe how many women don't have health insurance, and it's not just women that are homeless or unemployed. There are a lot of professionally employed women that don't carry health insurance because of the cost. Instead of electing for the insurance, they do without in order to handle some other obligations. No health insurance equals no medical attention.

"My mother passed away from cervical cancer when I was a teenager, and she would still be here today if she had the means to see a doctor sooner." Zack looked down at his hands. "After her death, I promised myself I would become a doctor someday and that I would do all I could to prevent another young man from losing his mother to cancer or any other illness that could be dealt with through early detection, medical attention, and care."

I was moved by the compassion he had for his profession. Zack truly had a calling over his life. Being a physician wasn't his job, not even his career choice. It was what God intended for him to do.

"Well, ladies, let me leave you because I've been known to have the skills to talk a pair of ears clean off."

One of the girls at the table leaned over and whispered to me, "I bet he can talk some panties clean off too." We snickered and laughed.

Zack caught us.

"Did I miss something?"

I gathered myself before responding. "Oh no, Dr. Stone, Everything's fine. Thank you again for taking a little time out to come talk with us."

"Well, you ladies enjoy the rest of your afternoon and thank you again."

When he walked away, I felt even more compelled to help these ladies that weren't able to help themselves. The time seemed to speed by after lunch. When 6 p.m. hit, we had serviced close to 200 women. To see the looks on their faces after they had received their services warmed my heart. Zack and his colleagues came out to thank us again for assisting them after the last patient was seen. I left that night feeling accomplished and blessed. I was reminded again of the old adage, 'It is better to GIVE than to RECEIVE.' Giving of my time gave me one of the greatest gifts I had ever received.

I called Stephanie the next day to ask her if the doctors would be hosting any more events and if so, I wanted her to let them know I would like to offer my hand to help out. Steph said that Zack would be over with Rodney later and that I should come by. I agreed to stop in after Jared picked up the girls.

As I hurried downstairs to grab my keys and jump in the car, I stumbled over a book Lily had left on the floor. Catching my balance, I stood up looking directly in the wall mirror hanging near the door out to the garage. I took a few steps back then looked at my reflection staring back at me. My eyes grew teary as I thought about how much my life had changed in the past few years. I had gone from being a married mother of two children just going through life accepting the daily hustle and bustle, lacking the one thing that I needed most to beinga fulfilled woman with new purpose, new meaning, and new love. Tears fell as I felt a sense of being, I was finally happy with my life.

The guys had already arrived by the time I got to Stephanie's house. When I walked in, they were sitting around listening to some music and having drinks.

"Hey, Geena!" Zack got up to take my coat. "How are you?"

"I am well. Thank you for asking. What are you guys doing?"

"Well I thought it would be a good idea to bring some wine over for you ladies. You DO like the blue bottle of Moscato?" He put the bottle and a wine glass right in front of me.

"I don't drink much, but I do enjoy sipping on a glass from the blue bottle." I noticed Rodney taking something out of a brown paper bag.

"What are you fellas sipping on?"

"Well, Rodney and I are having some Grand Marnier."

"What's that? Never heard of it before."

"Well it's a soft mellow drink that reminds you of a cognac. Would you like to try it?"

"No thank you. Brown liquor makes my head hurt, so I'll stick with this. Thank you. Hey, where's Stephanie!" I could hear her walking towards us, heels clicking on the hard wood floors.

"Hey, Geena! You ready to get this card game started?"

"Sure! Let's do it."

While we were there Zack went into greater detail about his childhood. He talked about the things he saw that he despised as a child, like living in poverty, drugs, gangs, early death, and crime. He vowed not to repeat any of those behaviors in his adult life. Living in the projects was hard, but he was fortunate to have a strong mother that placed him in programs that cultivated relationships with strong men that he wanted to emulate.. I was totally intrigued by his conversation. He was intelligent, warm, caring, and not to mention- he kept me laughing.

We became very good friends over the next few months talking on the phone more and more, playing cards at Stephanie's house, and working together to help the women of the community. He had the best sense of humor, and I enjoyed his company.

A Little Too Close for Comfort
Chapter 18

One Saturday afternoon as I was preparing for a board meeting, my secretary came in with a beautiful bouquet of flowers.

"Ms. G., these are for you!" I thought, *Michael! How sweet.* I couldn't wait to tear into the card to read what my sweetie had written me, but to my shock, the card didn't have a message from Michael and the beautiful bouquet wasn't from him either. The card read:

"Geena! Just wanted to share this beautiful bouquet with a beautiful person. Hope you are enjoying your day! Zack." I stood with the card in my hand reading it over and over and over.

"You are one lucky lady, Ms. G! Wow! To have flowers sent to you from across the country!"

I didn't even look up at Brittney. I didn't know what to say and I was so glad she hadn't seen what was really written on that card.

"Uhm, yeah, thank you, Brittney. Put these in water for me, please. I gotta get to this meeting."

"Yes, ma'am Ms. G! Should I put the card?" She was reaching for it, so I had to snatch it away.

"Uhm no, Brittney. I'll keep this one." Walking to

the elevator for my meeting, all I could think about were the flowers. Why would Zack send me flowers? After the meeting was over, I called him as soon as I got into my car. He didn't answer so I left a message. "Hi, Zack, it's Geena. Just wanted to say it wasn't really necessary to send me flowers, although they are beautiful. I, uhhmm, I'll talk to you later." I felt so dumb hanging up, why didn't I just say, "Hey, whassup with sending flowers to my job. I am engaged to be married in less than eleven months." But for some reason those words didn't come out. After I hung up, I immediately called Stephanie.

"Hello!"

"Girl, you are not going to believe this!"

"What?"

"How about I was at my desk today when Brittney comes in with these flowers that I assumed were from Michael."

"SO, who were they from?"

"You aren't going to believe this!"

"Don't tell me Jared!"

"Hell nawl, come on now, Steph! No! It's worse! Ya doctor friend, Zack!"

"WHAT! Zack sent you flowers? What did the card say?"

"It was something like 'you're beautiful, enjoy your day'!" Stephanie stopped me before I could finish my sentence.

"Geena, when was the last time you talked to Zack?" In that instance, I felt guilty, like I had done something wrong. I never even put too much thought into when or how long I talk to Zack. Until then.

"Last night."

"Last night? How often do ya'll talk?"

"Well, ever since we started doing that volunteer work with him, we've been kind of like talking every day."

"EVERY day? Since four months ago? Geeena! What are you doing?"

"What do you mean? What am I doing?"

"I mean what I said! Don't play with fire, Gee! You are bound to get burned!"

"Girl, please! I love Michael and no one else. Zack is someone to talk to in the meantime. He's a nice guy and all, but you know I have no intentions like THAT towards him."

"Well you may NOT, but it's evident that he does! Why else would this man send you flowers?"

My phone began to beep because someone was calling from the other line. "Hold on, Steph, let me catch my other line."

"Hello?"

"Hey, Geena!" It was Zack and I was ready to talk to him!

"Good evening, Zack."

"Whoa, that was dry. Is everything okay?"

"To tell you the truth, things are not okay. I'm confused as to why you sent flowers to my job." I had caught an attitude with him before I knew it, thinking about the conversation I was having with Stephanie.

"Ohh, that is what this is about? Look, Geena, it wasn't to offend you. I just saw the flowers and thought it would be nice to send them to you to thank you for your generosity over the past few months. Giving of your time is a precious gift and I thought the flowers would be a nice gesture."

Wow, did I feel like a butt hole! Jumping to conclusions like I always do. "Oh. I'm sorry, Zack. I read too deeply into it. Please accept my apology."

"It's no problem, Geena. Apology accepted." I had almost forgotten that Stephanie was on the other line.

"Oh, Zack. I gotta go. I forgot my other line."

"Well wait, I have a favor to ask of you."

"Okay, what is it?"

"I'm hosting a benefit in two weeks in Los Angeles, and I would love for you to go."

"In Los Angeles? What kind of benefit?"

"It's for the clinic that my partners and I are trying to start."

"Okay and Los Angeles is NOT in driving distance, so?"

"Well, of course it's an overnight trip, Geena, BUT you would have your own room and we would be back the next day."

"Overnight? I can't go anywhere overnight with you, Zack!"

"Why not? It's not like we'll be sharing a room."

"Well, why me? Isn't there someone else you could take?"

"There are many people that I could take, but none

of those people have made the connection that you have with the women at the shelter. Those women look up to you and I need to have you there to let my colleagues from around the world know how beneficial this FREE program is. Having you there to speak on your experiences will allow them to hear it, from the horse's mouth. We need other cities and states to jump on the bandwagon so we can help more people."

I thought about what he was saying and I really wanted to help out, but what would Michael think. "Okay, Dr. Stone, let me think things over and I will be in touch with you soon."

"Thanks, Geena, and listen. I really am sorry about the flower incident."

"No, Dr. Stone. I'm sorry for the way I acted. You have a good night, and I'll talk to you soon."

"You do the same, Geena."

I was afraid to click back over to Stephanie because I knew she was going to go off for keeping her on hold for so long!

"Hey, Chick! I'm back!"

"Dannnnnggg, who was that? JESUS?" I laughed at Steph; she loved saying if it ain't Jesus, then it shouldn't take that long!

"No girl, it was Dr. Stone."

"Ohhyeahh! And what did ole' Zack have to say? Did ya kuss him out for sending you those flowers?"

"Nah. I had, no, well we read too deep into it. He was just being friendly and trying to thank me for continuing to help out at the shelter UNLIKE some folks I know!"

"Oh, honey, don't do me. I told ya'll I be busy! I'll come down there when I can, but I have a life I need to service, just like ya'll service the community."

We both laughed. "Girl, you are crazy!"

"But seriously, Geena, I'm glad you have found something that makes your time worthwhile since the girls are with Jared a lot, and Michael is away."

"Yeah, volunteering is always a good thing and it takes my mind off things." I paused trying to gather my thoughts before I went deeper into the conversation that I had with Zack.

"Oh yeah, by the way, Stephanie, Dr. Stone asked me to go to a benefit with him to talk about my experiences with the women at the shelter."

"Sounds like a worthy cause, when is it? I'll probably go with you."

"It's in two weeks."

"Oh! That sounds like fun. I will definitely make plans to come and support ya'll."

"Well, that may not be so easy."

"What do you mean?"

I said a small prayer before I continued. "Because the benefit is in Los Angeles."

Stephanie screamed from the top of her lungs through the phone. "LOS ANGELES! Girl, have you lost your mind? I know you are not going out of town with this man!"

"Come on, Stephanie, you talk like you don't know

Zack. Haven't ya'll been close friends for about eleven or twelve years?"

"Well yeah, but I don't know, Geena. That sounds a lil too close for comfort. Ya'll talk all the time, spend a lot of time together, he sends you flowers, and now wants to take you to L.A.?"

"It's not like we'll be in the same hotel room!"

"I don't care. You will be in the same HOTEL! Out of TOWN!"

"Look, Stephanie! I know what I am doing! TRUST me on this!"

"Okay, Geena. You better be careful, and what is Michael going to say?"

I hadn't even put too much thought into that. I just planned to handle it when I talked to him. "I will tell him, Steph. I will."

That night I talked to Michael about what was going on with Dr. Stone, minus the flower delivery; he was so proud of me! He said he thought it was a great thing Dr. Stone was trying to do and he was honored that I would be there to speak on behalf of the women. Although he was all with it, I still felt kind of uncomfortable. I guess because of the flower incident and from listening to Steph rant and rave. So I asked him again for reassurance.

"So you really think I should go, babe?"

"Of course you should! Any time we are given an opportunity to bless someone, it is our duty to do so."

I was feeling guilty for the simple fact that I really wasn't being totally honest with Michael. Him not knowing how I met Zack and the fact that we had developed a friendship didn't sit well with me, but for the sake of the cause, I ignored those feelings and decided to go through with the trip. "You're right, babe. I'll let Dr. Stone know tomorrow that he can count me in.

"Okay, well I have to meet with a client in a bit, Geena, so I'll talk to you later. I love you."

"I love you more, Michael."

Dr. Zackary Stone
Chapter 19

The week before the event, Zack called to tell me that they needed us in L.A. sooner than they thought, and that there were three events requiring our presence. There would be one Friday night, one Saturday morning, and another one Saturday afternoon. This meant we wouldn't get back into town until Sunday evening. I was hesitant because of the sudden change in plans and having to stay overnight, but didn't want to pull out of the obligation since I had given my word, so I went ahead and kept my commitment.

We arrived in Los Angeles, checked in the hotel, and arrived just in time for the first event. It was great! I had such a good time and luckily all three of the events were spectacular! I met a lot of new people and everybody loved the ideas that Zack had about the free health screenings and his take on spreading the good News About Health. I was so pleased about how everything had gone and so was Zack. A few of the doctors had gotten together for lunch earlier and wanted to go out for drinks later that night. Since it was the last night in town, I agreed to go on the stroll

181

with them. We had the best time, laughing and talking, getting to know one another. I always had the misconception that doctors were stuffy and uptight and only used words like arteries, blood vessels, lungs, and kidneys. But to my surprise, they were real people that liked to have real fun. It was late when we left the club, so Zack walked me back to my room. I was pretty tipsy and being in a foreign environment, I was glad that he offered. Zack walked me all the way to my hotel room door as we exchanged a small conversation.

"I hope you've enjoyed yourself, Geena."

"Oh I have! Everything has been awesome! From the time we got off the plane till now, it has been a great experience and I'm forever grateful for this opportunity to do something I've never done before."

I turned away from Zack to open my room door, but couldn't get the card to slide through the slot. I think it was that last glass of wine. Zack noticed my inability to open my door so he leaned over to assist me.

"Let me help you with that, Geena."

As I turned back around to say goodnight and thank him for making sure I got back to my room safely, I was met by his lips, which were soft and tender and tasted like sweet mint mixed with a hint of vodka and lime. My heart and my mind told me to resist him, but my body said I should welcome him in.

"Wait. Zack, what are you doing?" After a few moments, I closed my eyes and returned the kiss that tasted like ecstasy. My hand began to lose the grip on the door handle as we fell back into my room. The door closed as Zack walked me towards the bed, pushing his body against mine until we were parallel to the pillows. I began to run my hands up and down the back of his bald head as he ran his large hands up and down my hips and thighs.

"Oh, Zack. what are we doing?" I whispered to him in between my pants and moans.

It didn't take long for his white button down to be off and my pink blouse unbuttoned. He kissed my neck with his soft lips, stopping ever so often to softly suck my diamond-pierced earlobe. *How does he know my ear is my spot?* My body began to boil over and the room was overheating. My skirt went to the floor as he unlatched my bra and pulled down the straps. I felt my pink lace panties being rolled down my thighs and watched as his crisp white briefs fell to the floor. His kisses were powerful and passionate and I couldn't get enough of them.

"Zack. Wait, we shouldn't be doing this. What..."

Zack put his finger to my lips and whispered, "Geena, take your mind off everything except this."

I don't remember how but our bodies fell to the floor where he grabbed and groped me vigorously until my body began to purr. His fingers danced around between my thighs as he suctioned my nipple with his mouth. Our eyes met and we stared at one another, clarifying that what we were about to do was all right. Feeling his large chest pressed against my hardened nipples made me want him inside of me. I pressed my hips up towards his from the floor, signaling to him that I was ready for all he had to give.

In a matter of seconds, my body was lifted into his arms as he turned me around and around in the middle of the room, cradling me like a newborn baby, kissing me passionately as he carried me across the room to a chair in front of the balcony that over looked L.A. I could see the lights as they sparkled like the Fourth of July. I was on my knees, and my hands gripped the back of the chair. My head was buried as he made my body tremble like a leaf. My moans were muffled by the pillow that Zack pulled from the bed. After the space became too small, Zack grabbed me from behind like a rag doll, lifting me into the air, as he sat in the chair, placing me directly on top of him. I could feel the warm sweat from his bald head drip down my back.

The pressure from his large hands around my hips had me incarcerated. Sweat matted my hair to my face, my neck, and my back. Zack turned me around so that we faced one another. He yanked my head back, holding me in place by my hair, letting his tongue dance from my chin to my cleavage then gnashing away at my rock-hard nipples. My small body was lifted into the air as he continued his tasting from my navel to my chin, taking his hand and latching on to one of my breasts, continuing to use the other hand as a vice grip forcing my sore hips in place.

I couldn't control myself. My body was hot, and his

body was hard. My legs became numb from the continuous bouncing up and down in the tight space of the chair. "Let's go to the bed," I whispered in his ear. Zack stood up, with my legs wrapped around his waist! I felt weightless as my body was being lifted up into the air back on to the bed, where Zack's strong arms took both of my legs and pinned them to the headboard. I could feel a pillow being placed under my lower back and Zack inside of me. It only took a few moments for Zack to find the exact angle that he needed to send my body into full climax. My body began to shake and it felt like mini-convulsions running up my spine.

"Wait. Zack. Wait." I begged for him to stop, but wanted him to go! He flipped me over onto my stomach and pressed his weight against my back while he pulled my hips up, taking my knees and holding them up off the bed. He began to push and I continued to moan. He pushed harder, and faster, and I began to scream. He dropped my knees, letting them fall back on the bed, pressing my body down on to the sheets with one hand, holding my hips with the other. He was thrusting until all we could utter was a soft whisper. I lay there, breathless, on top of the down comforter, unable to move or make a sound. I immediately fell asleep.

The next morning, I was awakened by rain drops tapping on the balcony window and a knock at the door. "Room Service!"

The room was a total mess, and I looked like I had

been hit by a whirlwind. I covered my body with the sheet from the bed and tried to fix my wildly matted hair. "Just a minute!"

The hotel attendant knocked a few more times then said she had fresh towels for me. I asked her to leave them by the door and I would get them later. To my surprise, I opened the door to a full breakfast with a note, which read, "*I will see you in the lobby at noon. Our plane leaves at two; Enjoy your breakfast.*" It was from Zack. It was 10:15 when I received my food, so I had to hurry! Eat, shower, dress, pack, and get out!

As I walked downstairs to the lobby, I could see Zack talking with the doctors that we had drinks with the night before. One of them noticed me as I walked up, and he tapped Zack on the shoulder. He turned around to greet me.

"Well good morning, Ms. Geena. I hope you slept well?" I didn't know how to respond. I felt out of place, embarrassed, like there was a sign on my back that said I had sex with him.

"Good morning, Dr. Stone, and yes, sir, I did. Thank you."

I immediately turned away from him to greet the other doctors. "Gentlemen."

"Good morning, Geena."

I could feel Zack stare at me, and I was doing all I could do to look away from him.

"What time does the plane leave?"

I looked down at my watch. "It leaves in 90 minutes so we should get a move on."

Zack nodded his head in agreement then walked towards the door.

"After you, Ms. Geena."

As he opened the door for me, the other doctors waved goodbye, and I did the same. The ride to the airport seemed like it took forever. We rode in complete silence all the way there. I didn't know if I should feel ashamed, angry, or what! I kept replaying the night in my head. How in the hell did I sleep with Zack? He finally opened the door for discussion.

"Hey, are you okay?"

"I'm fine."

"Well I haven't heard you even breath hard since we got into this car, so there has to be something wrong."

"No, I'm okay."

Zack looked at me in disbelief. "Look, Geena, let's get everything out in the open before we get back home, Okay. Let's start HERE: we're both adults. We're smart people. So there's no need for us to ignore what happened last night. I know we both agree there are no strings attached. You have your life, and I have mine. We are just two grown folks handling grown folks business." I was stunned. I couldn't swallow. I didn't know what to say. "Nobody has to know what goes on between us except us. I've wanted to taste your body from the first day I saw you at Stephanie's house, and I knew you wanted me from the way you looked at me the first morning you volunteered at the clinic. Once we became friends, I knew it was only a matter of time."

I couldn't believe what I was hearing. "WAIT! So you planned all of this?"

"Geena, I didn't plan it LIKE this, but this was a part of my plan. I'm a man who knows WHAT he wants and I go after it, no matter what the stakes are."

Before I could answer him, the driver was pulling up to the front door of the airport. "Have a great flight, Dr. Stone," the limo driver said to Zack.

Zack tipped the limo driver with a $100 bill. "Thank you, sir. You enjoy the rest of your day."

On the plane Zack didn't say a word to me. He kept his head buried in his laptop, answering emails, sending emails, reviewing reports, and making appointments. I sat there like a bump on a log, not knowing how to start a simple conversation. As the plane reached our destination, I started to get the courage to talk to him about what he said in the car leaving the hotel. But before I could say a word, he was motioning for me to pass him his briefcase.

"Are you ready? Geena?"

"Yes, I believe so."

"Well, let's do it!" Zack grabbed his briefcase out of my hand and instantly began walking away from me like he was about to miss his connecting flight. I hurried to stay near him, hoping I would muster up the nerves to talk to him about the previous night's events.

"Come on, let's go this way! I have to get home so I can prepare for tomorrow. Monday is gonna be hectic around the office."

I watched as he fiddled with his cell phone, walking quickly through the crowd of people with his head facing straight away. He was paying absolutely no attention to me. It was as if he was alone and I wasn't there. I watched as he reached the luggage carousel, grabbing his luggage then looking back for me, yelling out, "Take care, Geena."

As he winked then turned to walk through the double doors, I stood in a cold silence. I was rendered speechless and was wondering what had just happened. I wasn't able to comprehend what had just taken place. Did this man just sex me and leave me? I was furious! I headed out to follow him and demand some answers because he had some explaining to do! I wasn't going to stand for that kind of disrespect! I began to march in the direction that Zack had gone. I rehearsed my lines in my head, ready to give him a piece of my mind. I searched and searched looking for his Louis Vuitton briefcase and overnight bag. Each time I thought I was gaining on him, I realized that I was following the wrong person. Before I knew it, I was standing alone, in the parking lot of the airport with a sweat-stained top, a parched mouth, and a sense of hopelessness. At that moment, embarrassment settled in and I felt like every person that passed me in the parking lot was staring at me in disgust for what had taken place between Zack and I. I could feel myself welling up but I was too mad to cry. All of a sudden I felt a vibration. It was my cell phone. It had to be Zack calling to talk about what happened and finish our conversation from earlier.

"Hello?"

"Mommmmmy!"

It was Frances. I had forgotten that I told them what time to expect me at the airport. "Hey, my babies. How are you?" As they talked, I couldn't get what happened in the last 24 hours out of my head. I finally had to hang up with them because I was ready to get my luggage and get home. "That sounds like fun, Frances! Okay, baby, I'm getting my luggage and heading home. Ask your dad to meet me there. I love you!"

"Yes, ma'am. I love you, too!"

After the kids got home and we all got settled in for the night, I couldn't fall asleep. I tossed and I turned until I decided I needed to talk to Zack, so I called him. Each time the phone rang, my heart would stop beating. Finally, he answered.

"Hello."

"Hey, Zack, it's me Geena."

"Thank you for calling Dr. Zackary Stone. I am unavailable at the moment. Feel free to leave me a brief message, and I will soon return your call."

I couldn't believe it was his voicemail! Damnit! I was so upset! But I still left a message. "Zack, hey it's me Geena Uhm, would you please give me a call when you get a chance?"

After I hung up, I still couldn't sleep so I tried to read some of the book that I had started by Katrina B. Hill, the world-renowned author. That didn't work so I decided to listen to some music on Pandora. tThat didn't work either, so I reached for the remote from my nightstand to switch on the television. I must have flipped through one hundred channels before finding reruns of *Law and Order* to watch. With my head on my pillow, I watched only a few episodes before I allowed the episodes to watch me.

The next few days at work I was a total mess. I just couldn't get it together. I was fumbling, my mind wasn't focused, and I kept forgetting things. I was just all over the place. After a week or so, I was really starting to lose it. During an internal audit one afternoon, my Senior VP noticed my behavior and became concerned.

"Geena, is everything okay. Do you need any help with the Creek Side project?"

The project was due in the next two days, so I had to assure him that everything was okay and that I would have the charts ready for our next meeting once I received more information from one of our affiliate companies. After the internal audit that day, I decided to close my door to block everybody out and get some work done. Before I knew it, the day was almost over and I hadn't accomplished anything. I happened to look down at my watch and noticed that it was already 5 p.m., which was the hour that time began to stand still. It looked like it would be another all-nighter. Around 6 p.m. Brittney paged me to take a phone call on line three.

"This is Geena." Nobody responded. "Hello? Is

there someone there? Hello!" All of a sudden I heard a click, then a dial tone. I got up to open my office door to ask Brittney who was on the line. Before she could answer, I felt someone walk up behind me. I was afraid to turn around. When I did, Zack was standing in front of me.

"Did you forget our dinner meeting?"

I didn't know what to say or how to respond to him in front of Brittney. We didn't have a scheduled dinner meeting! What was he talking about? Before I could answer him, he motioned for me to follow him into my office. I closed the door behind us and began to question his being there, but before I could get more than two sentences out of my mouth, his hands were around my waist and his lips were on my neck. I couldn't resist him so I returned the favor, while thinking to myself, *What has this man done to me?* I missed him so much I just wanted to taste his liquor. We walked and kissed till we ended up close to the cherry-red leather love seat across the room. He continued to run his hands all over me. My mind was ordering me to stop him, but my body wanted him to continue. Before I knew it, both of my Via Spiga pumps were off and my Oscar de la Renta suit jacket was coming off. He used the weight of his body to part my knees as he placed his warm hands between my cool thighs. My body was hungry for him. I began to pant as he started to take off his jacket then I heard a knock at the door.

"Excuse me." I had to gather myself before I could

respond.

"Yes, Brittney?"

"I was just letting you know I was calling security up to walk me to my car and I'll see you in the morning."

"Ohhkay, Brittney. You be safe, honey, and I'll see you in the morning."

"Was there anything else you needed from me before I left?" I was trying to answer her as quickly as I could because Zack was unbuttoning my skirt.

"No, I'm fine. I'll see you in the morning."

I immediately turned to face Zack as he continued to take each layer of my clothes off like a ravenous bull. I stood there in the middle of my office wearing nothing but my purple-laced thong. He picked me up, straddled my legs around his waist and carried me to my desk, where he pushed my papers aside to clear a space to lay my head and my back down as he sat down in my swivel chair and wrapped my legs around his neck. The purple lace came off with a quick rip from Zack's teeth. Once they were snatched away, he tossed them to the floor then returned his head between my legs as he slowly tasted every bit of my innermost secrets. I rubbed my hands around his head like a crystal ball then gripped his neck, hoping he would never stop. My back arched as I headed towards my climax.

"Did you miss this Geena?" I couldn't make a sound. "Do you want me to lick it fast or suck it slow? I turned my head side to side, trying my best to hold in my groans. I bit my lip trying to muffle my moans and screams. Zack scooped me up, taking me back to the red leather couch where he pounded and pressed and pushed until I couldn't take anymore. My body was tossed back and forth just like my feelings had been all week long. I was weak after we were finished, lifeless, so I lay there naked, with one eye closed and the other slightly open watching as Zack put his clothes back on and was about to walk out the door.

"WAIT! What are you doing?"

"Oh, I have another engagement at nine so I have to get home and get showered. I can't be late. I'll call you when I get back in."

He then walked over to me, kissed me on my forehead, and then made his way out of the door. I sat up, pulling my skirt from the floor and covering my naked body, wanting desperately to chase after him, but I was weak. My legs couldn't move and I wasn't able to say a word. After I finally gathered myself, I paged the security guard to walk me to the car garage. Driving home, my cell phone rang. I was hoping that the number that flashed across my car radio screen would be Zack's, but instead it was Stephanie and I was in no mood to talk. I just let the call go to voicemail and decided I would talk to her later.

Once I got home, I went straight to my room and prepared my bath. I soaked for hours. It seemed that night, replaying the situation I found myself in with Zack, now twice. What was I allowing to happen? In all of my years, I had never been in a situation remotely similar to this one. I felt like I had become Zack's secret sex slave, giving in to his every desire. It was impossible for me to love him, because my heart belonged to Michael. So why on Earth was I allowing myself to be treated this way? After trying to wash all of my guilt and shame off my body, I crawled into bed waiting for Zack to call me. Midnight rolled around and I still didn't hear from him. Finally, I fell asleep.

The next few weeks went by pretty fast; I dived into things at work and started spending more time with my girls, trying to keep my mind off Zack and back on what was important in my life. I had totally neglected my wedding plans and it was time that I got back on it. While in the floral shop with my girls one Saturday afternoon, my cell phone rang.

"Hello?"

"Hey, Geena."

I asked the girls to give me a second to take the call and I stepped out into the plant area to talk. "You have some nerve."

"Excuse me?"

"How dare you call me? What do you want, Zack?"

"Oh nothing much. It's been a minute since we got together so I was wondering if you were free tonight."

"Wait, how do you figure you can jump in and out of my life when it's convenient for you?"

" Geena, Geena, we've been over this. We're adults. No strings attached, right.

I've been busy with my patients and some charity events, and this is my first free night, so I figured we could hook up."

"Hold on, Zack! Hook up? Look, I'm not some two-bit skank you can call whenever you want a piece of tail! I'm a grown woman, and I don't have time for games."

"Hold on, Geena, I didn't mean to disrespect you in any way. I agree that you're a grown woman and I apologize if I have done anything to make you feel that I think less than that of you."

As mad and as pissed as I was at him for how he had treated me, I agreed to meet him, BUT I was meeting him to get some clarity and nothing more. "Okay, look, I'm spending time with my girls right now. Once I get them situated, we can meet."

"Sounds like a plan. Call me after eight and we'll make plans from there. Okay?"

"Okay. I'll talk with you then."

We made plans to have dinner and discuss what was going on between the two of us. Driving to meet Zack, I had a laundry list of things to talk to him about. I met him at one of his friend's condominiums since it was closer to my house. Zack lived on the outskirts of the city and didn't want me to make the 45-minute drive. Walking towards the front door, I could feel myself getting madder by the second. Before I could even ring the doorbell, Zack opened the door and greeted me with a single pink rose. He invited me in where a table was set for two. A meal was prepared, wine chilled, candles lit, and soft music was playing in the background.

"You look gorgeous, Geena," Zack stated as he took my hand and kissed me on the wrist. "Let's hurry and eat dinner so I can get to dessert."

"Wait, Zack. Look, we need to talk about this situation we're in."

"Okay, Geena. Let's talk."

Silence fell on my lips because I didn't know exactly what to say. "Zack, ever since we came back from L.A. things between us have been complicated."

"And how is that?"

"Come on, you know what I'm talking about. Us and what we have been doing."

"Geena, like I said to you in L.A., we're adults so what we choose to do is our business. It's not like we're in high school and somebody is going to find a note that will expose us! I like you a lot and if I can be totally honest with you, I love the sex, but I've learned to face the facts. You have a fiancé, kids, and soon you'll be married. That's not the life I desire."

"So what? I'm just a convenient piece of ass for you?"

"No, Geena, that's not what I'm trying to imply. I enjoy your company, and I love the fact that you're intelligent; I get off on you being a real woman and that turns me on. There's nothing abnormal with what we're doing. I mean some folks like to spend time shooting pool and playing basketball. I'd rather play with you." He then took me by my hips and tried to kiss me.

"No wait, Zack. It's not that easy."

"Yes it is, Geena, if you allow it to be. Now don't go sticking rules and parameters into place. That's how things get sticky and end up ugly. Do you enjoy my company?" I sat there with my head turned away from him. "Do you?"

"Well yes, I enjoy it, but I have to remind myself that this can't go any further than where it is. I'll be getting married in less than seven months and this will have to stop."

"And that's fine with me, Geena. I'm not trying to steal you away from your soon-to-be husband. To be honest with you, if I were him, I wouldn't have ever left you here alone."

"Wait a minute, Zack. He didn't just leave me, he's away for business and if he had a choice in the matter, he would be here with me."

"Hey, I didn't mean to upset you. Look, Geena, there are no strings attached to what we're doing. I just want to fill the void while he's away. So can you please let me take care of you until he gets back?"

As much as I wanted to leave for the right reasons, I stayed for the wrong ones. What was Zack doing to me, making me act out of character the way I was? My heart belonged to Michael so why was I allowing Zack to have my body? Listening to Zack explain our situation, I accepted it for what it was. bBesides, it was just between us. We were both adults, capable of making wise decisions. Our business was our business and nobody had to know about it.

Zack and I had a ball that night. He fed me steamed

lobster tails and Greek salad for dinner. He served Moscato, my beverage of choice, to wash it all down. I, in turn, let Zack have me for dessert. There was definitely something different about Dr. Stone. His sex was rough, but gentle at the same time and he introduced me to things I had never experienced before.

SexTera
Chapter 20

The sultry sex with Zack continued for about three months with him introducing pornos and novelty toys into our repertoire. The feelings I had with Zack were indescribable. He knew that he had me where he wanted me and that if he asked me to follow him, I would go. One afternoon while I was doing some volunteer work at Zack's office, he came into the file room where I was finishing up some free med packets.

"Hey, Geena, have you heard of the new club called *SexTera*?"

"No, what's the name of it again?"

"It's *SexTera*. It's a club where couples go to party, drink, and if they like, have sex."

I stopped what I was doing to get clarity. "You said couples go there to do what? Is it a hotel, too?"

"No, it's not a hotel. But there are rooms available if you would like to go in to have sex with your partner."

I turned my face back to my work, signifying I had absolutely no interest in the club. "Oh hell nawl, that sounds nasty."

"Come on, Geena. What's nasty about fulfilling your fantasies? You said yourself that you had never watched a porno or used toys. Now how is the queen of porn and the vibrator afraid of a little challenge?"

Smiling at him in agreement and hitting him with a piece of balled up paper, I replied, "Okay, okay, okay. I guess it doesn't sound that bad."

"Of course not! What do you say we go check it out tonight?"

"Oh, I don't know, Zack. I don't think I'm ready for that."

"Come on, Geena. It won't be bad. You'll be with me and you know how WE get down."

I wasn't sure about what I was about to agree to, but once I had given my word, it was too late to back down.

Later on that night, we got dressed and headed out to *SexTera*. I was terrified because I didn't know what to expect. It was packed and people were everywhere. There was nothing left for the imagination with those characters. I saw a lady walking around with a mini tarantula stuck to her face like a piece of jewelry. I saw a few guys walking around with snakes around their necks, and I saw couples freely fondling each other as if their acts were equivalent to holding hands.

Zack could sense my apprehension, so he walked me to the bar to explain what to expect on each level of the club. I had never seen a club like *SexTera* before, not even in a movie or television show. The top level was designed as the bar, which stretched from one end of the club completely around to the other. The counter was shiny red marble accented with tiny black specks that sparkled, reflecting the light from the ceiling. Customers were seated in tall black bar stools waiting for the bartenders to fill their orders.

The second level was where the party got started. If you stopped on the second floor, your intentions were to dance! The floor was made of crystal tiles that lit up each time someone stepped on them. I was reminded of the seventies with all the disco lights and rays shooting from one end of the room to the next.

The third floor was the seminude floor; it was common to see a woman walk around with nothing on but her skirt or shorts, completely exposing her bare top, which I didn't think was too bad because I had gone to a nude beach while in college.

The fourth floor was where the big dawgs went to play. If you entered the fourth floor, everything had to come off except jewelry, purses, or caps.

The fifth floor was named "Fantasy Fulfiller" for obvious reasons.

The first few times Zack and I went to *SexTera* to party, we only went as low as the third floor. You could see women walking around with nothing but their pants or skirts on. Men were in their underwear and some were going as far as exposing themselves. Zack asked me a few times to take off my shirt, but I wasn't with it. I told him I would only go with the agreement that I didn't have to get naked. I wasn't about to take the chance of anyone ever being able to say that I was in a club with my shirt off. It was a weird club, but we had so much fun! We started to frequent the club regularly and after a while, just like Zack said, I started to get comfortable. Besides there was never anybody there that I knew, so if I got a little wild and crazy, who would find out?

It was Thirsty Thursday night at the club and I had a few drinks too many and was starting to feel pretty good. Zack walked me to the Fantasy floor and I got butt booty naked. As we walked around, I noticed rooms alongside the wall that had huge windows giving onlookers an eye-full. I stood in amazement as I watched couples perform sexual favors on each other while complete strangers watched. In one room, there was a man and a woman. In the room beside them there were three women. In a room down the hall there were two men and two women. I had never in my life witnessed such a thing in person, only on the porno that Zack and I had begun watching more and more frequently.

I guess Zack could tell that I was feeling a little uncomfortable by the way I started to tense up after looking into the sex rooms.

"Excuse me, could I have one of those, please?" Zack stopped a waitress and grabbed two fluted shot glasses of vodka. "Here, Geena, you need this to relax and unwind a bit. Remember, we're here to have a good time, so loosen up."

I took the shot glass from Zack's hand and threw it back as quickly as I could. Before I knew it, Zack was taking me by the hand and walking me into one of the rooms. To make me as comfortable as possible, Zack closed the dark purple drapes that covered the window for the onlookers. Once the drapes were closed, he pulled me on to the bed, burying our naked bodies in the silky gold sheets. It didn't take long for Zack to rub me right and once he did, our bodies collided!

As I took my time on top of him, watching as his eyes rolled into the back of his head, I felt a slight breeze on my back and eyes beaming on the back of my neck. To assure myself that no one had entered the room, I took my eyes off Zack to look over my shoulder. I froze in place staring into the eyes of a tall fair-skinned woman with long black hair wearing deep red lipstick. I screamed, jumped off Zack, and jerked away, not understanding what was going on. I fell to the bed, grabbing the gold sheets to hide my naked body.

"What in hell is going on?"

Zack sat up reaching for my leg. "Calm down, Geena."

"WHAT? Wait! You know her?"

Zack began taking this woman by the hand as if to invite her into the bed with us. He looked back at me and answered, "Yes. This is Char."

Her dark pitted eyes pierced my soul as she looked at me. She began walking towards the bed as I scooted away, making my way to the headboard until I was stuck and couldn't move any further. Zack leaned in to kiss me on my shoulder with reassurance that I had nothing to fear and everything was okay. He slowly pulled the covers away from my now trembling body and pushed my legs apart. He motioned for this Char person to come closer. She crawled up on the bed directly between my legs, licking my inner thigh until she reached the place that no other woman had gone before. I felt stuck; I wanted to get away but my body remained still. I didn't know what to do. Zack turned my face towards his and started kissing me, trying to take my attention away from what was going on between my legs. I had two options. I could run out into a club full of naked people that I don't know, or stay there with Zack, where I felt safe but awkward. I watched Zack as he watched Char. He stared at her every move then began to rub her hair as she continued to run her tongue up and down my body.

"Just relax, Geena. She knows what she's doing."

I closed my eyes and tried to take my mind out of my body. Her long fingernails clinched my waist as she used her tongue to lick me. As she continued, all I could think to myself was, *Does this mean I'm gay?*

After she finished, Zack took over by placing himself where her tongue had prepared a slippery slope. This rendezvous continued for at least an hour, and when it was over, Char was gone. It was like she disappeared into thin air. Zack took me by the hand and walked me through the club like nothing happened. We got upstairs, put our clothes on, had another drink, and then left the club.

The next morning when I woke up, I had a terrible headache. Zack was lying beside me still asleep, so I nudged him to wake him up.

"Heyyy. Good morning, Geena. You sleep well?"

"I hardly slept at all. I keep thinking about what happened last night."

Zack sat up in the bed to look at me as he responded. "Geena, what happened last night is over. It's in the past, never to be talked about again."

Now I was really confused. "What do you mean, it's over? I might be a lesbian."

Zack laughed at my response, kissing me on the shoulder. "Geena, you're not a lesbian. You just enjoy good sex."

"Well, Zack, let me ask you something. Do you let random men lick you?"

"NO. That's different. A man that allows another man to lick or suck them is gay as hell, but for women, it doesn't mean a thing. Don't sweat it, Geena. Like I always tell you, what we do is our business. You don't have anybody to answer to."

Zack pulled the covers off of us, stood and took my hand and pulled me up from the bed. "Come on, let's take a hot shower and get some breakfast. You'll feel a lot better then."

A few more months passed by and I found myself at the same club doing the same things. Having sex with another woman was never my intention, and I prayed constantly that no one would ever find out. What would people think of me? How could I explain my actions? That was one skeleton I didn't want popping out of the closet.

I never went to Zack's home because it was so far out. But to my surprise one night, he called me and said to get dressed because a cab would be outside to pick me up for a candlelit dinner at his home. I was excited because it had been almost seven months since I met Zack and I was finally going to see where he lived. By the time the cab driver arrived, it had started to rain; although I don't like to ride or drive in the rain, I was eager to spend time with Zack in his home so I hopped aboard. As we got closer, I could see the massive home from the road. It sat on what seemed like a mountaintop. Though the rain clouded my view a bit,I still could see the gorgeous masterpiece.

I had to run to the front door with my heels in my hands so I wouldn't slip and fall on the stone paved driveway. Once I made my way to the door, I began knocking with the huge brass door knocker that was on the fifteen-foot door. Zack answered the door and welcomed me in. I walked in and was blown away at the artistry in the home. The walls were draped with beautiful paintings. The floors were made of marble and the ceilings were made of gold. The room was dim and the only light that allowed me to see was from the fireplace and the candles.

"Welcome to my home, Geena. Allow me to take your coat. Come on in and have a seat. You're practically soaked; let me grab a towel for you to dry off." Before walking away to get the towel, Zack pointed to the table in front of the fireplace. "I have your favorite wine on the table already chilled and waiting for you." I took my time taking my seat because I was in utter amazement at how beautiful his home was. It was something I had never seen before in my life. I was speechless. Zack returned with a fluffy white towel and some slippers. "Come, let me dry you off, Geena."

"Thank you. These are some nice slippers." I sat down with my back turned toward him, allowing his strong hands to blot dry my rain-soaked body. His kisses skirted my neck and shoulders.

"That feels so good, Zack."

"I'm glad you like it. Here, take a sip of your wine. How was your trip here?"

"It was kind of scary to tell you the truth. With the rain and all, I could hardly see."

All of a sudden, I could hear what sounded like footsteps coming from another room. I thought it was odd because Zack lived alone and he hadn't mentioned that anyone else would be joining us. As he continued to run the towel over my body, I turned to see where the footsteps were coming from. I looked up and saw Char from the club, in red high heel shoes, and with much shorter hair than the last time I had seen her. "Hello, Geena. Nice to see you here at last. I'm Zack's wife."

As she made her way to the sofa where I was sitting, I felt sick as it registered with me that Char was Zack's wife. I could feel tiny beads of sweat popping out all over my forehead. My heart dropped to my feet, and a chill seemed to rush through my entire body. My thoughts were racing at what seemed like a mile per minute, and I could feel my blood pressure rising. After what seemed like an eternity, but had only been seconds, I dropped my glass of wine on the floor and stared at her in shock. Zack jumped up, looking at the glass that had broken all over his marble floor.

"Geena! Are you okay?"

I ignored him, still staring at Char. "You are Zack's WHAT?"

"I'm his wife." I turned away from her, looking at Zack with tear-filled eyes.

"What's going on, Zack? You have some explaining to do!"

"What do you mean, Geena? Explain what? Like I told you before, we are adults so what we do is our business. Char is a part of our business."

I burst into tears, crying uncontrollably. I couldn't catch my breath. I felt like I was dreaming. This could not be happening.

"You used me!" I turned to hit Zack, but he caught my wrists in midair.

"Wait a minute, Geena. WHO used WHO? If I can recall correctly, when I met you, you had just recently got engaged to your so-called high school sweetheart who was about to take a fifteen-month tour AWAY from you for a job. You, my dear, took it upon yourself to USE me while he was away! You Acted as if you were interested in charity when, in fact, you were a charity case yourself."

I couldn't believe what I was hearing. I cried

frantically. I could barely catch my breath. "NO! That is not how it happened, and you know that, Zack! How could you say that about me? You are a liar!" I turned to look at Char. "You are both liars! This was a set up from the start! I cannot believe you have done this to me! I should have known that something was up with you with all the' we are grown folks' talk, 'we can keep this between us', then I let you talk me into that *SexTera* place and getting with this dyke!"

Char cut her eyes at me, and if looks could kill, I would have been dead! "Wait a minute, now you will not come into my home, raise your voice at me, and degrade me. Like my husband said, you knew exactly what you were doing and NOBODY put a gun to your head to do ANYTHING that you did! I sure don't ever recall you asking me to stop; each night you wanted what I was giving. So if I'm a dyke, a lesbian, or whatever you want to call me, Geena, then what in the hell does that make YOU?"

I couldn't take it anymore. I ran to the front door, flung it open, and ran down to the end of the driveway. I ran and I ran and I ran until I couldn't run anymore. As my legs grew tired and my body grew weak, it seemed like the long winding road would never end. My adrenaline was dissipating and I could barely take another step. I fell to my knees and crawled in the rain, crying uncontrollably, asking myself how I had got to this place. I was embarrassed and ashamed. I prayed to God that would be the last time I ever saw or talked to Dr. Zackary Stone.

Ms. Sharon
Chapter 21

It had been three months since I'd seen or heard from Zack, and I was happy that our paths no longer crossed. I was getting on my feet and putting my focus on what was important, once again! I had to really pray about the situation with Zack, and I asked God to erase the pain and take away the embarrassment of what I had done. Although I felt guilty about the ordeal with Zack, I was happy to have Michael in my life, and in less than four months, I would be his wife.

Stephanie and I had taken a Sunday afternoon to finalize some details for the wedding. The night was drawing near so she left to get home before it got too late. Around the time she left, it was time for Jared to bring the girls home. Since I had just locked the doors, I was still standing in view of the driveway. As I stood in the great room near the window, I heard a car door slam. I peeked through the blinds before I unlocked the side door to make sure it was the girls. As I squinted, I noticed that my girls were getting out of the car with 'Ms. Sharon' and Jared wasn't present. I watched as they each hugged her, smiled, laughed, and waved before walking away from the vehicle.

I stood there in disbelief. Did I just watch my children get out of the car of a stranger? What in the hell just happened? Where in the hell was Jared, and why was he allowing this woman to drop my children off without him? The girls began to run up to me as I stood in the garage waiting on them to walk up.

"Heyyy Mama!" I couldn't even greet them like I should have because I was so angry. I stood there and eyed the heffa as she drove out of the driveway, she even had the nerve to try and throw her hand up to wave at me. "Mama!!"

"Hey. Oh, hey baby." Lily and Frances both were sweet as pie, always showing their affection and love to their mommy. "I missed you girls." I had to cool off before I asked them about what just happened. "Hey! Where was your dad?"

As Frances took a seat on the couch, picking up the remote, she responded, "Oh, he's at home."

"Ohhh, why didn't he bring you?"

"He was busy getting some work done, so he asked Ms. Sharon to bring us."

I could feel myself get a real attitude. How dare he be too busy to handle his responsibility, and furthermore, have that woman be alone with my girls!

As Lily took a seat on the other couch to join her sister, she interjected, "Mama, Ms. Sharon is so nice. She takes us to all of these cool places. sShe likes to listen to the same music we like, and she drives a silver sports car with a drop top. She lets us try on her clothes and shoes, and any time we all go to the mall, she picks out the cutest outfits for us." It seemed like they would never stop talking. They were boasting about this woman, so I politely cut off the 'I love Ms. Sharon' song and dance.

"Hey! How about we get a snack then work on those bouquets for the wedding. How does that sound? I can put some cookies in the oven and put on that new Fantasia or Nicki Minaj CD."

The girls jumped up from where they were sitting. "Mama! You do NOT have the new Nicki Minaj CD?"

"I sure DO! Well, the clean version of course."

"YaAAAaaAaYYYYy."

I was so glad Stephanie had left her CDs when she went home because I didn't know a Minaj from a collage, but I wanted to make my girls happy.

"Go upstairs and put your things away, and I'll turn on the oven!"

It was getting late so we didn't stay up too long.Plus I was ready to dial Jared's number. After I got the girls settled down, I went to my bedroom to call him. Of course, he didn't answer so I left him a message. "Hey, Jared, it's Geena. I noticed you didn't bring the girls home tonight, and I wanted to speak with you about that. Could you give me a call back at your earliest convenience? Thanks. I look forward to talking with you soon."

I didn't hear from Jared until around noon the next day. He agreed to meet me at the park so we could talk during our lunch break. On the way there, I promised myself I would only talk to him and not cause a scene, even if he pissed me off, like it is so easy for him to do. Driving into a parking space, I saw Jared's BMW so that meant he had beat me there. Before I got out of the car I took out my Mac compact to make sure everything was in place. Yeah, gotta always look my best I promised myself after we divorced that he would never see me looking like a lost fool. I was tight, so I got out of the car heading to take a seat beside him where he sat on the park bench. He had his head down so I had to speak first.

"Hey, Jared."

"Oh hey, Geena." He didn't even look up at me as I approached him. Instead, he looked at his watch then gave me a look as if I was late. "Look, I don't have a lot of time so can we just get to the reason we need to talk during my lunch break, TODAY."

I could tell he already had an attitude so I didn't want to prolong our time any longer. "Jared, I just wanted to talk to you about the agreement we made about the girls. I was under the assumption that you would pick them up and drop them off."

"No, Geena, the agreement was that I provide transportation for the girls and that is what I did."

"Well, I think there needs to be an amendment to that clause because I don't appreciate strangers driving my children around."

"WAIT. Is that what this meeting is about? And how dare you call Sharon a stranger? You know perfectly well who she is."

"CORRECTION! I don't KNOW her! And I don't

appreciate you allowing OUR children to ride around with her alone."

Jared stood up and picked up his briefcase and newspaper. "Okay, that's it! I've had enough of this! I'm OUT!"

I pulled his arm back trying to make him sit back down. "What do you mean, you're OUT? We aren't finished talking."

"Oh, you may not be finished talking, but I'm FINISHED listening. You know, Geena, you may as well get over this bitter taste you have in your mouth about Sharon. She isn't going anywhere, so you can either accept her willingly like an adult or continue to act like a silly kid."

"How dare you talk down to me, Jared! I'm the mother of your children, your first and your last born! And this is how you treat me?"

"Okay, so what now, Geena, you want a medal or something?"

"A medal? So now you want to be sarcastic and mean?"

"No, I'm just trying to figure out what you want from me. Are you saying that I have no say in how our children are taken care of?"

I was growing more and more frustrated with him. "Oh, you have some say in how they are raised, but you are forgetting they have TWO parents so I have some say so TOO."

"We have been apart for some time, Geena, and before we were separated we had already become strangers living in the same house. Now the divorce is finalized, you have a fiancé, and you are STILL tripping on ME? I mean, what is it? Do you honestly dislike Sharon, who you haven't even tried to have a relationship with?"

"Wait a minute, Jared! Tell me WHY I should have a relationship with the woman that destroyed my family?"

"There you go blaming Sharon because you didn't handle your business."

"I didn't handle my business? I didn't handle my business? What do you mean, I didn't handle my business?"

"Look, I'm not gonna go there. We both know what I am talking about."

"No, I think I need for you to elaborate."

"Look, Geena, like I was saying, you either get over it or continue to wallow in your self-pity and hide behind your pride! Even if you claim that you don't KNOW Sharon, you DO know me! And you know I would never put my girls in harm's way. So if I believe Sharon is capable of taking care of them, picking them up, dropping them off, or doing anything else for them, then that should be GOOD enough for you!"

"NO, Jared, it's not good enough. I don't want her at my HOUSE, period! Point blank! And I mean that!"

"Okay, Geena, let's be realistic. The real problem isn't the girls being with Sharon or Sharon picking them up, or whatever else you claim to be the case. You are still mad because we aren't together, so you try to FIND things to get in our way. You will find anything to nitpick about Sharon! You make it seem like you still want ME!"

I couldn't believe his accusation! "That is the last thing on my mind! I have a man that loves and respects me and treats me like a queen."

"Okay then, it shouldn't be an issue then. Have I ever questioned your reasoning for whatever YOU do? No, because I trust you will make sound decisions when it concerns the girls so I don't even come to you with anything like that. I have never had an issue with ole' dude being around the girls so there is no reason you should have any issues either."

"Well my ole' dude wasn't the reason we split up!"

Jared stood firmly this time with his newspaper and briefcase in hand. "Okay, Geena, you aren't going to listen to me so this is just a waste of my time. You have issues that you are going to have to deal with on your own. I'll be over to get the girls next weekend. Have a nice day!"

I sat there fuming in my seat watching as he walked away. I was so upset that I could feel tears fill my eyes. I had to shake it off because I was sitting in the middle of the park, we had already made a scene raising our voices at each other and I didn't want to make matters worse so I just got up and went back to my car. On the way back to the office, I couldn't shake how Jared stood up for that witch of a woman, Sharon. How dare he put her feelings before mine? I couldn't hold my tears back any longer. I wept quietly as I drove back to the office.

Later on that night as I washed the dishes with the girls, Stephanie called. I was glad to hear from her, so I could release some of the built up stress and tension I had about Jared and Sharon. I sent the girls out of the kitchen and asked them to go straighten the great room while I wiped down the counters. As soon as they were out of my view, I recanted the latest events with Stephanie, filling her in about the latest news on Sharon and Jared's audacity.

The next time I encountered Sharon would be the following weekend. Just like he always did, Jared came to pick the girls up for their weekend at Daddy's, but this time he had Sharon with him. I watched as he opened her door then held her hand as they walked up the driveway. When I opened the door, I cringed to see her standing beside him. The look on my face must have told the tale of how I was feeling because when I opened the door, their smiles soon left their faces. I couldn't believe Jared brought her to my door without speaking to me about it first. What didn't he understand about leaving her at home when it came to picking the girls up? In order to break the awkward silence, Jared started to talk.

"Hey, Geena. Are the girls ready?"

With my arms folded and looking directly at Sharon, I responded, "They are in their bedrooms waiting for YOU."

"Okay, could you let them know we are here?" I wasn't paying attention to anything Jared had to say. I just stood there with my arms still folded staring at the worthless piece of life standing before me. Jared started snapping his fingers in the hope of getting my attention. "GEENA, could you get the girls for me?" I continued to ignore his requests. After a few more minutes, I couldn't stand it any longer so I looked her directly in the eye to let her know I meant business.

"You know what, you have some REAL nerves to sashay your way up to MY door thinking you can just walk away with MY kids and do with them as YOU please!"

Sharon turned to Jared and whispered, "Okay, I'm going back to the car, I knew this would be a bad idea. This woman is crazy and I don't have time for it."

Wait, did she call me 'this woman' and say I was crazy? Oh she had pushed the right button with her last sentence. "Excuse me? What did you just say? Would that woman you are referring to be me?"

She turned to look me in the eye. "Yes, Geena, it's you. I am tired of trying to be nice to you. I'm always biting my tongue and ignoring your childish behavior."

I started walking towards her to make sure she could hear what I was about to say. "Hold on one damn minute. Bite your tongue? Be nice to me? You don't even KNOW me, and as far as I am concerned, YOU don't even exist!"

She turned and threw her hands up and started to walk away. "FINE! I'm out of here!"

I wasn't finished talking so I took off walking

behind her. "No, you are going to stand here and listen. For the past year, I've had to stand beside and watch you play house with my daughters and you know what, "Ms. Sharon," I am tired of it."

"What is it with you, Geena? I mean what is it going to take for you to swallow your pride and digest the fact that I AM HERE! Your daughters are a part of my life whether you like it or not. The divorce was finalized months ago. So WHAT is your problem with me? Jared told me about the episode you had with him at the park and you know, I tried to defend you. Yeah, believe it or not, I did! I had to step out of myself for a minute and put myself in your shoes.

"I thought she must feel as if she has lost her husband to another woman, her children love this other woman, and she's evidently unhappy with her own personal life so WHY would she embrace me? But after all this, I'm going to wash my hands when it comes to trying to deal with you."

I was growing angrier and angrier by the second. "Let me tell YOU something, SHARON. I don't know how or where you get the idea that I'm so miserable, but let's set the record straight. I am happy and I have a man in my life that loves me to no end, but if you want to put it all on the line, let's do it. What pisses me off about this situation that you have with Jared is HOW everything started. You came between our marriage and took away my children's security and the normalcy they once had. How dare you think I should treat you as a guest in my home when YOU were the one that destroyed it!"

I guess we had gone back and forth so long that we didn't realize the girls had walked up.

"Hey girls," Sharon called as she noticed them. As I turned to them, I could tell something was wrong by the looks on their faces and I hoped they hadn't heard the argument between Sharon and I.

"Oh, I didn't realize you all had come down so soon. Are you all ready to go with your daddy?" They weren't looking too enthusiastic like they usually are, so I asked Jared to wait there while I speak with the girls before they leave. We went back into the kitchen to talk. Before I could even speak, my youngest daughter got in before me.

"Mama, I want to ask you something but I don't want you to be mad at me."

"What is it, baby?"

"You promise you won't get upset?"

Frances' question baffled me. "You can ask me anything you wish, sweetie."

"Okay. Ummmm..." she paused, looking up at her older sister, then looking back at me. "...why don't you like Ms. Sharon, Mama? Is she a bad person?"

I was confused, not understanding where these questions were coming from. Had Jared filled their heads with mess trying to make me look like the bad guy? "Is there something you need to tell me about Ms. Sharon? Did she hurt you in some way? Say something out of the way?"

She looked at me with her soft brown eyes, full of

innocence and said, "No, Mommy, she is always so nice to us but every time I hear you talk about her, it's always something bad. I hear you on the phone arguing with Daddy about her, and I hear you cry talking to Auntie Stephanie." She fell into my arms, drowning me with her tears. As I embraced her, trying to calm her, she looked up at me and added, "I don't want to like anybody that makes you sad."

My heart broke because for the first time I realized that my actions were teaching my daughters to hate someone, and that was a message I never wanted to convey to them. What kind of mother was I to allow my hurt to transcend as anger towards another person and have my child question the goodness of another human being based on my actions? I was filled with emotions. Tears fought to escape my eyes as I looked at my beautiful daughters.They were the innocent parties in this ugly situation. All I could do was hug them tightly, wishing I could turn back the hands of time. There were so many things I would do differently.

"Mama, why are you crying?" Lily asked as she pulled my hair back trying to dry my tears with her shirtsleeve.

"Well, you know what, girls, sometimes adults do some things they aren't proud of and no matter how old you are, some hurts aren't easy to get over. You won't understand right now, but in due time you will. Just know that I love you girls with all of my heart. Okay?"

"Okay, Mama!"

"Now give me a hug, let me see those pretty faces. No more tears, promise?"

"Promise!"

"Okay now, go ahead with your daddy. He's been waiting for you long enough. I'll call and check on the two of you tomorrow."

They cleaned their faces, grabbed their bags, and headed for the door. I waved to them, blowing kisses as they walked through the garage with Jared and Sharon.

That night I lay in bed thinking about the blow up between Sharon and me. I asked myself what it was about that woman that made me despise her so. I had never harbored that much anger in my heart towards any other person and I didn't like the feeling. It made me look like the crazy ex-wife and that was a title I didn't want to hold. I was happy with Michael, so why did the thought of this woman still make my flesh crawl?

The next day, I called my girls over to help me get my mind off of all the drama and talk about the wedding plans. I couldn't contain my excitement! I only had about sixty days before I was back in Michael's arms, and soon after I would be his wife. There were so many last minute things that had to be handled and I was running around like a chicken with my head cut off! It was time I called in my reinforcements. I planned a night of drinks and eats with my bridesmaids to knock the bulk of the things out of the way. Stephanie, of course, was the first to arrive. I could hear her banging on the door and ringing the doorbell at the same time.

"Whooo izzz it?"

"Itzz MEEEY!"

I opened the door for her. "Come on in, MEEEY."

"Hey, Gee! Whassup, girl!"

"Trying to get this stuff together for the wedding. The other girls should be here in a minute. Come on in the kitchen, and let's grab a drink."

Stephanie and I laughed and talked about her new friend and their eventful excursions until the doorbell rang.

"Heyy Girllsss." Hugs and kisses started to flow within our small circle. Kim, Rachel, CJ, and Erica, the rest of my bridesmaids, had arrived.

"Come on in, ladies! Stephanie and I were just having a drink while waiting on the rest of you to get here.Come on and join us!"

Kim was still walking around marveling at the house and all of the upgrades that I'd done. "Geena! I love what you've done with the house! It's so nice in here, I love the earth-toned colors, the greenery, the paintings; everything is so warm and inviting and these floors are gorgeous! Who did your tile work?"

"One of Michael's groomsmen did them, believe it or not!"

"Oh really? He did a magnificent job. Is he single?"

We all burst into laughter and I knew where the night was headed. CJ was Lily and Frances' godmother. She was the more stable one out of the group, other than myself, of course; we didn't spend a lot of time together because she lived so far away but whenever we got together, it was like we just picked back up where we left off. She couldn't keep her eyes off of my walls.

"You like what you see, CJ?"

"Yes, Geena, these pictures look like paintings. The lighting is precise, and you can see a different angle of the shot anywhere you stand in the room. Tell me, WHERE did you find these?"

"Well, a good friend of mine named Keema started her own photography business about ten years ago, and this is some of her "virgin work" from when she first started out. If you think this is something, you should go to her website to see her latest work on her site, www.thesweetestthingsbykimaphotography.com; she's a master at what she does. I'll give you a card before you leave."

"Thanks I'll have to give her a call, does she do couple shots?"

"Yeah, as a matter of fact she did some work for this couple by the name of Brad and Trina Hill, and their pictures were hot, steamy, and sexy."

"Okay, I'm sold. I'll be calling Ms. Keema tomorrow."

It had been more than ten minutes since Stephanie had spoken a word, so I knew I would hear her voice very shortly.

"Hey! Enough talk about floors, walls, and pictures;

it's time to get to BUSINESS, ladies. My best friend is getting MARRIED!"

"You're right, Steph, come on, girls let's get to business."

As we worked on the invitations, bouquets, and wedding favors, we chit-chatted and caught up on the latest gossip, which was Kim's cup of tea.

"Hey! Have any of you ever heard of that new club called *SexTera*?"

I took a deep gasp, but didn't utter a word.

"It's supposed to be a sex club if you can believe that or not!"

Stephanie and Erica had heard of it. Rachel had heard of it, but CJ had not. I never gave a response.

Out of curiosity, CJ asked, "Why would someone want to open a sex club? What do people actually do there? Do they have sex? Is it like a whore house or something?"

Kim had all the answers. "Well from what I hear, it's a nude bar where couples go to get naked, and some even are BOLD enough to have sex!"

They all stopped what they were doing and looked up at Kim. "At the club? Come on, Kim!"

"NO, I'm serious, Stephanie. One of the girls who works in the shop where I get my hair done has been before. She said you will see just about anything in there! It puts you in the mind of those Miami night clubs. It has like four or five different levels, bars, dance floors, and private rooms where people have sex. And get this: they DO IT in FRONT of complete strangers!"

CJ gasped. "WHAT! You mean to tell me people actually do that? Isn't that against the law? That is SO nasty? I don't believe it!"

Kim had to cut her off before she went on and on. "I don't know if it's illegal or not, but I do know it is the so-called happening place right now, and as big of a freak as I am, it's way too over the top even for me."

All of the girls laughed while I sat in silence. I instantly got sick to my stomach thinking about the events that took place in that club between Zack, Char, and myself. CJ noticed my silence.

"Hey, Gee! Are you okay?"

"Uhhmm, yeah, I think that drink is trying to give me an upset stomach; I'm feeling kind of lightheaded. excuse me while I go get a drink of water."

I jumped right up and ran into the kitchen. My heart was racing and I could feel the back of my neck getting wet. My stomach was nervous and I felt like I needed to throw up. I stood there long enough to calm myself down, and after I gathered my thoughts, I went back to the great room to join the girls.

"Are you okay, sweetie? You look like you just saw a ghost."

"I'm fine, CJ. I think I didn't have enough to eat today, and drinking that wine was making me feel sick." CJ handed me a small sandwich from her plate, but I couldn't even eat it. I had lost my appetite and all I wanted to do was go to bed, but I had too much work to be completed and my time was quickly ticking away.

"Hey, Erica, how far have we gotten with the invitations?"

"Let's see here. We're almost completely finished. The wedding favors are the biggest job and that's what's going to take us a little more time."

"Okay, well let's focus on finishing the invitations up tonight because I need to get them in the mail this week. Before I know it, the wedding day will be here and..."

Steph put down her pen. "Geena! Calm down. We got you, girl! No panicking! That's why we're here so this can be a smooth transition. Now take a deep breath, and exhale. Okay. Now you're good. Okay!"

"You're right, Steph. Thanks girls!! I really appreciate you all coming over to help and spend time with me tonight."

It was time for me to change the topic of conversation before they continued the club talk so I asked CJ about her kids; she had a son and a daughter that were around the same age as my Lily and Frances.

"How are the kids doing now? Are they in high school yet?"

"They are doing great! Patrick is a sophomore and my baby girl Taysha is in the eighth grade. I'm blessed with some great kids, girl. I think I was on God's good side the day he gave them to me."

"That is a blessing, CJ. My girls are some angels, too. They help to keep me going on the days I want to give up. The divorce wasn't pretty. I thought it may have taken me out, but to my surprise they were real troopers. Their ability to adapt made it so much easier for me. Does Patrick have any plans for college yet?"

"Well, you know he has always loved school, so I have never had to worry about him doing well with his studies. He's never been a real sports buff but his athleticism increased in a major way about three years ago, so now he's working hard with a trainer to perfect his skills in the hope of getting a Division 1 scholarship, go to college, and make it to the NFL, just like every other young boy that plays football. What I love about him is that he is a realistic thinker and always has plan B on the other burner just in case the NFL doesn't come through for him."

"That's awesome, CJ! I know you are proud of him. What are his plans if he isn't the next Reggie Bush?"

"He wants to be a doctor, a gynecologist to be exact."

My mouth instantly got dry as the Sahara, but I couldn't let on that I was bothered by her response so I tried to play it off. "Oh, really? A gynecologist? What made him want to pursue that?"

"Well, Stephanie has a friend named Dr. Stone that took Patrick in as an intern during spring break a few months ago, and he just fell in love with his work and he totally admires him."

Stephanie turned from her conversation with Erica to interject. "Oh, Geena knows Zack!"

"Oh, do you?"

"Uhmm, not really. I just..."

"Not really? Girl, stop playing! As much time as the two of you spent together!"

CJ looked at me, confused. "Did you date Dr. Stone Geena?"

I snapped at her before I knew it! "NO! I have never dated him!"

Stephanie stood to walk over towards CJ and I. "Hold up, let me clarify! Ya'll know that Geena is the world's greatest community service advocate. Well last year she met Zack at my house while he and another friend of mine, Rodney, were visiting me. Shortly after that meeting, Zack asked me if I had any friends who would like to volunteer at the shelter where he gives free medical attention to the ladies in the community that can't afford to pay for it on their own. Of course, I asked Geena and of course she jumped at the opportunity. After the initial community service event, ole' Geena here became a regular. She participated SO much that Zack took her to Los Angeles on an all-expense paid trip to a convention!"

"Whoa, Geena! How was it? Sounds exciting? Did you do a lot of site-seeing? Any shopping?"

I was silent with my head down, concentrating hard on the invitations praying they would just drop the subject, but of course that was not about to happen. "No, CJ, it wasn't a pleasure trip; it was all business, no frills, no fun."

Kim chimed in from across the room. "How does he look?"

Again, I remained silent, but of course Stephanie

was sure to take over for me. "How does he look? Girllll, that man is fine!! Bald, beautiful white teeth, broad shoulders, sensual lips, and a body you could never get enough of! Isn't he sexy, Geena?"

I tried to ignore the question.

"I know you hear me. She knows he's a masterpiece, but she had to play hard to get because she had recently got engaged to Michael."

I instantly looked up from my writing pad. "I did not have to play hard to get, Stephanie. I was there on business, I have a fiancé' and furthermore, doesn't he have a wife?"

Steph and CJ both burst into laughter.

"A what? A wife? Girl, please. You know Zack isn't married; that man can have his choice of woman each day and night of the week. Those kind of men don't settle down, they settle up."

"What does that mean, Stephanie? They don't settle down, they settle up?"

Erica interjected. "I got this one, Steph. Geena, I don't even know this dude, but from sitting back and listening to everybody give their two cents about him, I can tell he is NOT the relationship type. His money, fame, reputation, and looks carry him so he can settle up with any woman he chooses and not be questioned about his whereabouts, the decisions he makes, or the company he keeps. He is UNTOUCHABLE!" She turned to look at the other ladies. "Am I right, ladies?"

Stephanie replied, "Yeah, I would say you hit the tail on the donkey! And on top of all what Erica just said, he is fiiiinnnneeeee!"

I could feel myself getting irritated. Zack said Char was his wife. Was she really his wife or just another part of his little game?

Stephanie got up and started walking towards my lap top. "Hey, Geena, how do you turn on this laptop? Everybody isn't as fortunate as you are to have a MacBook Pro."

"You turn it on like any other lap top, Stephanie-with the power button. Why are you getting on the laptop anyway?"

"Because I'm going to show the girls a picture of Dr. Stone from my Facebook page." I just looked at her. "And don't say a word, Geena. We know how you feel about Facebook, so I won't be on your lil laptop long."

I didn't want her to pull that picture up. I did NOT want to see Zack. "Stephanie, must you stop what you are doing to get on Facebook? I really want to get a lot of this stuff done tonight."

"Goodness! Okay, okay, okay! I won't look him up right now, but, ladies, when you have some time, go to my page and look him up, his name is spelled D–R–Z–A-K, hey! When was the last time you talked to him, Geena?"

"Uhmm, I can't remember."

"You can't remember?"

"Well, have you done any volunteering at the center?"

"No. I've been busy with the wedding stuff so I had to give that up."

"Oh! Okay."

By this time, Stephanie had caught on to my snappy responses because she soon changed the subject. After we finished up and the ladies were leaving, Stephanie remained behind. "Hey, Gee! Is everything okay?"

"Yeah, all is good."

"Well from the time we got here until now your demeanor has changed. Are you SURE everything is all right?"

"Yes, Stephanie, I am fine. Just a little tired that's all, ready to get this wedding behind me."

"You aren't being honest with me, Geena. Did something happen with Zack that I don't know about?"

"No. Why do you ask that?"

"Because the entire night when his name was being spoken, you were fidgety and soft spoken. So that tells me that SOMETHING is up."

I couldn't dare breathe a word of the Zack ordeal to Stephanie, so I had to continue to just play it like it was nothing because I promised myself that NOBODY was going to ever know about that.

"Look, Stephanie, it's a few weeks before I marry the man of my dreams. Don't I have a right to be a little crazy?"

"Okay, Geena, if you say so, but please let me know if there is something I can do."

"Thanks, babe, but I'm good AND I appreciate you."

"All right then, Geena, give me a hug. I love you

girl, now lock up and I'll talk to you later."

"Thanks, I love you too. Goodnight, Stephanie."

Erica and Derek
Chapter 22

I was really happy to see all of my girls that night, especially Erica. She and I met in college so she was really my friend; the other girls met her through me. It had been three or four years since I had seen her. Our only means of communicating was through an occasional text or email. I was so pleased that she accepted my invitation and agreed to be a bridesmaid because she had vowed to never be involved in a wedding again after her ugly divorce. I can still remember the conversation I had with Erica walking in the yard talking about her engagement to Derek like it was yesterday.

"Geena, look at this!"

I stopped in my tracks almost spilling my bottle of water on the grass. "Erica! Is that what I think it is?"

"Yes, ma'am, it is! I'm getting married."

We dropped our books and started jumping up and down, screaming and hollering with excitement.

"Let me see it! Let me see it! OH, Erica, girl it's gorgeous! Okay, tell me how it happened. I want to know every detail. I'm so excited for you!"

"Well, you know that Wednesday nights are our

usual date nights so last night we went to our favorite Italian restaurant. Derek suggested I order Chicken Marsala because I always get the same thing, and I needed to try something different."

"What's Chicken Marsala? Sounds like lettuce and chicken to me. How is that so different?"

"No silly. It's a dish with chicken breasts, mushrooms, and marsala gravy."

"Oh. I was about to say..."

"Anyway, when the food came out the cook had forgotten to put the gravy on the side. And you know how I am about sauces and meats together. Well, Derek and the waitress started going back and forth about it. I was like, okay, it's not that much of a big deal, just take it back and put the sauce on the side. But when the waitress came back, she had the chef with her. The chef apologized profusely. And I was looking like, are you serious? Over some chicken?

"Then in the middle of all the commotion, the chef started feeling around in his pockets as if he was looking for something very important that he needed. Then he looked at me and said, 'Ma'am, we apologize for any inconvenience and would like to give you this small token hoping you will continue to dine with us in the future.' He then took out a red velvet box and placed it in my hand. I was confused, thinking, gift cards have really changed. Then, all of a sudden, I looked up to see Derek scooting his seat back, standing up to walk towards me. He got down on one knee. I was still clueless. Then I thought, 'Oh my Jesus.' I started hyperventilating. He took the box, opened it, and then said, 'All my life I have waited for the moment to feel as I do today. I am happy, I am content, and I am complete. Will you marry me?' I was speechless."

"Speechless? Girl, what did you say?"

"I said YES!"

"Erica! Are you serious? Oh my god! That is like the best love story I have ever heard."

Erica lifted her hand, marveling at her shiny diamond ring, shimmering from the rays of the sunshine. "I know, Geena.He is so romantic, sweet, and kind. That is why we've decided to get married in the Spring."

"You are getting married when?"

"In the spring."

"Uhm, Erica. You do realize that we are still in college, don't you?"

"Yeah."

"We're only sophomores. This is our second year in college. Our second year of being out on our own. We still don't know how to boil water to make grits from the package. Do you really think it's a good idea for you and Derek to get married so soon?"

"Why not, Geena? We love each other, and we don't want to be with anyone else. So what's the big deal?"

"The big deal is that neither of you have had time to live your lives. Why not graduate, start your career, get on your feet, then get married. You know, the logical thing to do."

Erica wasn't listening to anything I was saying. Her mind was made up and that was that!

The first few years of their marriage, things were kind of tight because both of them were still trying to finish school and Erica was the only one working. Derek couldn't land any real work, but that didn't bother Erica because she believed as his wife, it was her responsibility to hold things down while he got himself established. Derek was an architect and after many dead-end deals, he finally landed the granddaddy of them all. Soon their financial struggles were over.

When the money started rolling in, so did babies. By the time they celebrated their fifth year wedding anniversary, they had four of them: three boys and one little girl! Everyone warned her that having those kids back to back may not be the best idea, but she assured them that she and Derek had talked about it and agreed that they both wanted to have a large family. All was perfect in Erica's world until Derek found his new love for tennis.

"Hey, babe, watchya watching?"

"Oh, this is the Australian Open. Roger Federer and Rafael Nadal are playing. It's getting intense."

Erica kind of snickered at him as she walked to open the refrigerator door. It was cute how he had jumped head-first into this sport that he always claimed he hated. "You want some juice or something?"

Derek didn't respond to her because he was so

enthralled with the tennis match.

"Babe, did you hear me?"

Erica was surprised by Derek's newfound love for tennis because he always described it as a sport where the men run around in booty shorts swinging after some balls. He was more of the football type, a sport where the men wear tight Capri pants and run after each other. But lately it seemed like every time he turned on the television, he was watching tennis. A few weeks later he started receiving the *Tennis Magazine* through the mail. Eventually he bought some balls, a racket and some booty shorts. Shockingly, he even joined a local league that met twice per month. As time rolled on and he progressed in the sport, he was gone once or twice per week. Soon tennis was taking up all of his extra time.

Although Erica missed him, she never spoke a word about his absence because she didn't want to stand in the way of him having some free time with his friends. With Derek on the courts, Erica was stuck at home taking care of their four kids. True enough, he provided for them financially and Erica didn't have to work, but she was still being bombarded with a great burden on her shoulders. Since he was rarely home, she nor the children hardly spent time with him. She felt like the children didn't know him because by the time he came in at night, it was late so the children were either already asleep or about to go to sleep. Erica spent more time driving around in her Mercedes mini-van than she did in her homeShe grew frustrated at times because she had earned a degree inbiology, not taxi driving. If it weren't for her mom, Erica may not have made it.

Derek had always been a huge sex fiend, hence the four kids they had back to back as soon as they were married. With the responsibilities of five-year-old DJ, three-year-old Caleb, two-year-old Alexis, and eight-month-old Taylor, Derek's busy schedule at work, plus his newfound passion for tennis, sex was pretty much obsolete between the two of them. After the birth of Alexis, Erica didn't really have a desire for sex because she was always so tired from taking care of the home and the babies. By the time Taylor came on the scene, it was game over on the love-making team. The last time Derek rolled over to get some of her "goods" as he called it, Erica was tired. So it wasn't pretty.

"What are you doing, Derek?"

"Trying to kiss my wife."

Erica took a deep sigh, pulling his arms away from her waist. "Not tonight. I'm tired and Taylor's in here with us."

"Well, I'll put Taylor in her bed."

"No. Don't move her because she'll wake up then I'll be stuck sitting up with her the rest of the night while you sleep."

"Look, Erica, I've tried to be patient with you but something has got to give. I'm tired of having to beg you. I should be able to just roll over into some ass! Hell, we're married."

"What! Roll over in some ass. Are you serious?

After I've been home all day running behind four babies while you are out skinnin' and grinnin' in your lil drop top convertible? Oh, I don't think so! Trade places with me for ONE day, Derek, and we'll see if you are up for me rolling over in YOUR ass!"

"Fine. I'm going back to sleep." He snatched the cover, pulling it over his body. "By the way, with all of your screaming, you woke Taylor up. Good night."

Erica was pissed! Once again she was stuck rocking the baby while Derek slept like one. As the months passed, Derek became completely enthralled with tennis, even joined a traveling team, which took him out of town most weekends. Erica didn't like how things were going at all, but there was really nothing she could do.

After putting the kids down for a nap one Saturday afternoon, Erica began washing and folding clothes. Shaking out a pair of Derek's tennis shorts, a card fell out; it was from an OBGYN's office that practiced near Derek's office downtown. There was a name on the back of the card that was unfamiliar. She thought, *Who is Lauren Greer?* Her gut instincts told her that something wasn't right, but instead of confronting him with it, she decided to put the card back into Derek's shorts, fold them, and place them in his drawer. The rest of the day Erica was just sick! She didn't know what to do! Derek was out of town and wouldn't be getting home for another two days so she used that time to strategize.

The evening of Derek's return home, Erica planned

a welcome home dinner for him, hoping she could bring back some of the intimacy they had once shared. She had taken the kids to her mother's house so she and Derek could have some much needed alone time. While she was checking on his favorite meal still baking in the oven, she heard the garage door. So she snatched off her oven mitt, quickly looked into the microwave to put on her gloss, and ran her fingers through her long straightened hair, making sure everything was in place. She hurried to make her way into the dining room, lighting the candles, and turning on some soft music. When he came into the house, he was shocked to see Erica standing in the dining room wearing the chocolate lingerie she hadn't worn since their wedding night.

"What's all of this for?"

Erica began walking towards Derek to greet him. "It's for you, baby. I missed you and wanted to give you a suitable welcome home."

Without even taking a second to thank her, he said, "Ohhh, where are the kids?"

"They are at my mom's house, she's going to keep them for us tonight." Erica took her finger and started to play with the ribbon that ran through the lace on her lingerie, hoping that her sexy attire would entice Derek like she remembered it used to. But to her dismay, he acted as if he didn't even notice what she was wearing and walked towards the stairs.

"Hey! Wait a minute! Don't I get a hello hug or something?"

"Oh yeah, sorry, Erica. You know I'm used to coming into a house with whiney babies and kids running around everywhere. Forgive me." He put his briefcase down only for a second and gave her a hug that resembled an embrace between two strangers, lacking all compassion. "Is that better? I need to get upstairs and get showered. I'm starving! I hope you have something good to eat!"

Derek turned to make his way up the staircase. As he reached the top, he turned back and called down to her. "Hey!"

Erica was wishing desperately that he was about to ask her to come upstairs with him, but instead he asked. "Is that the lingerie from our wedding night? You must have lost some weight."

Erica stood at the bottom of the stairs as her heart sank down to the bottom of her soul. There was a lump in her throat that made it almost unbearable to breathe. She was losing him and she knew it. Walking back to the dining room seemed like it took forever. After each step, flashbacks of Lauren Greer's name popped into her head. She finally reached her destination, turned off the soft music, blew out all of the candles, then walked into the kitchen. Erica took a few seconds before preparing Derek's dinner plate to gather herself. Standing near the wall, facing the stove and looking at the meal she spent four hours preparing for him, her body became weak. She slowly slid down to the floor, trembling from grief and despair. With her legs crossed and head bowed, Erica sat alone in her pool of tears, knowing in her heart that her marriage was over.

The following morning while she prepared Derek's breakfast, Erica kept trying to figure out how she could bring up the card and Lauren Greer. She sat quietly eating her oatmeal and grapefruit while he scarfed down a bowl of cheese grits, sausage, eggs, toast, and orange slices, screaming at the television because of the report he was listening to on ESPN. After he finished his coffee, Erica stood to take his cup and plate away. He was about to head to the bathroom with his newspaper so it was then or never.

"How was your breakfast?"

"Oh it was great. Just how I like it."

"Do you have a minute?"

"I have about five. It's almost 8 a.m. and I need to get to the office early."

"This won't take long." The fear of finding out the facts was terrifying her. What if he confirmed something that she really didn't want to know. She took a deep breath and went for it. "I found a card while I was doing the laundry the other day; it had someone's name on it. Lauren Greer. Do you know her?"

Derek placed his newspaper on the bar before answering the question. "Yeah, I know her. She's a young lady on my tennis team, why?"

"I was just wondering why you would have her card from the OBGYN."

"Oh well, Lauren started with the league around the

same time I did. We were put on the same team because we were both novices. Talking to her from time to time, I found her to be a nice girl, but she's caught some tough breaks. She's a single mother trying to make ends meet, and she needed some help. I was just trying to be there for her."

That news crushed Erica. "Wait a minute. Let me clarify before we go any further. You were doing what? Trying to help her out? When was the last time you helped me out around here?" The thought of her husband taking time out for some girl on his tennis team who he just met when he didn't take time out for his own family sent her anger into overdrive. "Wait a minute, Derek. Help me understand how you have time to help her, and what exactly do you help her with?"

"Simple things like taking her to the doctor, an occasional ride to the store." Erica cut him off before she knew it.

"How dare you disrespect me like that?"

"Disrespect you how?"

"Having her in the car with you? There is no telling who has seen you and what they have said!"

"Why would someone have anything to say about who's in the car with me? That's ridiculous!"

"No, you are ridiculous to even think that would be okay! Why haven't you ever mentioned her to me?"

"I really didn't think it was that big of a deal, Erica. All I did was take the girl to the store a few times, goodness."

"Well, let me explain something to you. The last time you drove her around was your LAST time."

"What? Why are you so tensed over something so innocent?"

"Come on, Derek! That doesn't even look right! I'm home going crazy with YOUR four children and you have time to ride some chick around in OUR car?"

They argued back and forth that morning, that night, and for the next few weeks. Finally, Erica decided to just let it go and try to continue on with life as she knew it. As the time was approaching for her and Derek to celebrate their 12th wedding anniversary, they decided to renew their vows. The ceremony was beautiful and Erica was on cloud nine. Towards the end of the evening, a young lady approached Erica as she walked out of the restroom.

"Excuse me. Your name is Erica, right?"

"Yes. Is there something I can do for you?"

It was really noisy in the hall so it was hard for either of them to hear one another. The young lady looked around first then asked Erica if they could talk somewhere in private. She noticed that the young lady was carrying an envelope in her right hand, so she thought it was, time for her to pay some of the caterer's. Erica motioned for the young lady to follow her into one of the empty banquet rooms.

"That's much better! Whoo! Couldn't hear you well out there with all the noise. You must be with one of the caterers?"

The young lady gave Erica a look that proved she

wasn't. "No, Erica. I'm not with one of the caterers."

"My apologies. Well, what can I do for you?"

"I just came by to bring this to you." The girl handed Erica the envelope.

"What is this?"

The young lady took a deep breath then said, "Oh. I guess he STILL hasn't said anything to you yet."

"Excuse me? Who hasn't told me what?"

"I think you should open the envelope."

Erica was scared to death to open the envelope but she did anyway. "What's this?" she asked as she pulled out a piece of white paper.

"It's the report from the lab."

"The lab?"

Immediately, Erica remembered the card from Derek's shorts. She stood frozen, wishing she could close her eyes and disappear. She feared what was about to come out of the young lady's mouth next.

"My name is Lauren Greer, and those are the results from the DNA test that prove my daughter, Andrea, is Derek's daughter, too."

The shock from the news was too much for Erica. She fainted and had to be rushed to the emergency room. While at the hospital, Derek was able to convince Erica to forgive him; even with that huge blow, Erica let Derek back in. Her friends all told her she should let him go! Who has a child with someone else when he is married? But even with all of the urging, she didn't take any advice. Erica felt like she had to take him back for her children's sake. How could she raise four children on her own, with no job, and no place to go.

Once their oldest son, DJ, turned fourteen, Derek took him under his wing to learn the family business. He had plans of going to college and becoming a great architect just like his father because in DJ's eyes, Derek was his hero and he wanted to do everything his father did. One summer, Erica started to notice that Derek and DJ's relationship had started to shift from great, to good, to not good at all. While pulling the covers back and getting prepared for bed one night, Erica questioned Derek about it.

"Hey, have you noticed anything different with DJ lately?"

"Nah, what do you mean?"

"I don't know, he isn't himself and since you all work so closely together, I figured you would pick up on it more than me."

Derek pulled the covers up on his shoulder after climbing in bed beside Erica then nonchalantly responded, "He's a boy, Erica, and he's just starting to feel himself. His attitude is just a part of him growing into a young man."

Since Erica had no experience with teenage boys, she took Derek at his word and tried to leave the situation alone, but as the days continued to pass she watched as the relationship between them became more and more strained.

"Hey, DJ, hand me that pen over there."

"Man, please, you better get it yourself."

Erica couldn't believe the type of disrespect she was witnessing and what made matters worse was that Derek would just let it go. Him being a stickler for chastisement and having respect for elders, she couldn't understand how all of a sudden DJ could get away with murder.

"Are you going to let him just walk away from you like that, Derek?"

"He'll be all right. DJ is just mad because I didn't give him $20 today when he asked for it. Don't pay him any attention."

Erica was confused, but believed in letting the man of the house be the man, so she just let it go with the hope that her once sweet and gentle son would revert back to the person that he was. After shopping with a friend one afternoon, Erica rushed home to prepare Derek and DJ's favorite desert, thinking maybe they could at least be civil over some food. When she pulled into the driveway, she noticed Derek's car was there and the garage was still up. She got out of the car and started to go up the walkway when she heard voices in the backyard that sounded like some people arguing. She hurried to see what the commotion was all about. The closer she got, she could hear the voices more clearly and realized it was Derek and DJ. Instead of trying to stop the arguing, she decided to duck behind some trashcans so she could listen and hopefully find out what had really been going on between the two of them. She stooped quietly as they went back and forth and finally it all came out.

"Look, son, I'm getting sick and tired of your blatant disrespect! You're going to stop with this nasty attitude and foul mouth if you're going to continue to come up to the office to work. I sign your paychecks at the office, and I make the rules here at home. You're going to have to show some level of respect in both places. You need to learn soon that in life there are some things that won't be tolerated, and your attitude is one of them. You need to fix it and handle yourself accordingly or suffer the consequences. I'm tired of people asking me what is wrong with you! I'm done with you raising your voice at me like you've lost your mind, walking away from me while I'm talking to you and never doing anything I say."

Erica couldn't believe what she was hearing! How dare DJ show such disrespect to his father? He was raised to honor his mother and father, what had gotten into him? After a few seconds of silence, she peeped around the corner to take a closer look at what was going on. As she turned the corner, she watched as DJ stepped right in front of Derek, look him up and down, then directly in the eye before he began to speak.

"DISRESPECT you? Man, are you serious? Do you even hear yourself? You know what, Dad, I mean Mr. Woods or whoever you are today, you can go straight to HELL with that! I don't care what those people at the office say or think about me! For the past eight months, I've had to sit back and watch while you take extended lunch breaks to meet your mistress at hotel rooms, how you flirt with every skirt that passes by, and how I have stood by and watch you LIE to my mother about your whereabouts, how she continues to bend over backwards for you and all you do is kick her in the ass!"

DJ turned away and dropped his head before continuing. "I am sick of it, I am sick of the disrespect you have shown me as your son, and I am pissed off for the way you have treated my mama!"

Erica was numb because she was so angry she couldn't even cry. She clutched her stomach with her sweat-drenched palms. Slowly, she stood up from where she hid behind the trash cans, trembling as she made her way around the gate. Silent tears rolled down her cheeks as pain rolled around in her heart. Slow motion was the pace she chose to make her way to Derek. Erica was too weak to even scream at him. She could only muster enough strength to stand before him.

"So this is what DJ's attitude has been about?"

"Wait, Erica, look. I can explain. What you just heard was..."

Erica didn't want to hear any more excuses, she was tired of the lies, and she was done with the betrayal.

"Look, Derek, I know you have played me for a fool all these years, but rest assured that I'm far from being one. I remained in this marriage for my children's sake, fighting teeth and tongue to make our relationship last, knowing that I was doing it alone. I should have walked away when I had the chance years ago after I found out about Andrea, but no. I wanted to honor my vows, and be a good role model for my children, so I sucked up the embarrassment, the disappointment, and the disgrace to stay by your side. But it's over, Derek. Bravo on a job well done. You got me, for the very LAST time."

Erica started to walk away. Derek tried to stop her.

"Wait a minute, Erica, we need to talk about this. You can't just walk out on our marriage."

"I don't have to, Derek. You already did."

Erica didn't waste any time. A few weeks later she hired a divorce attorney, gathered all of her information proving Derek's infidelity, and went forth with the proceedings. Derek didn't protest anything. He agreed to give Erica everything she wanted in the divorce decree. Although he thought she would, Erica didn't want the house. She said there were too many emotions tied to it. She wanted and desperately needed a brand new start, so she found some land and planned to have a smaller home built to suit the needs of her and the children.

While leaving the courtroom that afternoon, Erica headed towards the front door to leave. Derek jogged up behind her to get her attention so they could talk. He apologized to her for the way he treated her during their marriage and explained that he didn't mean for things to turn out the way they did. Although she was hurt, she wasn't angry.

After he was finished, she said, "You know, Derek, for twelve years I've had to search deep within myself to figure out how I should handle your adulterous ways. There were numerous occasions that I was in so much pain that I needed to leave, but being the mother of your children, I wanted to stay. I thought sticking it out for the children's sake would make me a better mother, feeling as though my staying would mean I wasn't greedy and thought only of my feelings and how much I needed to be loved.

"But after today, I finally realized that sticking it out as long as I did was only harming the children. Staying with you, I was teaching our daughter to allow a man to treat her with disrespect, lie to her, cheat on her, and lose herself in distress. Staying with you, I was teaching our sons to marry someday only to disrespect their wife, lie to her, and mistreat her thinking that there will be no repercussion for their unrelenting behavior.

"After that epiphany, I know that divorcing you is my only option. My children mean more to me than a big house, nice cars, and a lot of money." Erica turned to make her way down the steps, Derek followed after her pleading for her to wait. She turned back to give him an opportunity to speak his last piece. With tear-filled eyes, he looked at her and said, "Erica, I'm sorry."

Erica took a deep sigh looking up at the sky, then looked back at him. She didn't say a word, but the look in her eyes said it all. After a brief moment, she turned her back to him and walked away.

Since the divorce, Erica hasn't even talked to

another man on the phone. It's sad but she gave up on love. She told me that love hurt her, and she couldn't deal with that kind of hurt again.

In Honor of Me!
Chapter 23

The girls had decided to give me a "lovely ladies luncheon where we all dressed in heels and hats to celebrate the soon-to-be union of Michael and I. They rented one of the largest rooms at the Country Club and had it adorned with white and silver pieces of artistry. The chairs were covered in white linen and silver bows. Three dozen white roses sat as centerpieces on each table. There were ice sculptures and wine fountains around the room. Pictures of Michael and I from high school, college, and present day were being played on a big screen while soft music played in the background. As I walked into the room, I literally felt like I had entered heaven. There were over 50 of my dear, sweet friends in attendance. All of my bridesmaids were there, some of the ladies that I grew up with, some from my office, a few from my social club, and some from my church.

As I mingled and made my way around the room to greet my guests, I couldn't help but notice one woman that stuck out more than the others seated next to Rachel. There was something peculiar about the way Rachel and this woman interacted with each other.

They giggled a lot, their chairs were pushed close together, and they touched hands frequently, almost in the way that I interacted with Michael. I couldn't enjoy talking with my guests for watching them out of the corner of my eye as they went to the bar together, walked around the room together, and stood alone talking to each other. Before I could make my way over to where they were standing, they started walking up to greet me. I could feel someone tapping me on my shoulder as I was about to walk away from one of the sisters from the church.

"Hey, Geena!"

"Well, hi Rachel!" She started motioning for me to look at her friend. "This is JayJay."

The woman extended her hand to shake mine. "Hi, Geena. I've heard so much about you. It's great to finally put a face with a name."

"Hi, uhmm JayJay, right? How are you?"

"I'm great and this place is gorgeous! It shows how much your friends think of you and love you."

Rachel chimed in, "Yeah, Geena has always been everybody's favorite."

"Oh, girl, stop it! I am not."

"Come on, Geena, you know everybody loves you! And there's nothing wrong with that. You are like the big sister that none of us ever had. You always have the best advice, you're able to give us direction when we find ourselves lost, you always offer the sweetest words to help soothe our pains, and of course the occasional scorching you give us any time we needed it. You've always been such a great friend to everyone, so people can't help but love you!"

"Awwhhhl. Thank you, Rachel, I love you too, honey! Look, you girls go ahead and take your seats, by the looks of it, the program is about to start."

Everyone had already begun scrambling to their seats as Stephanie began to speak from the podium.

"Could I have your attention? Ladies, Ladies. Thank you! Good afternoon, everyone. I would like to first thank each of you for taking time out from your Saturday to share your love with my best friend, Geena." The ladies began to clap as I smiled and waved, thanking them.

"Geena and I have been friends for a very long time and I'm very thankful for the friendship we share. I know there are many of you here today that could stand and tell a story or two about a time where Geena came to your rescue, but due to time constraints, I'll be the only one sharing today." The ladies begin to laugh. "No seriously, Geena has been a rock for many people, and I can't thank her enough for being a rock for me. When my mother passed away a few years back, Geena was the only person that I could depend on to help me stay afloat." Stephanie paused as tears began to fall. "She was there for me when I felt like my world was coming to an end. Being an only child, I didn't have siblings to help me cope, so she pulled me under her wing and made sure I was okay. I will forever love her for that.

"Geena and I have been through a lot and I'm

grateful, that with her, I share some very special memories. I was there for the birth of her two beautiful children and she was there when I bought my first Bentley. "The crowd chuckled. "But on a serious note," Stephanie turned to look directly at me. "I'm so happy and excited about this new phase in your life, Geena. I feel in my heart that this marriage will be blessed and nothing but good will come from it and I feel fortunate to be a part of this special union. This kind of love gives all of us hope that love is real and that each of us can have it."

Every person in the room stood to clap as I walked up to take the podium, hugging Steph then taking a deep breath preparing myself to speak.

"Good afternoon, my dear friends, I won't take up too much time talking because I know that you may be hungry and I hear the chef here can get down in the kitchen." The ladies chuckled as I gathered my thoughts to continue. "I would like to take just a few moments to share with you how happy and blessed I am. First, I must give honor to God for allowing me the opportunity to be given a chance at this kind of love. You know, as a little girl I always dreamed of being a wife. I wanted to have somebody I could share my whole life with the way I watched couples on television. I remember watching husbands and wives as they interacted with one another, taking mental notes, and putting them in my back pocket so that I might capitalize on their strengths as well as their faults when I became a wife. Although all I ever heard from older people was that marriage is hard, it's tough, it's a lot of work, it's not all fun and happy times like you may think it would be, I believed in my heart that it could be blissful and rewarding.

"It's no secret to anyone in this room that I was married previously and after ten years, that marriage demised. Everybody goes into a marriage with the expectation that it will last forever. Sadly, in many marriages, that's not the case. As much as it hurts to admit it, I fell into that statistic. Divorce can be devastating, and drain what little life you have completely out of your body. The embarrassment of a failed marriage sends many people into a whirlwind of depression. I know without a shadow of doubt that my close relationship with God is what gave me the strength to stand behind this podium speaking to each of you today.

"Even with all of the tears I shed, all of the sleep I lost, all of the pain I endured, my divorce gave me a strength that no man can ever take away. I'm strong because of my weak nights and I'm happy because of my sad days. Through those dark valleys that I had to travel, God reached down, pulled me up, and blessed me in a way I never thought was possible. You see, each of us DESERVE to feel loved each and every day of our lives, and do not let anyone tell you different!

"This is what I have been blessed to learn from and feel with Michael. He is my sunshine, he is my life preserver, he is my breath of fresh air, he is my safety net, and, through God, he is my everything. I love him with my whole being and I'm grateful that God saw fit that I experience this kind of love that I was led to believe didn't exist. Our hearts share one rhythmic beat, and our souls have become one.

"Do you all remember playing Hide and Go Seek as children? We'd pick the person that would do the countdown by the tree as we ran to find somewhere to hide. We could hear them count as we scurried to find our hiding spot, five, four, three, two, and one, ready or not, here I come! I can remember standing behind the old shed at my grandmother's house as my older cousin ran to look for us. My heart would be pounding as I stood as still as I could, hoping he wouldn't find me. Even to this day when I close my eyes, I can still hear his footsteps in the dried leaves right beside the shed. I start holding my breath hoping he couldn't hear me breathe. Then as soon as I think the coast is clear and he has passed on to find someone else, he jumps around the shed and screams, 'I gotchya!'

"He would pick me up, toting me back to the front of the house where the rest of the cousins were standing, laughing and pointing because I had been caught. As he put me down, he whispered to me, 'You're safe now, Geena.'"

I started to get choked up, my voice cracking as I tried to continue my speech.

"During that time, I just thought we were playing a game. I didn't realize what was going on, but even then as a seven-year-old little girl, God was speaking to me, letting me know that if I can just hold on, He was going to send someone to find me, and when he comes, I was going to be SAFE. And in Michael, I have found my safety."

I put my head down, as tears fell, wetting the podium. A wail of emotions came flooding out of me. I tried to pull myself together, but I wasn't able to. After a few moments, Stephanie stood to hug me and the ladies began to stand and clap.

"Please forgive me. Thank you, thank you everybody. Wow, where did that come from?" I giggled through my tears trying to stop them from flowing.

"I have some thoughts that I call personal prayers that I would like to share with you today and I hope that you will hear and hold on to them. To my unmarried sisters that are in the dating process but are looking to find a husband, my prayer is that you seek first the face of God, pray without ceasing that God prepares you for your mate. Make sure that you are ready to be a wife. Handle all things that concern you. Be certain that your credit is intact, your business is handled, and that you are accountable for your actions. I beg of you to stop walking around professing that you are looking for a man to take care of you. Have your business in order, so you can take care of yourself. Then when God sends whom He intends, you will be able to complement each other, grow, and build a prosperous life together.

"You don't want to marry because of looks, financial gain, the length of time you have been together, the number of children you may already have, or because you are being coerced by a family member or friend. You should accept his hand in marriage after you have prayed and received confirmation from the Lord.

"To my engaged sisters, my prayer is that you pray individually as well as collectively with your partner for understanding. In order for your love to be successful, you must first understand one another. Take time to find out his desires and openly share yours with him. There is nothing wrong with compromising; there is nothing wrong with change. If it benefits your relationship, then DO IT! You don't want to go into a marriage blindsided thinking that you know everything or go into it having ill intentions. Ill intentions will lead you straight to a divorce.

"To my married sisters, my prayer is that you accept nothing but the BEST from your spouse each and every day and that you give your BEST in return. Now don't go turning your lips up and rolling your eyes." Giggles came from the crowd. "I know many of you are saying to yourself, He does NOT deserve my best, and in many cases I have found that to be true. But I honestly believe that we get what we give. And now I know many of you are sounding like Jeffrey Osborne singing, 'I gave my best, but I guess my best wasn't good enough.' The ladies laughed and slapped hands with one another in agreement. "Let me explain to you what I mean and why I say what I say. In my first marriage, I wanted nothing more than for my husband to spend time with me. I loved his company and wanted to share any extra time that I had with him. I wanted us to go places like the movies, a play, or a concert from time to time. I wanted to still date him although we were married because I was told that is one component of a successful marriage.

"Instead of taking me out and spending time with me, he would always tell me he couldn't go because he had practice or a game and after having to beg him time after time, I grew agitated. He coached a little league baseball team and he loved it. As a child he always dreamed of making it to the Major Leagues, but when that dream was deferred, he committed his life to working with the youth of the community to try and help their dreams come alive. After many years of begging him, I started to just pour my all into my children, my work, and things I could find to occupy my time, which eventually caused a divide in our marriage. He was living one life and I was living another.

"I realize now that maybe if I had taken some interest in the things that he enjoyed, he would have taken more interest in what made me satisfied. Maybe I should have showed some interest in the things that made him happy. I could have volunteered to take the score for them, or I could have given the players water and Gatorade after the game, instead of making him wash his own uniform and never attending any of his banquets. I was bitter and it didn't make things better.

"When I say the BEST, I mean that you plan to be

happy every day. How many of you know and believe that preparation is important? Well for those of you that may not know, it is one of the keys to success. You see, as a leader in my organization, I preach all day to my team members about how important it is for us to be prepared when it's time to make presentations to our potential clients. If we're prepared for the presentations, they go smooth and questions are answered swiftly and, in most cases, we receive their business. Whenever there is a time we're unprepared, we suffer and lose money and, in some cases, clientele."

I had to pause to take a deep breath. "It wasn't until I met Michael that I realized the same concepts I use at work should be used at home because I want to be successful in both arenas."

As I finished my last statement, I stepped away from the podium to take my seat. The ladies and I dined, I opened my gifts, and we ended the day on a happy note. My heart was content and my soul was satisfied.

Rachel and JayJay
Chapter 24

L ater on that night after the luncheon, some of the girls decided they wanted to meet for drinks. We all went home to change so we could meet back up at the cigar bar club near the airport; it wasn't your usual cigar bar because on Saturday nights the owner allowed his son to come in and handle the music. The room was cloudy from all of the smoke filling the air, which is one of the reasons I hated going there, but to spend time with my friends, I didn't mind. One of the waiters pointed Stephanie and I in the direction of the V.I.P. section that had been roped off for us. We ordered our drinks as we waited for the others to arrive.

Soon Erica surprised us and came through the door, shortly after her Kim and CJ came in. Rachel and JayJay were the last ones to arrive. We were having a ball, dancing and laughing just like we used to when we were in school. We danced and laughed until our feet were numb and our voices were practically gone! The entire night, I couldn't help but notice how Rachel and JayJay continued to dance all up on each other. I guess it didn't bother anyone but me because everybody around us ignored them like it was normal. After a while, I couldn't take it anymore so I pulled Stephanie aside and asked if she saw anything awkward about the relationship between Rachel and her new friend.

With her glass in her hand and continuing to dance, Steph yelled out, "Huh?"

I had to take her to the bar away from the music so she could understand me.

"What's wrong, Geena, another drink coming your way?"

"Ha ha ha, very funny, Stephanie! No, I want to ask you about Rachel and JayJay."

"What about them?"

"Doesn't it seem suspicious how they... you know?"

Stephanie looked at me, confused. "How they what?"

"How they are grinding all over each other and stuff."

"Uhm, no because everybody over there is smashed in that tight space so it looks like everybody is grinding to me."

Before I knew, it I had my hands on Stephanie's chin, snatching her face to look in their direction. "Stephanie! I'm being serious! There is something up with this JayJay. Look at them! Where did she come from? Do you know her?"

"She seems to be cool. Rachel brought her to my house a few weeks ago. I think she said they work together or something."

"Okay, and what else? Is that it?"

"I mean, I didn't ask any more questions. She seems to be a nice girl to me."

"So you didn't pick up any type of vibe from them?"

"What kind of vibe, Geena?"

"Okay, like at the luncheon today. They were all giggly and googly and it made me feel uncomfortable. Then when she introduced her to me, it just didn't seem right. Now that we are here, they are..." I turned my attention back to the V.I.P. section where they were all dancing. "Stephanie! Look! They are kissing!"

By this time, we were both sitting with our mouths wide open. Rachel and JayJay were kissing the way Michael and I would kiss one another. I couldn't move.

"Oh my goodness, Geena! Did you see that?"

I couldn't talk because I was still in shock. Stephanie elbowed me. "Geena! Geena!"

"Ouch! That hurt! Yes, Stephanie! I saw it!"

"So now what do we do?"

"I don't know!"

After some time passed, we both decided we would let the night end then talk with her the next day.

Confrontation Day
Chapter 25

Stephanie and I decided to invite Rachel and Kim over for lunch so we could all talk. We met at my house so we could remain private and keep Rachel's business discreet. After all the girls arrived, we started drinking wine and having small talk. We laughed and had a good time like we did each time that we were all together. After an hour or so passed, I decided to open the floor.

"Rachel, we all brought you over here today to talk about JayJay."

As I spoke, Rachel began to look around at us puzzled. "Okay, what do you want to discuss?"

"Well, we wanted to know what your relationship with her is."

"What do you mean, Geena?"

Stephanie took the floor. "Look, Rachel, we want to know if you are sleeping with this chick, JayJay!"

I looked at Stephanie, wanting to knock her in the head. "Uhmm, thank you, Stephanie, for just putting it out there."

I turned and took Rachel by the hand. "Look, honey, we just wanted to reach out to you to see what's going on."

"What do you mean, what is going on? If ya'll have questions, you may as well start asking them."

That was the door Stephanie needed open. "Okay, well tell us about JayJay."

"Okay, no problem. She and I work together. We met about four months ago, and we enjoy hanging out with each other."

"We understand all of that, Rachel, and that's cool. It just seemed like there was more going on than just friendship when you all were at my luncheon."

"Something like what, Geena?"

I turned to look at Stephanie for some help. "I'm just going to come out with it. ARE you sleeping with her, Rachel?"

"Well, ladies, I will put it to you like this. We are all adults here. We all have our own opinions and beliefs. Each of us can make up our minds to do as we like. And my belief is that I can do as I wish. JayJay is my friend and if you would like for me to be totally honest with you, YES, we are sleeping together."

Kim blurted out, "Rachel. You're GAY?"

"No, Kim, I'm not gay. I'm a woman that knows what she wants and is not afraid to get what she needs."

Stephanie spoke up. "And what exactly does that mean, Rachel?"

"It means that I'm not going to spend another day on God's green Earth being unhappy and miserable to satisfy other people."

"Rachel, please don't use God and gay in the same sentence."

"See. That is what I'm talking about, narrow-minded people. God loves all of us. He's not like man. He doesn't discriminate due to the color of your skin, your level of income, your status in society, OR your sexual preference. My relationship with JayJay is not just about sex, although it is really good." We all squinted and squirmed like we had just drunk a pint of pickle juice. "No, seriously, she understands me. She listens to me. She makes me feel appreciated. She helps me whenever I need her, and she's always there. I've never felt this kind of security with Cedric and quite frankly, I doubt if I ever will. And furthermore, I didn't know that you all were so homophobic and judgmental!"

Stephanie stood up from her seat, drink in hand. "Hold on, Rachel. I think I can speak for all of us when I say we don't believe in same sex relationships." She walked right over to where I was seated and looked directly at me. "Right, Geena?"

My mind immediately went back to the situation with Zack and his wife. How could I judge Rachel when I didn't want to be judged? There was no way I could let them find out about my situation though. I had to be quick on my feet.

"Geena! Right?" She didn't even give me time to respond. "Yeah, she agrees, Rachel! That's just nasty and we ain't down with it." Stephanie turned to look at Kim, who was sitting in her chair with her mouth wide open. "Right, Kim?" Kim remained silent.

"Well honestly, Stephanie, I didn't come over here asking for the three of you to give me your approval. I received the invite to come over here to talk openly amongst my closest friends. I talked. Now I'm being mistreated because of what I believe in? Because of my choice?"

I couldn't just sit there and allow Rachel to be ridiculed and treated so unfairly. I had to speak up. "Okay, okay, okay, LOOK! There's no need for us to get all uptight about something that's really none of our business, and by all means, we don't need to raise our voices. Look, Rachel, Stephanie makes a valid point, although she may not be 100% right. We have never agreed with same sex relationships, BUT I do believe that everyone has a right to love whomever they choose."

Stephanie interrupted me. "Wait a minute, Geena! So you mean to tell me you're okay with Rachel bumpin' this chick?"

"Stephanie, all I'm saying is we need to be more compassionate about her feelings. It doesn't mean we have to agree with her, but as her friends, we have to respect her."

Rachel stood to hug me. "Thank you, Geena. Thank you. Thank you. Thank you." She turned to Stephanie. "Can I have a hug Steph?" Stephanie stood, Kim followed and we all embraced. "Look, girls, I know this relationship is something new and I don't expect anyone to understand. That's why I kept it a secret for so long because I was afraid of having to deal with a situation like this. I know what the bible says, and I understand you feel like this is not of God. But I do know that God is LOVE and the God that I love wants us to feel His love and for the first time in my life, I feel it."

Rachel began to cry as she continued, "I have had to settle for less all of my life. Stand back as my friends enjoyed relationships with men that respect them, treat them well, and make them feel like queens. I have always envied how a man and a woman held hands, sat close to one another, were able to share a soft kiss, and give a gentle touch. For as long as I can remember, I have had to put up a front like I'm okay with the way my life has played out. There have been many times when I had to walk around wearing a smile, while in reality I was crying inside.

"None of you know how it feels to have a husband that openly cheats on you, lies to you on a regular basis, and talks to you like you are worthless. I have lived in a lonely dark hole for so long that I figured I would never see the light again. Meeting JayJay, I finally have at least a small ray of hope. She is good to me and I feel she is good for me; all I ask from the three of you is your support."

By this time, there wasn't a dry eye in the room. I stood to comfort her, and Stephanie and Kim joined us. "We love you, Rachel, and only want the best for you, so if JayJay is your choice, we will respect it."

Michael Is Home
Chapter 26

L eaving the tiebacks on my drapes the night before allowed the sunshine to make its entrance, waking me up early that morning. The warmth felt like God Himself had kissed me on my cheek. I rolled out of bed with a smile in my heart just thinking that the separation between Michael and I would be over in about four hours. In the shower, I sang *Love Me In A Special Way* as loud as I could, filled with excitement and bubbling over with joy. Lily and Frances were gone with Jared, so I had all the time I needed to prepare for my big day.

Walking out of the shower, I could hear my cell phone ring. It was Michael letting me know his plane had landed early and he was at the airport waiting on me. I jumped into my little black dress, bumped my hair, rubbed on a little eye makeup, and glossed my lips as I slipped on my Louboutin sling backs. I was so excited to see Michael. his time away seemed like eternity, and I couldn't help but fantasize about finally being able to feel his arms around me again, to smell his cologne, and feel his lips against mine. I had arranged for a limo to pick us up and take us to brunch because I didn't want to have to wait to cuddle with him after we left the airport.

The driver was already in my driveway when I walked out of my front door, standing beside the rear passenger door, holding it open for me to get in. As we drove closer to the airport, I got butterflies in my stomach from the anticipation of seeing my love. Once we parked, I took a trolley car to the entrance gate. I could see Michael standing with his luggage waiting for me. I was able to sneak up behind him and whisper in his ear.

"Are you waiting for someone, sir?"

He turned to me, dropped his bags, and grabbed me, holding on for dear life. It felt so good being in his arms again and I couldn't wait to get back to the limo.

"Geena! Baby, it's so good to be home."

"I know, Michael. I'm so happy you're finally here. I've missed you so much. Are you ready to go?"

"Sure, where did you park?"

"Oh, I parked near the entrance on the other side. We can get a trolley car to take your things so we won't have to carry them so far."

As we gathered his suitcases and loaded them on the cart, I grew more anxious to see his reaction when he saw the limo.

"Okay, babe, let's get out of here." As we got closer to the limousine, Michael began to look around for my Range Rover.

"Where's the truck, baby?"

"Oh! I didn't drive it."

"Well, how are we going to get home?"

I looked to the side of me where the limousine driver was standing with one hand behind his back and the other on the handle of the rear door.

"You didn't, Geena?"

"Yes I did, Michael."

Michael grabbed me and gave me another long passionate kiss. "I love you, baby!"

"I love you, too."

Inside the limousine, we had champagne and chocolate-covered strawberries all chilled and ready for consumption.

"So where are we going, Geena?"

"We are headed downtown to have brunch at the complex where we're scheduled to have the reception. We only have one week before the wedding so I didn't want to waste any time getting the last minute things done."

Michael began scooting closer to me. "Well, how far is the complex from here? And how dark is that window tinted up front near the driver?"

I smiled thinking to myself, *Do I know my man or what?* "We have about a thirty-minute drive there and all of these windows are VERY tinted. I asked them for the blackout special." We both giggled as I placed both of my hands around Michael's face, pulling him in to kiss me. Michael turned me around so that the back of my neck was facing his lips. He unlaced my black halter with his teeth, rubbing his gentle hands up the side of my dress only stopping when his fingers found their place inside of my lace panties. He seduced me with warm kisses all around my neck and shoulders, getting me ready for all that we had in store. I had to put my champagne glass down so that I wouldn't spill anything with all of the excitement. I turned around to face him, allowing my lips to meet his. We kissed until I was flat on my back, legs opened, and Michael in between them. As he continued removing my halter with his right hand, he unbuckled his belt with the left. The temperature was rising in the back of that limo, and I was ready.

My mind was on what I had been missing and that was Michael making love to me. I missed the feel of his weight pressing against my body. I missed the smell of his cologne. I missed the warmth of his breath on my neck. I missed his lips. I missed his hands. I missed his love. As I prepared my mind to receive all that his body was about to give, I felt the limo slowing down.

"Hold on, wait a minute, Michael. I think the limo is about to stop."

"Are we here already?"

I sat up to look, holding my dress against my chest, just in case there was someone passing by. "Hold on one second, let me take a peek out the window. Oh goodness, we're here! Hurry! Put your clothes on."

We rushed trying to get ourselves together before the limo driver came to open the door. We were going as fast as we could, giggling so much that we almost got caught.

"Geena, here! Put your shoes on!"

Michael and I pulled it all together just in the nick of time. Within seconds, the limo driver was opening the door for us to get out. Walking to the front door of the complex, we laughed about how close we came to getting caught just like the time we were almost caught in his grandmother's living room when we were teenagers. I loved the fact that Michael had a lot of good memories to share.

The meeting with the complex coordinator went great. Michael loved everything about the complex from the food, entertainment, the reserved rooms for our guests, and of course the master suite for us. After we finished brunch with the caterer, we hurried to the limousine so we could finally get home.

Once we arrived, the two of us immediately hopped into a warm bubble bath, sipped on some wine, and talked about the life we looked forward to living together. Later, after we made love, Michael fell off to sleep with one arm around his pillow and the other wrapped around me. It felt so good being in that place, lying in bed, being held by the one man that I knew in my heart loved me more than he loved any other woman in the world. I felt safe with Michael, free from worry, sorrow, disappointment, and pain. I quietly lifted his arm away from my waist, careful not to wake him, so I could turn and face him. Watching him sleep so peacefully warmed my heart.

I sobbed as I prayed for our love, for our union, and for the life that God was blessing us to share. The drapes were pulled back just enough for the light from the moon to rest directly on Michael, illuminating his uncovered body. I stared, in awe of the flawless beauty of this man. Not only was I attracted to his physical attributes and outward appearance, I was drawn to him like a magnet because of his spirit. Never in my life had I been that happy. I realized in that moment that although I had been in love before, I had never experienced real love. Tears continued to fall from my cheeks as I smiled thinking about this new chapter in my life, where Michael was the leading man and I his leading lady. Before I drifted off to sleep, I took another peek out of the window, up at the shiny moon and thanked God for allowing me to finally be completely happy with my life.

Our Wedding Day
Chapter 27

ICouldn't stop sweating. I was so nervous! The church was packed and the overflow room was overflowing. My wedding coordinator was doing all she could to calm my nerves, but no matter what she tried, I still couldn't settle down. All of a sudden, the door to my dressing room opened and there stood Mrs. Forté, my Sunday school teacher from the church I grew up in as a little girl. My heart skipped a beat when I saw her because I hadn't seen or talked to her since I was in the fourth grade.

"Hello, Geena." She sounded just as she did all those many years ago.

"Mrs. Forté, what are you doing here?" She began to walk towards me as I stood to embrace her. Mrs. Forté was one of the ladies from the church that always had her stuff together, dressed to a T, and knew her Word! We all loved her, envied her, and secretly wanted to be her one day.

"Well, I received your invitation in the mail just like I did for each of your graduations, the birth of your babies, your first marriage, and all of the other special moments in your life. During those times, I was unable to travel, but this time the Lord made a way."

"I'm so happy to see you, but what made this time different from the rest?"

"Well, I have a great-nephew who recently moved to the area, and when I told him I was invited to a wedding up here, he surprised me with a plane ticket to come. This way I will be able to visit with him and come to your wedding."

"That's wonderful, Mrs. Forté. I'm glad you were able to come this time."

"I'm happy to be here too, Geena. Look at you!" She took me by the hand and twirled me around like it was Easter Sunday back at the old church. "You are one beautiful bride. I know that your groom will want to fall to his knees once he sees you. You are radiant like an angel."

"Well thank you, Mrs. Forté. I feel beautiful today."

"Well you should, honey. I told your wedding coordinator that I wouldn't tarry long, but before I go, would you mind if I prayed with you?"

"Yes, ma'am, I would be honored if you did."

"Give me both of your hands baby. Now close your eyes.

"Dear Lord, we come to you humbly as we know how. First thanking you, Lord, for being a God of a second chance, a restorer of love and a sustainer of life, for being a faithful God to the faithless, and a hopeful God for the hopeless. I pray now, Lord, that this union be blessed and that these two people will never forget what brought them to this day. Rough times may come, tears may fall, and even feelings

may be hurt, but my prayer is that even during those times, they will be able to reflect on you knowing that the love of God is all they need to stand the test of times. I pray that Geena is the wife you have created her to be. To love and honor her husband. I pray that Michael is the husband you have called him to be. To cherish and protect his wife. Now, Lord, we give you all the glory and all the honor for you alone are worthy. Amen."

By the time she finished the prayer, my face was streaming with tears and my heart was filled with love. "Amen! Mrs. Forté, thank you, thank you. Thank You."

The wedding coordinator walked through the door. "Geena! We have ten minutes, are you ready?"

"Yes! Let me freshen my makeup. I'm ready!"

As I walked into the church that day, all I could remember was seeing Michael. I don't remember the preacher, any of the wedding party, the flowers, candles, or anything else. My heart was full and my eyes were fixed on the man that I would live with, love, and cherish for the rest of my life. Never in a million years did I think that I would end up being Mrs. Michael Sullivan. It's funny how life throws you a punch then suddenly everything you thought would last forever fades and what you thought could never be becomes reality. How many people marry their high school sweetheart or their one true love? I was about to embark on a journey with the person that I wanted to share everything with and never lose his love.

The ceremony was a blur because my focus was on waiting to hear, "And now I present to you, Mr. and Mrs. Michael Sullivan." After those words were uttered, it was time to celebrate! The wedding reception was a huge party. Our families and friends hit it off great. And my daughters absolutely loved Michael. After the wedding reception was over and all of our guests were gone, Michael and I sat in the middle of the ballroom floor, he in his Armani tux and I in my Vera Wang gown, looking around in a daze.

He leaned down to whisper to me, "What are you thinking about, Mrs. Sullivan?"

I turned to look at him, kissing him on his lips. "Oh, just thinking about how happy I am, and that being your wife makes me the luckiest girl in the world. . I'm living a life that I never thought was possible. I love you, Michael."

"I love you too, Geena."

It Can't Be Me!
Chapter 28

I could hear my cell phone ringing from the inside of my briefcase.

"Hey, Michael, could you grab that for me?"

"Sure, I'll get it. Hello? Oh hey, what's up, man? Yeah, they are ready? Okay, that's fine. Well, we were about to leave out ourselves so we could drop them off. All right, cool, we'll see you in an hour or so."

I could hear Michael talking on my phone as I walked out of the bathroom. "Who was that, babe?"

"Oh, that was Jared."

"What did he say?"

"He was saying that he and Sharon were kind of tied up and wanted to know if we could bring the girls by on our way out."

I could feel my temperature rising. "I hate it when he puts her over his children! That really raises my blood pressure."

"I *don't* understand that, Geena."

"You get me? I don't understand it either."

"No, I'm not saying that I don't understand Jared. I don't understand you."

"Excuse me?"

"Yeah, I have watched how angry you still become at even the thought of Sharon, and I don't understand why she is able to anger you the way she does."

"It's not that she angers me, Michael. It's just that I... Well, I don't like it when Jared puts her before the girls."

"But that's just it, Geena. He isn't putting her in front of the girls, he just called and said he was running behind schedule."

"That's my point! If he wasn't over there trying to cater to her, he could handle his business with the girls."

"Listen to yourself, Geena!"

"What do you mean? I can hear myself!"

"CAN you? Do you hear how bitter you sound?"

"Bitter? Me? I am far from bitter. What makes you think I am bitter?"

"It's not what I think. It's what I know. We've been married for almost five years now and Jared and Sharon have been married for almost two. Over the course of time, I have sat back and watched how you allow the relationship between Jared and Sharon to affect you."

"No, Michael, that's not the case. I could care less about the relationship Jared has with her! I just don't approve of the relationship she is trying to have with the girls."

"Oh, I see now. That is what this is about. You still want the girls to hate her."

"NO! I don't want them to hate anyone. I just want

to make it plain that I'm their mother! I was the one in labor for a total of 38 hours with those girls, not ANYONE else."

"And both of them know very well who their mother is." Michael held his hand out for me.

"Come sit here with me, baby." He could tell that I was about to get a really nasty attitude with him because I felt like he was siding with them.

"Look, I think it's time the four of us sat down and talked things out because there are a lot of underlying issues you are trying to deal with on your own. I think the only way you're going to be able to get beyond this is if we work through it together."

"Wait! You mean you want me to sit down and talk with Sharon? And Jared? Oh no! I don't think so!"

"And why not?"

"Look, Michael, I know you have good intentions and you want to try to fix everything for me. I love you so much for that, but this is one problem I don't think you're able to solve. Like I said, I don't feel I need to have a reason why I don't want to talk with them. I just don't want to. Especially Sharon. What is there for me to say to her anyway? All I have for her is a quick hello and an even faster goodbye!"

"Wait. Hold on, Geena baby. Listen to me and hear me out. That is the problem. To have that much animosity against anyone isn't healthy. Why can't you all have more dialogue than hey and bye? Jared and I can talk and hold a conversation with no problem. So what's the real deal with you?"

"Okay, Michael. Let me put it to you like this. The real deal is that YOU didn't come into my life and tear me away from my daughters, so Jared has no reason to have ill feelings towards you. That's why the two of you can still laugh all up in each other's face with no problem. And furthermore ya'll men are different from us."

"And how are we different? Is it because we don't allow petty issues to stand in the way of our ability to handle business? Or could it be the fact we are able to look beyond the surface of a problem and work to find a way to get over it, rather than holding grudges? Or is it because we can find it within ourselves to let the past go in order to be peaceful towards one another?"

"All of that sounds good, Michael, but you don't understand how it feels to watch your life be turned inside out at the hands of another person."

"So you have ill feelings towards Sharon because you think she took Jared away from you?" I sat there looking away from him, not wanting to answer the question. I mean, who wants to admit that someone was able to destroy their marriage?

"Is that it, Geena? You have allowed your bitterness to grow into resentment over something you had no control over? Let me explain something to you. There is no woman on this Earth that can TAKE another woman's husband. I know most women think that the other woman must be doing more in the bed than she did or she must be cleaning up behind him because she wouldn't. Men don't always leave for those reasons alone. In some cases he leaves simply because he has made the decision to leave. It's true that sometimes people just grow apart from one another. Sharon coming into Jared's life when she did just happened to be the time he wanted to get out of the marriage. If it hadn't been Sharon, it would have been Tiffany, Lisa, or Nikki."

Michael took his finger and turned my face towards him before he continued, "All I'm saying to you is that you cannot blame anyone else when your relationship fails. There are always a series of events that led up to the end result."

Ohhh, I was fuming. Contrary to what Michael believed, there are some trifling women out there that are waiting, plotting, and scheming to find ways they can step in and have a married man step out. I had to whoo-sah a few times and take a few deep breaths before I continued. I didn't want to cuss my husband out for trying to be helpful.

"I don't totally believe that, Michael. If it was a case of Jared so called making up his mind already, well, I know women, and I know that broad did her part in helping him with the decision and that is what pisses me off. If she wasn't flaunting herself around him the way she did, he never would have left."

"Well let me put it to you like this: if he had never left, we wouldn't be sitting here having this conversation today."

I looked down at my wedding ring then up at Michael. He was right; I had allowed myself to become married to my anger. The relationship was making me bitter and it was taking over. I was letting my anger towards my last marriage negatively affect my present marriage and I didn't want that to be the case.

"Okay, Michael, I see your point. But how do I even begin the process to get over this?"

"I have the solution."

"And what is the solution, Michael?"

"Don't worry yourself with that, just trust me. I have it."

Meeting Day
Chapter 29

One Saturday afternoon while I was cleaning the great room, the doorbell rang.

"Who is it?"

"It's FTD ma'am." I smiled while opening the door; Michael was surprising me with a bouquet of fresh cut flowers.

"Hi, Mr. FTD. How are you?"

"I'm fine thank you, ma'am. Is there a Mrs. Geena Sullivan here?"

"Yes sir, I am Mrs. Sullivan."

"Then these are for you."

"They are beautiful. Thank you so much. Hold on, let me grab my purse for your tip. Here you are. Thank you again."

"You are very welcome, ma'am. Enjoy your day."

I was smiling from ear to ear, putting the long-stemmed yellow and white flowers on the kitchen table when I noticed there was a note attached.

"Geena, look behind the bedroom door, there is a bag there for you."

I went upstairs to look behind the door and sure enough, there was a bag there. In it I found a sexy yellow dress and a pair of strappy heels. I immediately grabbed my phone to call my baby. He answered after the third ring as always.

"Hello."

"Hey, Baby."

"Hey, Geena."

"I got the flowers and I found my surprise. So what's next?"

"You think you can be ready in about an hour?"

"I sure can. Where are we going?"

"You are going on a date with me. Isn't that enough?"

"It sure is. See ya in an hour. I love you! And thank you for the flowers and the nice gift."

"You deserve it, Geena."

"But I haven't done anything."

"You don't have to do anything as long as you continue to be you."

Michael was always so tender and kind. We left the house a little after three o'clock that afternoon heading for a late lunch at the Wharf. It was beautiful out that day so we took our seats outside to enjoy the nice weather. I was enjoying the nice breeze and conversation with Michael until I looked up and saw the back of a man's head that looked like Jared. I sat frozen, hoping that he and Sharon wouldn't be coming to dine at the same restaurant as Michael and I. My hopes were shot to shambles when I saw Sharon's head peep around the corner looking for a place to sit while the hostess took their names for seats.

I never understood what Jared saw in her. I mean, what man wants to share the same style haircut as his woman? I guess Jared had turned into one of those guys that were into the Amber Rose type. You know, the wannabe supermodel with a little boy cut. What do they do? Go on dates to the barbershop for fun? The presence of Sharon turned my stomach! There she stood only 30 feet away from me, with her big fake boobs that resembled two melons being suffocated into her too-small shirt in dire need of air. I tried to turn my attention away from them, praying they would pass us and never look our way. As the hostess started to walk towards us, Michael looked up. He and Jared made eye contact and then Michael stood to greet them.

"Hey, Jared. Hello, Sharon, how are you all doing this afternoon?" I sat in my seat in shock wondering why in the hell Michael was greeting them like they were some old, dear friends that we were happy to see and were about to join us for lunch? Jared even had the nerve to look at me to speak. I gave him a look like, please do not waste your breath. I was not in the mood. But, of course, that didn't stop him because he spoke anyway!

"How's it going, Geena?"

"It's going." I was blunt and straight to the point, hoping he would catch my drift and run along with his boyfriend-looking wife.

Michael spoke up to break the friction that was building at the table. "Why don't the two of you join us."

291

I stood up from my seat. "Michael, could I speak to you for a moment. NOW! Please?"

"Well, of course, sweetheart. Excuse us, we'll be right back. You all go ahead and take your seats, get comfortable, and we'll return shortly." I couldn't move my legs fast enough to get down the steps away from them.

"What in the hell was that?"

"What was what, Geeena?"

"Okay, Michael, let's cut to the chase, you know very well what I'm talking about. Why in the world would you invite them to sit with us?"

"Well actually, it isn't a coincidence that they came here today." I couldn't believe what I was hearing. I looked away from Michael for a few seconds before returning my gaze, staring him in the eyes. "I invited them here, Geena, so we could finally talk things out."

"What?" I was outraged! How dare Michael invite them without informing me? How did he know I was ready to talk to them? "Talk things out? I told you that there's nothing to talk about. I can't believe this! I'm ready to go, let me grab my purse. I want to get out of here."

"Wait a minute, come back. Don't walk back in there just yet. Listen to me, Geena. I knew you wouldn't approve of this meeting. That's why I decided to do it the way I did. There has been too much time wasted on arguments and disagreements between you and Sharon. This unresolved pain needs to be dealt with. Once it has, the mending process begins. Then before you know it, the ugliness of the pain is gone away! Jared and I agreed that this was the best thing for the two of you so the healing process could begin."

"Healing process? My pain? So what, now you are discussing me with Jared? Of all people?"

"Geena, listen. I'm not going to go back and forth with you about my decision. As your husband, I have your best interest at heart so I would never make a decision that wasn't good for you. This meeting is long overdue. Now, like it or not, the two of us are going back to our table. When you get there finish your drink, and get your mind right because the four of us are about to talk."

I was so upset. I could feel steam coming out of my ears. Walking back to the table, I could see Jared and Sharon laughing and talking, playing around with each other. I wanted to run up to her from behind and just knock her out of her chair. He never laughed and talked with me that way.

"We're back." Michael had to make an announcement of our arrival to get their attention.

"Hey, man! Sharon and I were just sitting here talking about how nice this place is. Do you and Geena come here often?"

WHAT! Jared had the nerve to look at me with a smirk on his face. I wanted to get up and just slap fire to his face, but I was trying to be an obedient wife and follow my husband's instruction.

"Matter of fact, we do frequent here often. The food

is great. If you are a shrimp and crab lover, then this is your spot."

They continued to go back and forth like old army buddies while Sharon and I fiddled around in our purses, looking at our cell phones and scanning the short menu as if it had a million choices on it. I was so glad when the waiter finally came to take our order. After the orders were taken, Michael and Jared continued on and on and on. I nudged him under the table trying to get his attention to Shut Up already! He was working my last nerve. He politely ignored my nudging and went further into La La land with my ex-husband. After the food arrived, he finally took a second to converse with me.

"How's your food, baby?"

"It's fine." I had an attitude and didn't really want to talk and Michael knew it. He scooted his chair close to mine and opened his mouth for me to feed him from my plate like I always do. At first I just gave him a look to get away from me, but then decided to drop the attitude so I could enjoy my date with my husband. Once the meals were complete, the waiter asked if we would like another cocktail or dessert. I was ready to go, but of course, Michael was not.

"Yes, I would like another drink. How about you, Jared? Yes, bring both of us a rum and coke, please. We're going to be here for a while."

I couldn't believe what I was witnessing. My husband was ordering and buying drinks for my ex? I turned to look at him. "We're going to do what? And be where?"

Michael ignored me until the waiter had walked away. Once the drinks arrived, Jared and Michael picked them up, excused themselves from the table, and walked away, leaving Sharon and I at the table alone. The silence was so thick between us you could have cut it with a knife. After a long and ugly stint of quiet time, Sharon started the conversation.

"Look, Geena, I know that you don't want to be here alone with me, any more than I want to be here alone with you. But what do you say to at least making it worthwhile? Can we talk?"

I sat there for a moment before I responded to her, thinking, *Is she really opening her mouth speaking to me?* "What is there to talk about, Sharon?"

"If we're honest with ourselves and with each other, I think there are a lot of things for us to discuss and I think you can agree with me, Geena, that they are all important."

I took a deep breath, put my cellphone back into my purse, and tried to give her my undivided attention. "Well go ahead, I'm all ears, talk."

"Okay, I guess the best place to start is with my relationship with Jared."

I took a deep breath knowing this was going to be a discussion I would regret. "Fine."

"Geena, it's not a secret that you don't care for me and that's something I'm willing to live with. I'm not here for you to like me, but I would like for us to at least be cordial with one another since we're in a situation where we have to deal with one another.

"It's been communicated to me that you feel as though I waltzed into your life, plotted to take your husband, set my sights on destroying your family, and planned to end what you knew as your happy life. And if all that I'm saying is true and you do feel that way, then I sincerely apologize and I can assure you that is not what happened. I didn't come into Jared's life to take him away from you or the girls. I'm a woman of faith, and I believe that nothing happens by coincidence. I believe that everything happens for a reason. My transfer here was scary. It was a leap of faith for me, but as the years have passed, I understand now that God brought me here for a reason. Do I know all of those reasons right now? No, but He has showed me many of them. This may be hard to hear coming from me, but I have never had a man to love me the way that Jared does."

"Well honestly, Sharon, your innocence plea doesn't move me and I don't care how you try to sugar-coat it, fix it up, or try to make it look nice and pretty. You had every intention of doing exactly what you did. You're no different from all of the other men-hungry women out there looking for a man you can seduce away from their families. You saw a nice-looking man that was established, a leader at his firm, a role-model amongst his peers, and you wanted a piece of the action."

"Excuse me?"

"Yeah, and don't give me the 'Oh I never' look

either. You're not fooling anyone but yourself. Jared was perfectly fine with the life we had made with each other until you came and stuck your ass in his face."

"Okay, Geena. Look if you want to take it there, we can take it there. I was trying to stick with the facts but if you want to pull out all the details and make it plain, oh, we can do it. I'm going to explain to you exactly how everything happened.

"When I came to the firm, Jared was one of the first people I came in contact with. Did I find him attractive? Yes. Did I enjoy being trained by him? Yes. I had never worked with someone that was so passionate about his career. It was easy to learn from him because he knew how to teach in a way that you couldn't help but understand. Did I want to deal with a married man? No."

I had to interrupt her right there. "So if that wasn't your intention, how did the two of you end up in a relationship?"

"Although you may think we started dating upon my arrival, that wasn't the case. The first day that I stepped foot onto the campus of Miller and McBride Institute, things got really hectic, really fast. There were a million things already set for me to do. The agenda that my VP had set forth for me was outrageous. It was full of meetings, conference calls, and deadlines. On top of that, I was still trying to get acquainted with the fact that I was here all the way from Los Angeles. During my initial "welcome to the firm" meeting, my VP was called in to handle an emergency situation that couldn't be put on hold. Since I needed more instruction, he suggested I get with the guy down the hall named Jared because he would be the one to give me some direction. I didn't know what to do. I was fresh out of grad school, new to the area, new to the position, didn't know anybody, and I was being thrown to the wolves and still was expected to make a good impression.

"I walked down the hall to find Jared's office that day scared to death knowing that in corporate America, a woman's work is sometimes not respected. When I got to his office, the door was closed, which made me apprehensive to knock. He answered the door with a pen in his mouth, one on the side of his ear, and a few highlighters in his hand. I apologized for interrupting him because from the looks of it, he was pretty busy. I told him who I was and why I was there, and although he was busy with his own work, he allowed me to come in.

"Even with all the chaos of the day he had the girls with him, was attentive to them, and I was impressed. I thought, either his wife is deceased and he is a single father, or his wife is one lucky lady to have a man that takes such good care of his daughters. Jared had spreadsheets all over his desk, and the girls were lying around on the sofas in his office reading. He really didn't have time to help me, but being the type of person he is, he did anyway.

"During lunch later that afternoon, I saw them downstairs in the café eating. Lily noticed me as I paid for my meal and asked if I would like to sit with them. Since I didn't know anybody else there, I graciously took her up on the offer. I had a great time with them at lunch that day, listening to all of the great stories they had to share with me about their wonderful mommy. Jared was there co-signing with them all the way, singing your praises. He talked about how much he loved you and the girls and he bragged about the life the two of you had worked so hard to have together. I was in awe, thinking this must be a pretty magnificent woman to have a wonderful husband and beautiful children that love her so much."

"I'm still not moved, Sharon. If you were in awe of what you were hearing and seeing, let's skip all of this fairytale talk and fast-forward to the day when you went in for the kill that destroyed my family."

"Geena, are you listening to anything I just said? Let me continue. Jared and I worked very closely together. Being on his team, I admired how focused he was and how driven he was to meet the needs of the clients. He was on point at all times, never slacking when it came to work, and our superiors sang his praises. I was told by many of my peers to stay close to Jared and learn as much as I could if I planned to move up in the ranks. My intentions were to emulate him as a leader, not to follow him. A few weeks after you came home from your trip to Miami, I noticed a difference in Jared at work."

I had to interrupt here there. Miami? "Wait. How did you know about my trip to Miami?"

"Remember the day that I had lunch with Jared and the girls? They told me that was where you were. Since that time, I noticed that he wasn't focused like usual, and he was forgetting things that should have been second-nature for him. One morning after an executive board meeting, I asked him if he was okay. It must have been weighing really heavy on his heart because he laid it all out on the line right there in the conference room. He just poured his heart out to me. He said there wasn't anyone else he could go to about the situation for fear of embarrassment and he was tired of holding it all in."

"Embarrassed about what? Jared and I discussed everything.Why couldn't he talk to me about his feelings?"

"Evidently, Geena, he felt like you weren't listening. He said there were a few occasions where he tried to discuss things with you, but you would always pull away from him and he felt like there was nowhere else for him to go. I can tell you this, Geena, Jared noticed a difference in you after that trip with your friends. He said that it almost seemed like you had met someone while you were away."

I immediately thought about Michael and I in Miami. "Did he say that?"

"No, he didn't say that. He didn't know for a fact you met someone, and he didn't have any proof that you had.

, He just had his speculations. He said with the kind of chemistry the two of you shared he could easily pick up on the slightest difference in your demeanor. He said the shift was great once you came home. It was scary and what made matters worse was that it continued to weigh heavily on him as the days and weeks passed by. Jared loved the way things were when you were dating and first married. He said that the relationship that he enjoyed with you took a turn for the worse soon after the girls came and you moved up in your firm.

"He complained that your focus was totally on them, work, and other things that tied you to various committees. He felt like it was no use to complain to you about how he felt because you didn't see anything wrong with the way things were being handled. After a while, he decided to come to grips that he would accept things as they were and just try to be okay with the way your lives were playing out. Being roommates and co-parents was okay with him as long as Lily and Frances were okay, but the day he found your diary everything changed."

"My diary? When did he read my diary?" I immediately tried to think back. What had I put in that book of memoirs? Oh my goodness. What did Jared read?

"He said that he was about to surprise you with tickets to a play that you had been talking about seeing for months. He'd planned to present them to you after dinner one night, but you were too busy helping the girls, talking on the phone, cleaning the kitchen, and putting away laundry. Jared's feelings were hurt because he felt like you had completely taken away all of his responsibilities as a dad, all the way down to going over a simple homework assignment with one of the girls. He said you seemed happy doing it all because you were always the one that handled it ALL for everybody. From your family, your friends, your co-workers, and even down to the little ladies that cooked on Saturdays at the church. After trying for many years to be the man that he felt you deserved, he settled for taking a back seat to your strong personality and focused more on his career, allowing you to handle it all."

The memory of that night came back like a tidal wave in my mind. The play was *The Way We Were,* one of my all-time favorites and I wanted desperately to see it. The night he tried to give me the tickets, I was busy with the girls and brushed him off, unknowingly pushing him away. That was one of the few nights that Jared beat me to bed. I remember pulling the comforter back to climb into bed beside him, finding the tickets on my pillow. The date of the play conflicted with another commitment that I had made, putting me in a tough position of having to choose quickly between the two. Instead of going to the play with Jared, I chose to attend the gala for my women's group. We never even discussed the play or the tickets. I guess we both just let it go.

While I was away at the gala that evening, I remember leaving my book of memoirs on my nightstand, never thinking Jared would ever read it because it resembled a day-planner more than a diary of secrets. I felt my eyes sting as tears formed, thinking of a snippet from a poem I wrote back when I finally realized I had been a large part of the reason my marriage fell apart.

I am at a very low time in my life, seeking desperately to bury my hurt, hoping that it will resurface no more. I carry a stifling pain in my bones having no one to turn to who can help me grapple with my emotions and the constant emptiness that feels pinned to my soul. I am longing for something or someone to fill me up again. I have become everything to everybody, but there is no one left to be anything for me. My heart has become my well, my love has become my water, and my life's experiences have become the pump line that is slowly draining me dry.

Looking back on my relationship with Jared for the last few years, I realized that my flawless hair, makeup, and designer clothes had not done a very good job of protecting me from pain. I was embarrassed to let anyone know that my black leather book was my lifeline. Being that I was always the one that spoke of God's redemptive power and saving grace, how could I possibly let people know that I had struggles, too? In between those white pages were specific details of how I had grown to despise my relationship with Jared and even at times myself.

I didn't put any explicit details on those pages, but I guess what I did say was enough. I began to think back. Had I treated Jared differently after I came back from my trip to Miami? He was the one that had changed! Wasn't he? I was confused. Could it be true that I pushed Jared into another woman's arms?

"I tried to talk to him about working things out with you, if not for anything but the children's sake. Geena, I understand that you don't trust me, but I give you my word that I never thought Jared and I would end up in a relationship. After a few months of spending time to reflect on what he wanted for his life, he made the decision on his own to leave. I was not a determining factor."

"What I still don't understand, Sharon, is why you continue to say that you didn't have any intentions of getting with him, but the two of you ended up together? Why didn't you just walk away?"

"I ran into Jared at the gym one night when he was coming in as I was headed to an aerobics class. This was after the divorce was finalized. All the time that we worked together, we never realized that we were members at the same workout facility. That night, we only spoke briefly at first because I was asked to teach the class and he was headed to lift weights. Once class was over, we saw each other again at the smoothie bar. He and I talked for an hour or so before we knew it. A few weeks later as we were walking out to the cars, he asked me if I wanted to grab a salad, so we did. Never once did we talk about anything other than work at the office, but after a few months of seeing each other at the gym, we became really good friends. We found that we had a lot in common, making it easy for us to want to spend time together. He never disrespected your marriage. There was no sex involved because I believe in karma and I would never want another female messing around with my husband behind my back."

"Didn't you feel any remorse for destroying our family, Sharon?"

"I wish there was something I could say or do to help you understand that I never wanted to hurt you. I played the situation over in my head many times. I kept thinking about how I would feel if I were you, and to be perfectly honest, I would probably feel the same way. That's why I've never allowed myself to get upset when you were nasty to me. I could have easily retaliated, argued, and made a fool of myself, but I refrained from doing so because I knew that your anger came from a hurting place. Anyone on the outside looking in at the three of us would deem me the problem, and if the problem could be eliminated, things could go back to normal. But on the inside, I know that the problem was never me. The problem was derived from all the things that you and Jared did long before I came into the picture. I didn't take Jared away from you, Geena. When you pushed him aside, you pushed him away."

I sat there in my seat boiling over with emotion. I wanted to cry but fought hard to hold back my tears. I gripped my dinner napkin as if it were an anchor, able to keep me from sinking. As my gaze left Sharon's face, it slowly fell to the floor. My heart was aching with indescribable pain, and my feelings were rumbling around in my chest.

"Geena, are you okay?"

I couldn't look up just yet. I had to try and gather myself. I closed my eyes hoping the tears would dissolve and not come down my face. Before I could respond to Sharon, she got up from her seat to come and sit next to me. As she sat down, she scooted her chair close to mine, putting her arm around me. I couldn't believe what was happening. Sharon was consoling me? After the awful way I had treated her? Tears rushed from my eyes as I played my life back in my mind. Although I didn't want to admit it, Sharon was right. Jared was right. Michael was right. I was the one in the wrong. I gasped for air, trying to get enough wind to answer her.

"I'm going to be okay."

Sharon took the napkin from my hand, placed it on my face, and dried my tears. By this time, the guys were walking back up.

Michael noticed my tear-soaked cheeks. "Geena, baby, is everything okay?"

It was still hard for me to speak so Sharon spoke for me. "We had a much-needed talk. Things got pretty emotional, but we both are going to be all right. Right, Geena?"

I smiled and nodded in agreement.

Jared interjected. "Well, can somebody fill Michael and I in?"

"Sure, babe. Geena and I have an understanding that we never had before. We both realize as women we carry burdens that are not ours to carry. We lose all sense of hope because we are too afraid to communicate with one another. Hurt is powerful towards the spirit. Left unattended too long, it turns into resentment. Once resentment is present, it opens the door to everything else that is damaging to our soul."

Jared took his seat and scooted in closer to the table, making eye contact with me.

"Geena. I think this would be a good time for me to say some things to you that I should have said a long time ago." He paused, taking a deep breath. It seemed as if he was tearing up. "First, I apologize for the way that I left. On our wedding day, I made a vow and promised that I was going to stay in the marriage until death do us part. I'm so sorry that I wasn't able to keep that promise. I know that to you, it felt like I was running away because I couldn't have my way, but that was far from the truth. Although we had a lot of problems in our marriage, I wanted desperately for us to work so I was constantly looking for ways to add to our years rather than take away.

"The truth was that I finally realized that although we vowed to be as one and had two beautiful daughters together, things between us would never work out. I didn't want to spend another day living under a roof where love wasn't present. We had love for one another, but we had fallen out of love far before I made the decision to leave. I also allowed anger and a bad attitude to lose sight of what I know is important and that is communication. Had I communicated with you better, things wouldn't have gotten so out of control between you and Sharon. Although it may seem like it, she had nothing to do with the reason I left.

"To be honest, to get back at you for the way you were acting, I allowed you to think whatever you wanted. I couldn't believe you acted the way you did about the girls spending time with Sharon and saying that I lost focus on what was important because of my relationship with her. That was one of the things that burned me up the most during our divorce because you know that I take my responsibility as a father seriously. Then on top of that you acted like Sharon would actually harm them and, Geena, you know me better than to think I would allow anyone to hurt our children. Sharon has not done anything except love those girls. Not having any children of her own, she pours her all into them so to hear you say things negatively about her pissed me off."

"Jared. I'm going to be honest with you. It wasn't that I felt like she would hurt them. I was just afraid that one day, they would love her."

Michael interjected, "Why wouldn't you want the girls to love Sharon, Geena? Isn't that what we all should do? Love one another?"

"I know it's hard for any of you sitting at this table to understand where I'm coming from, and the reason you're not able to comprehend my feelings is because none of you are mothers. Only if you have carried a baby in your belly can you empathize with what I have had to deal with. Birth is one of the most magical things a woman can experience in her life. Our bodies go through a metamorphosis; we are able to house, protect, feed, and nurture our babies from the pit of our bellies. When I see my daughters, I sometimes stare in amazement thinking about how God allowed me to participate in such a miracle.

"Once you came around, Sharon, I was harboring a lot of anger towards life in general with all that had transpired between Jared and I. You being a part of the picture intimidated me, not so much by who you were, but the threat I felt because of your presence. I was torn. I was in disbelief, and I was broken. It pained me to watch my girls love you. I witnessed how quickly the relationship between the three of you grew stronger each time they came back home. I had to listen to them talk about the things you did with them that I had never thought to do. You took them places I would have never thought to go. They loved you, and it wasn't fair. And I hated you for it." I broke down into tears. "My heart was breaking because I had to swallow the fact there was another woman in their life that could tickle their hearts with her touch, just like I was able to."

I continued to sob. Michael reached out to console me.

Sharon started to speak. "You're right, Geena. I haven't carried a baby in my belly, so I'm not able to empathize with what you've had to go through. But I can assure you of this one thing: although I haven't birthed a baby from my womb, it doesn't mean that I don't know how to love." She reached down to touch my hand. "You've done a great job raising them, Geena, and I think that's why I fell in love with them so quickly. Anyone that knows me, knows how I feel about children. I've never had a lot of patience with them, but there was something special about Frances and Lily that helped me to change. I love those girls, and there is nothing in this world that I wouldn't do for either of them. I feel fortunate to be a part of their lives, and I'm grateful that God allowed me to have such an opportunity. I believe that a child can never overdose on love, so if you would allow me, Geena, I would love to have your permission to love them."

I reached out and placed my hand on top of Sharon's, giving her the assurance that it was okay without speaking a word. I then turned to Michael as he started to speak.

"I can agree with that, Sharon. I don't have any children either, but I love Lily and Frances like they are my own. I have also been blessed to experience fatherhood because of my union with Geena. God has a plan for each of us. Many times, we can't understand what He is doing and that's okay because I believe in allowing God to have His way and to let things happen in His timing. Can you all imagine the kind of future the girls are going to have with two awesome mothers and two great dads?"

We all laughed and I turned to Michael, put my

arms around his neck, and kissed him on the lips. "Thanks, babe."

"What was that for?"

"For being you."

Later that night as I lay in bed, I thanked God for my union with Michael. Had he not insisted that I talk to Sharon, I would have still been in that empty place full of rage and anger, hurting no one but myself. I learned that hurt binds us to a lot of ugly things if we let it.

My heart was light now, my burdens were gone, and finally my mind was set free. I chanted that phrase to myself as I drifted off to sleep with a smile on my face, and Michael's arms around my waist. Joy was in my heart and I was ready for a brand new start. *I am free. I am free. Thank you Lord, I am free.*

Mrs. Sullivan
Chapter 30

I could hear my office phone ring as I walked through the door. Brittney wasn't at her desk, so I had to run in to catch it.

"Hello, this is Geena Sullivan."

"Girl, it's ME! And we all know you are Mrs. Sullivan! You've been Mrs. Sullivan for years now. What happened to answering the phone, 'Hi, this is Geena'?"

"That was when I was just Geena. now I am Geena Sullivan, the wife of Mr. Michael Sullivan." Stephanie blew her breath through the phone as if I was working her last nerve.

"Okay, Mrs. Sullivan, do you think you can make a lil' time to have lunch with your best friend that you haven't seen in over a month?"

"It hasn't been a month, Stephanie!"

"Yes it has, Geena. I still haven't seen you since you met with Jared and Sharon.!"

"Oh, well then you may be right. I'm sorry, Steph. Please forgive me. How about you get Rachel and Kim together and we all have lunch Thursday. It's time for all of us to catch up. Being married has me so busy."

"Whatever!" We both burst into laughter. "That sounds like a plan, Geena. I'll get with the girls and confirm with you later."

"Okay, well let me get off the phone. I have a lot of work to do before I can leave the office for today."

"Cool, Geena. Have a good one, babe!"

"You do the same." My phone beeped as soon as I put the receiver back down.

"Yes, Brittney."

"I'm sorry, Geena, but you have another call on line three. I think it's the guy you are meeting with next week from Indonesia."

"Do me a favor, tell him I'm with a client and I'll get back with him later today. I know he probably wants to know about the forecasts I'll be presenting at the conference. Let him know that I will send him a copy of each of them before noon tomorrow."

"Yes, ma'am. I'll let him know."

"Thank you."

"You're welcome."

The time began to fly, and before I knew it, it was after six. Michael was expecting me home by 6:30, and I still had some more work to do. My cell phone rang as I was about to dial his number.

"Hello!"

"Hey, baby."

"Hey, love. Look, I was calling you because I'm going to be a little late coming home from the office tonight. How much more do you have before you can get out of there?"

"Uhmm, I should be able to leave by 7:15. How about you?"

"It's gonna be a little later for me, maybe nine or so. I have a mixer to attend that my C.O. just informed me about today at lunch. I got so busy I didn't get a chance to let you know sooner."

I took a deep sigh. "Okay, Michael. That's fine. I'll grab a salad or something and head home. I'll see you when you get there."

"Okay, Geena. Thank you for understanding, sweetheart."

"You're welcome. Now hurry and get home. I miss you when you aren't there."

"Will do. Will do."

Later that night, I climbed into bed to catch up on reading one of my books when I heard Michael come in. He came straight into the bedroom, threw his briefcase down on the chaise lounge, took off his sport jacket, and jumped on the bed beside me, giving me a kiss, then sniffing my neck.

"Uhhmm, you smell tasty." I giggled.

"Oh stop it." I pushed him away softly, not really wanting him to stop.

"I know what that means." We both laughed.

"How was the mixer, babe?"

"It went really well, Geena." Michael stood up to take off his clothes. This was the part of the night that I loved. I admired his body as I watched him take his suit jacket off then unbutton his dress shirt before he dropped his trousers to the floor. Did I mention that my man was fine?

"You know, when my C.O. asked me to go to the mixer with him, I was dreading it, but I'm glad he urged me to attend. I met a really interesting group of people that we're about to start doing some partnering with in the near future."

"Oh yeah?" I stood to come help him finish getting undressed.

"Yeah, these guys have some great ideas that are going to blend well with our practices. I exchanged business cards with the gentleman I will be working closely with as the merger happens. There was one of the guys that I took to more than the others. He seems to be a pretty smart guy. He's classy. I like him. He reminds me of myself.

"I'm about to jump in the shower. You want to join me?"

I took my reading glasses off, dropped my robe to the floor and gave him a wink to seal the deal. "Baby, you didn't even have to ask. I would love to join you."

For the next few months, Michael was really busy working on the big merger. I missed him but understood it was imperative for him to be away in order for everything to work out the way he intended. He helped the situation greatly by calling me or texting me to let me know if he would be home later than usual. After many months of extended work hours and loss of sleep, Michael came home excited with some big news! The merger was a big success and to celebrate, the company had invited all of the associates and their guests to a huge ball. He was so excited. I was happy for him, and very proud of his accomplishments.

A huge ball meant that it was time for me to make a stop at the Galleria to find a sexy dress for the occasion. One of Michael's favorite colors was cranberry, which is also his favorite cocktail chaser, so I went out and found the most seductive but classy cranberry evening gown I could find. I didn't let Michael see the dress till the night of the ball when I walked into the great room wearing it. I cleared my throat to get his attention.

"Excuse me, sir, but are you waiting for someone?" He turned to me and reached his hand out to meet mine.

"You look amazing, sweetheart. Almost as amazing as you did the day I married you."

"Awwhh, thank you, baby. You're looking pretty debonair yourself." And he was with his tailor-made tuxedo and cranberry and black striped bow tie.

"Shall we?" He folded his arm for me to grab hold of it.

"Yes, we shall." On the way to the ball, Michael couldn't stop telling me how much he appreciated me for sticking things out with him while he completed the project. It made me happy to see how happy he was. Approaching the ball, I was shocked to see so many people.

"Hey, Michael. Is this ball only for the associates locally or was the invitation extended to partners and associates elsewhere?"

"The invitation was extended to everyone, so there's a great possibility that close to 400 people will be here."

"Really? This is going to be something else then, huh?"

"Yes, the night should be very interesting."

After entering the ball, a young man escorted us to our table. The program was very nice, short and sweet, but the partying afterwards was off the chain for a corporate event. I was shocked to see so many people on the dance floor. Everyone looked so boring and dignified when we first arrived, but after a few drinks, I think everybody started to get a lot more comfortable!

Michael and I loved dancing, but after our last dance, I was hot and it felt like my dress was stuck to my body. I asked Michael to get me a glass of water from the bar. He walked me back to our table before heading to grab the water. There were some nice ladies at our table, so I had small talk with them while he was away. We compared wedding rings and stories about our children. My mouth became more and more parched, so I looked around to see if I could see Michael coming back with my water.

After a while, I could see him walking back towards the table, not realizing there was someone walking towards me with him. I turned my head for just a second, then looked up to take my glass of water only to drop it and watch it break into hundreds of small pieces all over the floor. Water splashed all over my dress, the table, and the nice lady sitting beside me. My heart felt like it stopped beating, and my lungs felt like they had just collapsed.

"Geena! Are you okay?" I was far from being okay. Michael turned to his companion, "I apologize. Did any water get on you?"

"No, I'm fine. It's water. It'll dry." Michael's new friend extended his hand to shake mine. "This must be your wife, Geena?"

"Yes, this is Geena.. Geena, this is my new partner that I've been bragging about for the past few months. Please meet Dr. Zackary Stone."

Oh Lord, He's Back!
Chapter 31

E ver since the night of the ball, I had been a nervous wreck. How in the hell did Zack find his way back into my life after over five years of avoiding him?? How should I deal with the fact that he was hanging around my husband at work and afterwards? Lord, how did this happen?

My fear of Zack telling Michael about us haunted me with each day that passed. With the two of them working so closely together, I hoped that Zack had let bygones be bygones and decided to keep his mouth shut about what happened while Michael was away. I prayed daily that things would stay under wraps because I wouldn't be able to deal with him finding out, and couldn't imagine what would happen to us.

Michael never questioned me about the water incident at the ball and I never brought it up either. Each time he came home talking about Zack, I would remain silent trying my best to find a way to change the subject. Michael was enjoying his new position with the firm, and I didn't want to do anything to jeopardize his happiness.

One afternoon as I was driving home from work,

Michael called me to let me know that we were invited to a dinner with some of his colleagues later that night. As much as I didn't want to go, I agreed to go with him, praying fervently that I wouldn't run into Zack. On the way to the dinner, I couldn't help but think about seeing Zack's face. What would I say? Would I clam up again? Would he make me feel uncomfortable? I couldn't stop questioning myself and I hated that his relationship with Michael had started to consume me. As soon as we arrived, we pulled up behind a silver Bentley with a car tag that read "DRZAC" and my heart fell to the floor. I was so nervous.

Walking into the dinner, I saw everybody except for Zack and I was relieved. We sat down for cocktails and the night was going well. Some of the wives and I had really great conversations. Dinner was good and afterwards we stayed around talking, trying to get a little more acquainted with our new friends. The doorbell rang, which caught everyone's attention because of the magnitude of the sound. After the door was opened, in walked Zack and his wife! Michael went to the door to meet him.

"Hey, Zack." They shook hands and gave each other a 'man hug.' "I was wondering what happened to you."

"Yeah, man, I had to handle some business with my wife, so she came to pick me up as soon as I got here." He then looked up at the man of the house. "I apologize for missing dinner."

"No problem, Dr. Stone. The two of you are just in time for cocktails. The guys are all on the terrace and the ladies are sitting in the great room." Michael started to walk towards me with Zack and his wife, but I could barely look at them. My heart began to beat faster and faster.

"Hey, sweetheart! Remember Zack?"

"Geena, how are you tonight? Looking beautiful as ever." I couldn't even respond to him. He pulled his wife around to stand in front of me. "This is my wife, Char."

Char smiled and extended her hand. "Hi, Geena! It's so good to finally put a face with a name. I've heard so much about you."

I couldn't move. I couldn't believe what was happening. Michael could sense that something was wrong with me.

"Geena! Baby, are you okay?"

"Uhm, excuse me for a second. I need to use the ladies room."

Zack motioned for Char to follow me. I went straight into the bathroom and leaned against the sink. As soon as the door closed, I heard it reopen. Char walked in behind me.

"Geena, is there something wrong?"

"What do you want from me? Why are you here? What's the meaning of all of this?"

She interrupted sarcastically and giggled at me. "Why, whatever do you mean, Geena? My husband and I are here to mix and mingle, just like you and your husband. Is that some sort of crime?"

I turned to walk out. "I'm out of here! I don't have time to entertain this!"

Char pulled me back by my arm. "Not so fast! Where do you think you are going?"

"I'm going back out there, get my husband, and we are leaving!"

"Well, I don't think that is a good idea."

"Who gives a flying flip about what YOU think?"

"Well, Geena, if you storm back out there and demand Michael leaves all of a sudden, he's going to wonder why. Then there's a chance that he'll think back to the night of the ball when you dropped your glass of water." She walked up to me, looking me directly in my eyes. "Now I know that you don't want him to start putting two and two together, do you? If you continue with this behavior, he's going to start wondering why you aren't able to sit still once Zack and I are around."

I was so angry and upset! I snatched my arm away from her and walked to the other side of the bathroom. "Well, WHAT do you all want from me? Why did Zack befriend my husband, and why are you in there acting like you want us to go over apple pie recipes?"

"Look, Geena, the meeting between Zack and Michael was innocent. Zack's great-aunt called us a few years ago talking about wanting to attend the wedding of some girl she knew from her church."

I immediately thought back to my wedding day. I couldn't believe Zack was Mrs. Forté's great-nephew.

"We had planned to surprise you at the wedding, but had some other business to handle and weren't able to make it. The night that Zack and Michael met, he couldn't stop talking about you. At that time, Zack didn't know that you were his wife; once we found out, we wanted the opportunity to say goodbye properly because the last time we were all together, you left so abruptly we didn't get a chance to leave on a good note."

Char walked up to me and I backed away from her. After she cornered me, she put her hand on the wall over my head, leaned in, and whispered in my ear. "Now if you play along like a good girl, like Zack and I want you to, your husband will never have to know what happened between the three of us."

I pushed her back away from me. "You are out of your mind. Do you think you can blackmail me?"

Char leaned back towards me, rubbed her index finger down the side of my face, and replied, "That or tell your dear sweet husband about us. You see, Geena, the choice is yours."

Book Club Questions

1. How do you feel about Geena's concerns about going out of town with her friends for an entire week? Do you agree? Disagree? Why?
2. What are your feelings about the decisions that Geena made while in Miami?
3. Do you think Jared should have stayed with Geena and tried to work it out although he felt like it was over?
4. How would you handle the situation with Cedric and Rachel if you were her cousin? Would you try to make him stay, why or why not? Would you remain close to Rachel and take on the attitude that blood is thicker than water?
5. Do you think Sharon had ill intentions toward Geena? Was she really innocent?
6. If you were in Geena's shoes, would you go with Dr. Stone on the trip? Why? Or Why not?
7. Do you think it is a good idea to remain in a relationship for the child(ren)'s sake?
8. Do you think Sharon and Geena should try to be friends?
9. Should Geena tell Michael about Zack and Char? Or should she keep it to herself?

About the Author

Katrina Butler Hill, born October 15, 1975, is a native of Columbus, Georgia. Affectionately called "Trina" by her family and friends and "KBH" by her supportive clients, she is a brand new author excited about the art of expression and has been writing since the age of 16. She has found that a piece of paper and a few words can be powerful, uplifting and exhilarating.

The fresh new author graduated from Hardaway High School in 1994, completed her undergraduate degree in Computer Information Systems in 1999 from Columbus State University and her master's degree in education in 2011 from Western Governors University. She has been a certified personal trainer since 2002 and owns KBH Fitness alongside her life partner and husband Mr. Bradley S. Hill, Jr.

She is a believer in God and works actively in her community to serve the underprivileged. She and her husband, with the support of her extraordinary clients, launched a campaign to partner with the House of Mercy in November of 2010. The House of Mercy supplies food, shelter and necessities to individuals who have fallen on hard times and are homeless in the Columbus area. She says that the beautiful thing about the partnership is that each person that is a part of the

KBH family understands that giving to those that cannot give anything back to you in return is a blessing, and each month they, along with many others, give freely.

Katrina believes in empowerment. As a personal trainer, aerobics instructor and boot camp instructor, she has learned that each of us has the potential to be or do whatever we want, as long as we have a strong desire and a serious support system.

Not only is Katrina compassionate about expressing her creativity through her novels, she is also crafty when it comes to putting life's experiences together in a poem.

She is the daughter of Mr. and Mrs. Willie James Butler, whom she feels have been her biggest supporters and greatest cheerleaders her entire life.

She is empowered by her many clients whose intriguing life stories have enlightened her about a world that she was unaware of, but glad to know exists. The characters in her book are all fictional, but they have a voice that will speak volumes to any audience.